THE *Wolf* OF MY EYE

TERRY SPEAR

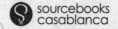

sourcebooks
casablanca

Published by Sourcebooks Casablanca, an imprint of Sourcebooks
P.O. Box 4410, Naperville, Illinois 60567-4410
(630) 961-3900
sourcebooks.com

Printed and bound in the United States of America.
BVG 10 9 8 7 6 5 4 3 2 1

To Elizabeth Marie Labare,
thanks so much for loving my sense of humor in my
wolf books and enjoying the Highland Wolf books in
particular, which is why I dedicated this one to you!

Chapter 1

ROBERT CAMPBELL JOINED HIS TWIN SISTER, EDEEN, and her mate, Lachlan MacQuarrie, for breakfast at their kitchen table in the manor house, where he'd been living while his own home was being built with the vet clinic right next to it. His place was on their property, within walking distance of their manor house, and was finally finished. Edeen's home was formerly an inn, originally built in the 1700s, and had always been owned by the Campbells in the Highlands of Scotland, though it had been called a manor house for years.

"Thanks again for giving me fifty acres of your one hundred to build my clinic and home on the property."

Brushing a red curl of hair off her cheek, Edeen smiled at him. "We would have given you much more than that to entice you to leave your veterinary practice in Edinburgh and join us here."

"The decision was easy to make." Robert's sister was four months' pregnant, but Lachlan's brothers both were sitting on pins and needles waiting for their own mates to have babies any day now. "Besides delivering both your babies and Lachlan's brothers' sets of twins, I can't wait to be at your wedding to Lachlan in a little over a week."

"Oh, absolutely. I'm so excited about it." Edeen had made Robert a grand tux and the works to wear to it. His twin sister had a successful business creating faux vintage gowns and menswear, tartan kilts, and other garments out of the manor house, while Lachlan worked with his brothers, Enrick and Grant, the leader of their wolf pack and clan business, which meant anything concerning the pack, the castle, and their grounds.

Besides, Robert loved the wolf pack, and he'd always been close with his sister, so he couldn't imagine living that far from her long-term.

"Have they found a replacement for you at the vet clinic there yet?" Edeen asked.

"No, but I'm sure it won't be long. The other two veterinarians there can manage the workload until that happens."

"Well, we're so glad to have you here," Lachlan said. "We feel really lucky."

Robert had been a practicing family physician for a few years before leaving his practice and becoming a veterinarian, which meant that they now had a doctor who was well versed for most scenarios.

"Happy to be here." Robert loved working with animals, though now that he was living among his kind, he loved taking care of the shifters also.

"Hey, we're having some weapons training in the inner bailey tomorrow afternoon. Edeen says you're going to come join us." Lachlan buttered his toast and coated it with grape jelly.

Robert glanced at Edeen. She smiled sweetly at him. His sister wanted him to be immersed in the same things that the other men in the wolf pack were. Robert wanted to be part of the pack in that way, but he didn't want to look like he could barely hold a sword. He'd always been busy getting degrees and working. Sword fighting just hadn't been part of his agenda, and he hadn't had any wolf friends to practice with over the years, even though it was part of their heritage.

He had a sword that had been handed down from his grandfather, but he worried about actually being able to do well in "weapons training." He would be required to wear his kilt and the rest of his attire, as if they were ready to go to war. He told himself it would be fun, but he was too alpha to want to admit he could be a failure at it. These guys had been doing this training for years.

"And fishing next week." Lachlan took a sip of his tea.

That was another thing Robert rarely did. "Uh, right."

Lachlan nodded, serious as could be, and began eating his eggs. "Good. You're part of the pack now, and you're my brother."

Robert appreciated that all three brothers treated him like he was one of their own. "I agree. I've been enjoying getting to know all of you."

"Good. We sure love having a new brother in the family." Once he finished eating his breakfast, Lachlan said, "I have to go." He gave Edeen a hug and kiss.

"Love you." She stepped outside with him to say goodbye.

On a beautiful summer day like this, Lachlan would walk up to the ancient stone dike between the MacQuarrie and the Campbell properties to reach Farraige Castle to do his duties, whatever they were for the day. Robert had had a hand in installing the wrought-iron gate they'd erected between the two properties.

When Edeen reentered the manor house, she said to Robert, "You know you don't have to worry about looking like you're clueless at sword fighting. They want to teach you, and they know you haven't trained in swordsmanship like they have."

"And fishing?" Robert finished eating breakfast, then got up to help her clean the dishes.

She laughed. "You will have to do an archery match with them. Then you can show them how good you are."

"Lachlan never mentions that. It's like he knows I might best him."

Edeen hugged her brother. "I did let it slip that you were good at it."

"Ha! I knew it."

"So what are you going to do today?"

"I'm going to fish."

She arched a brow.

"Just to get a little practice in before I have to fish with the others."

She smiled. "You know they love you no matter what. You don't have to prove anything to anyone. Okay, well, I have to work on my wedding gown. You have fun fishing."

"I will."

"And bring something back for dinner!"

He laughed. If he had luck, he would.

Later that morning, Robert was sitting in the boat off the western coast, where he could see the MacQuarrie castle and battlements sitting high up on the cliffs—a spectacular sight. The water was calm as he listened to the seabirds calling out above while casting his line out again. He knew the birds were waiting for him to catch something, just like he was. He was trying to enjoy the fishing trip, the solitude, and the summer day before he opened the clinic in three weeks and would be too busy to do something like this. He'd had to wear a waterproof jacket and pants over his T-shirt and jeans though, the wind off the water a wee bit chilly for soaking up any of the sun's rays.

He was moving into his home tomorrow, first thing, giving Lachlan and Edeen their much-needed privacy, even though the manor house was set up with two complete living areas. As gray wolves, that meant they'd only want to lease to other wolves, and Robert fell into that category, as well as being family. But he was ready for his own space and was also thinking about the grand opening of his vet practice.

Then he got a nibble on his fishhook. Hell, he'd caught something. He began reeling in the fish, careful not to lose it, giving it slack, reeling it in again, but damn, it was big and struggling to get free. He continued to reel in his catch, and it continued to fight him. He was afraid he'd lose it. But then the sky was darkening. Storm clouds were building and moving in his direction. Winds were whipping the water up in a frenzy. Hell, he was facing a fierce squall, and he had to hurry.

The wind was blowing hard, the waves starting to swell. Robert needed to return to the MacQuarrie beach. He still couldn't see what he'd caught, but as he pulled his catch closer, a hand reached out of the water and grabbed on to the fishing line. The first thing that came to mind was a mermaid, but then logic caught up: He'd caught a person?

That's when the diver came up with the hook caught in her arm. Och, he was a worse fisherman than he thought he could ever be.

She glowered at him through her face mask, her beautiful blue eyes spearing him. She pulled out her regulator. He at once smelled that she was a wolf, though also wearing the scent of the sea and salt air. He felt awful that he'd hooked her but couldn't help but be interested in the pretty wolf.

"You were under my boat?" He held his hand out to her.

"I was swimming out there!" She motioned with her good arm to a point a long way off, where he'd tossed the fishing line out in the first place. Of course. "Ohmigod, we've got to get out of this weather." Lightning was striking the ocean off in the distance, thunder following. Gale-force winds were blowing the boat about, the waves capping.

"Here, let me get you into the boat and I'll remove the hook. Is it just caught in your suit?" He prayed it was.

"No. It's also in my arm." She sounded furious with him, her eyes flashing with indignation.

He didn't blame her. Here she'd been diving, minding her own business, and he'd ruined it for her. "I'll get the fishhook out, but we have to hurry. I'm so sorry. Here, let me take your tanks." But as soon as he leaned over to grab them, a rogue wave hit the boat and capsized it. He went into the water, swallowed seawater, and came up coughing. Aww, hell. Panic washed over him in that moment because he didn't see the woman.

He dove under, but seeing in salt water without a face mask was nearly impossible. Everything was blurry. Then he felt her bump his leg, and he dove down and grabbed her good arm, pulling her out of the water.

She coughed up water, and he held on to her until she could get her bearings. If the boat had hit her, he couldn't tell because of the wet suit hood she was wearing.

They would have to swim around the cliffs and reach the beach on the other side. The water was cold, and he wasn't wearing the right clothes for it. Plus, he wasn't wearing fins like she was. He worried about having to pull her from the water. Had the boat hit her and knocked her out momentarily? She could have a concussion, but at least her wet suit should keep her warm enough.

His hook was still in her arm. His phone and fishing pole had sunk to the bottom of the ocean. The ice chest and overturned boat were floating on top of the churned-up water.

She pushed the inflator button closest to the air inlet to add air from her scuba tank to the buoyancy control device, or BCD, that essentially served as a life vest when needed.

For a moment, she just stared at the upside-down boat, him, and the bobbing ice chest—and then she took a picture with her dive camera.

The storm was getting worse by the second. Yet for one

crazy instant, he wanted to ask if she was single and seeing anyone else.

She pulled a diving knife out of its sheath and handed it to him. "Don't drop it. Cut me free of the fishing line. I'll go to a doctor to have the fishhook removed."

"I'm a veterinarian. I worked at a clinic in Edinburgh. I can remove the fishhook." He cut the fishing line free of the hook and handed the dive knife back to her.

She sheathed it. "Not out here, you can't, and I can't help you with your boat. Can you make it to the shore okay?"

"We'll swim around the MacQuarrie castle coastline and get to their beach. That's where I launched the boat. Come with me."

"You're going to get hypothermia before long."

Man, he did not want his soon-to-be in-laws to know about the disaster he'd had. They would have to help him retrieve his boat once he and the mysterious wolf made it to shore. "Hopefully, we'll make it in before that happens. Are you okay?" he asked.

"Aye. I wasn't out for long, was I?"

Hell, so the boat had hit her and knocked her out. "Only for a few seconds. I had to bring you to the surface."

"Uh, thanks. I didn't know I'd nearly drowned. Let's swim hard. You might not make it otherwise."

———————

After the dinner date Maisie MacTavish had had last night with a guest at her and her sister's inn, a man named Gus

Anderson, she felt he took the number one spot for the weirdest date ever. While taking the marine wildlife photos for her magazine assignment, she'd kept mulling over the circumstances and wondered if Gus had been having another date after that. She could have taken a look at their security video footage last night, though it didn't really matter. He was just a guest who happened to be from her hometown of Glasgow, not anyone she figured she would ever see again. Besides, if he were meeting another woman after Maisie's dinner at the pie shop with him, it didn't mean the woman would have seen him at his guest room, so the security video wouldn't have told her anything.

Then a fishing wolf had caught her on his fishhook, and now she was swimming to safety with him. The gale-force winds, lightning, and torrential downpour were slowing them down.

She could get to the beach, no problem. But the wolf who had caught her was falling way too far behind. She knew he had to be suffering from the early stages of hypothermia. She swam back to him and pulled out her regulator. "What's your name?" She felt bad that he had been trying to help her when that huge wave had overturned the boat.

"Robert Campbell," he said, his words slurring.

"Maisie MacTavish."

Then another rogue wave headed their way. "Watch out." She placed her regulator in her mouth and quickly grabbed his arm, not wanting to lose him. They were tossed about under the wave and then finally resurfaced.

He came up coughing.

She pulled her regulator out, though she hated to because the seas were so rough and she kept getting mouthfuls of water. "I need you to hold on to my belt, and I'll pull you along." She had already dumped her weights.

Once he was holding on to her, she put the regulator in her mouth again. They just weren't making enough progress against the currents and waves, the rain pouring down in sheets, the lightning still striking everywhere around them, and she had to swim hard to reach their destination.

She was trying to avoid the rocks below the cliffs, where waves were leaving millions of bubbles in their wake, when she finally got a glimpse of the beach. She was certain that, unless Robert was a beta wolf, this had been grandly humiliating to him.

Every time she looked at him, he was shivering, and now his lips were beginning to turn blue. She swam as fast as she could, though pulling him along was like dragging an anchor. Then she managed to get to the shallower area and they were on their knees. The storm had moved off, and the sun began to peek out between clouds. A rainbow appeared across the water, a light rain still coming down.

Maisie pulled her fins off, stood, and removed her regulator, the water tugging her and Robert back out to the ocean as the surf withdrew and then the waves pummeled them again. She helped him to his feet, and they stumbled up onto the beach beyond the water. They collapsed on the wet sand just as the rain quit, and they soaked up the sun for a moment. That was good for him. But she was getting hot now. She stripped off her mask and BCD. She was going to

THE WOLF OF MY EYE

pull off her wet suit because she was wearing a vest, sports bra, and long swim shorts underneath, but she couldn't because of the darn fishhook.

She couldn't fault him for that too much. Seeing the rugged wolf filled with regret and wanting to take care of her so badly, it'd been easy to remind herself he hadn't done it on purpose. She had caught herself once while fishing, hooked the back of her shoulder, silly mistake on her part, so she knew how fishing accidents could happen.

She glanced in the direction of the castle and saw what seemed like a million stairs going up to it from the beach. Then she howled, though as a human, hoping someone up at the castle would hear her. In the meantime, she laid down on top of Robert to try to warm him.

"Do you know the MacQuarries?" She did because she'd bought an Irish wolfhound pup from them, but she also wanted to keep him awake and talking.

"Sister mated to Lachlan." He was still stuttering from being so chilled.

"Okay, good. If no one comes at the sound of my howl, I'll shift into my wolf and race up the stairs to get help." She could go up them so much faster as a wolf. Then she remembered about the darn fishhook again. She howled again instead. It was a distress call, and this time a wolf howled back. She was grateful to hear the beautiful call of the wolf.

A wolf and three men appeared at the edge of the cliff and peered down at them, then they disappeared. Good, they had seen them. They would get help.

The next thing she knew, the wolf was running down the

steep, ancient stone stairs with speed and grace, hurrying to Maisie and Robert. She didn't recognize the wolf, but she figured he knew Robert. Then she saw a dozen men running down the stairs. "Thank God. They're all coming for you, Robert."

The wolf woofed in agreement.

When the men finally reached the beach, they headed straight for them. "His color is returning. He was mildly hypothermic," she said to Lachlan and his brothers: Enrick, the middle triplet, and Grant, the eldest of them and their pack leader.

They began taking care of Robert right away.

Lachlan got on his phone. "Edeen, Robert's on the beach below our castle. He has taken a dip in the ocean. He's reviving, but he's really cold. We're carrying him up the stairs to the castle now. See you soon."

The guys quickly began hauling Robert up the arduous stairs.

"What happened exactly, Maisie?" Grant asked.

Thankfully, one of the guys had grabbed her fins, tanks, and face mask. She was so worn out, she wasn't sure she would even make it up all those steps.

"He caught me fishing." She realized the whole time the other guys had been close by, she'd hidden the hook in her arm from them, as if she was afraid they would think it was her fault she'd gotten caught while Robert was fishing.

Grant waited to hear the story.

She didn't say anything more except, "He had a mishap with his boat. A rogue wave capsized it."

"Oh, that explains a lot. He was fishing?"

"Aye." She planned to go with them, and when Robert was feeling better, he could remove the fishhook. She could have gone to a doctor, but she wanted to give Robert the chance to make things right between them. Then she would go home. One of the guys would undoubtedly drive her back to her car.

When they finally made it to the castle, she was trying not to huff and puff. She wasn't used to walking up that many steps! The guys took them in stride. They probably did it all the time.

"How is Conan doing with his training?" she asked Grant. Maisie loved the Irish wolfhound that she and her sister, Anne, had bought from the MacQuarries, but in his exuberance to see them, Conan had knocked her and her sister over so many times, she'd finally signed him up for training at the castle. In three weeks, he was supposed to be perfectly obedient.

"He's doing well. The Irish wolfhounds take to obedience training really well, but they can need a firm hand to begin with. They can be stubborn."

That's exactly what she and her sister had learned. "That's great." She couldn't even imagine Conan greeting her in a mannerly way. She knew he would just go crazy like he always did. He had another week of training before she did a transitioning training with him so she could work with him on the basics he'd learned and she would learn them too. She couldn't wait. She really missed him—he was a big goof and so sweet.

She went in through the bailey with the others and joined them inside the castle.

Colleen hurried to greet her. As Grant's mate and pack leader, she escorted Maisie into the great hall to have some hot tea. Colleen was so pregnant, she looked like she was ready to deliver at any moment. "Do you want to remove your wet suit?"

"Uh, I need to visit Robert as soon as he's able to see me."

Colleen closed her dropped jaw and then nodded. "I'll check and see how he's doing. They would have taken him to one of the guest rooms."

"Can I come with you?"

"Yeah, sure." Colleen smiled. "So you know Robert?"

Now that sure sounded like Colleen believed there was something romantic going on between Maisie and Robert. Maisie sighed. As if that were the case!

"No, not really. We met quite by accident." She still needed to have the fishhook removed.

Chapter 2

LACHLAN AND ENRICK HAD REMOVED ROBERT'S WET clothes, and he was in bed shivering in one of the guest chambers, buried under a ton of blankets, before Edeen arrived. She had brought him some hot tea.

Lachlan was watching him, his arms folded across his chest. "You know you shouldn't be swimming out there unless you're wearing the proper clothes for it."

Enrick agreed.

Robert gave his brothers-in-law a half smile. He loved that the brothers ribbed him about things, which made him feel as though he was one of them. His relationship with his sister was so different. They were close, but it wasn't the same as being one of the guys.

"I know what I'll be getting you for Christmas," Edeen said.

"Oh?" Robert couldn't wait to hear what she had to say. He swore she was picking up some of the MacQuarrie brothers' habits.

"A dry suit."

Robert smiled. "I already have one. I just never thought I would wind up swimming while I was fishing."

"We can hold off on training you to sword fight tomorrow," Lachlan said, frowning, sounding serious.

"I'll be fine for that. As long as I don't get heatstroke during the practice."

Lachlan laughed. "We'll have plenty of water to drink, and it's supposed to be overcast tomorrow, so it won't be too hot while we're getting a good workout. This is our regular time to spar, and we want you to join us, but seriously, if you don't feel up to it, you can bow out and everyone will understand."

"I'll be there."

"We're having lunch first," Lachlan said.

"All right."

"Edeen's coming too. She said she doesn't trust us to go easy on you the first time." Lachlan smiled.

"You're right about that," Edeen said.

Robert chuckled.

"But we wouldn't do that to you. We don't want you to avoid other practices," Lachlan said. Footfalls headed toward the guest chamber. "Sounds like you have some more visitors."

———————

Colleen and Maisie headed down the long hallway after climbing the circular stairs—Maisie swore she didn't want to look at one more stair today—and reached a chamber. The door was open, and Colleen knocked on it. A pretty redheaded woman with beautiful green eyes was in the room standing beside the bed where Robert was buried under blankets. Lachlan and Enrick were there too.

"Hey, is it okay if we check on Robert?" Colleen asked.

"I'm fine." Robert rubbed his forehead, his dark-brown hair dry now. The color had returned to his lips and face, and he gave Maisie a small smile, his blue eyes sparkling in the sunlight streaming through the window.

Maisie was glad to see he was looking better.

The red-haired woman eyed Maisie, measuring her up. Was she interested in dating Robert? Or was she his mate? Maisie shouldn't have cared one way or another, but it bothered her just the same.

She was a sucker for beautiful blue eyes and a wolf who was apologetic—especially as she wasn't used to an alpha male apologizing to her for anything.

"Do you have a first aid kit?" Maisie said.

"Yeah, sure," Colleen said.

"I'll go get it," Lachlan said.

"And wire cutters and a pair of pliers," Robert said.

Lachlan frowned at him, then said, "Okay," in a drawn-out fashion.

"I'm Robert's sister and Lachlan's mate, Edeen. And you are?" Edeen asked.

Colleen jumped right in with introductions. "Oh, I'm so sorry. I thought you had already met each other, Edeen. This is Maisie MacTavish, proud owner of one of our Irish wolfhounds from the same litter that your Ruby came from. Maisie and her sister, Anne, own the MacTavish Inn down the coast. Maisie also does photography for magazines. Edeen creates faux vintage gowns and other beautiful clothes out of her and Lachlan's home."

"Oh, how wonderful. I would be happy to do a portrait of Ruby for you, Edeen," Maisie said. "I take a lot of animal photographs." She loved doing them, and she wanted to do one of Conan too, though he wouldn't sit still for her yet.

"That's right," Colleen said. "She took the Christmas pictures of the litter to help us sell them on our breeder's website. Of course, then she fell in love with all the pups and picked out one of them for her own."

"Aye, the unruliest one, so it seems. I had to bring Conan back here for obedience training for three weeks," Maisie said to Edeen.

"Oh, Conan, sure. I've seen him in training," Edeen said. "He's a beautiful brindle and doing a great job."

"That's wonderful to hear." Maisie was truly pleased, as she'd thought the dog would be hopeless to train, but then that made her wonder if his owners were the ones who were not very good at making him mind.

"I would love to commission you for some animal portraits for our fox terriers, Ruby, our Scottish fold cat, and Highland calves too," Edeen said.

"That's great." Maisie wondered if Edeen was trying to set her up with her brother, which she thought was cute.

Carrying the first aid kit and the other items they'd asked for, Lachlan walked back into the chamber.

"Um, could Robert and I have some privacy for a few minutes?" Maisie hated to propose such a thing in front of the others, but she preferred doing this without a big audience.

Edeen, Lachlan, and Enrick looked surprised, but Colleen

smiled. "Yeah, sure. Come on, everyone." Then they walked out of the guest chamber.

Once Colleen shut the door, Maisie said, "Okay, take it out."

Robert pulled the covers aside.

He was totally naked! And he looked perfectly alpha in that moment. Then she remembered he'd been hypothermic and they'd had to remove his wet clothes. "Sorry, I don't have anything to wear." He really didn't sound apologetic, just like he wanted to take care of her as quickly as possible. He was the perfect specimen of a male wolf in human form. "Luckily, I don't have to traumatize the area any further; the barb went all the way through the skin on your arm. I'll just cut it here."

She had totally forgotten about the fishhook and was still thinking of his beautiful physique.

He snipped off the barb, then laid it on the bedside table. "And pull this out this way."

After he removed the hook, she pulled her suit off so he could sterilize the wound and apply a bandage. At least the fishhook appeared to be brand-new, not rusty.

"How are you feeling now?" He began to clean the wound.

That stung like crazy. "Much better, but I'm glad I'm not swimming in seawater anytime soon."

"I'll say."

He applied the bandage with such finesse and caring, she looked back up at his beautiful blue eyes framed by the most luscious black eyelashes. To her surprise, he began to examine her head. "Where does it hurt?"

She felt the top of her head, and he put his hand gently on it.

"You have a contusion. I recommend an ice pack and a day in bed."

With him? She was ready. What was wrong with her that she was thinking of such a thing right now when he was still recovering from hypothermia and she had a head injury? Well, maybe the latter was the reason.

"Have you had a tetanus shot recently?" he asked.

"I have, aye."

"Good. If you have any trouble with either the head injury—nausea, dizziness, blurring vision—or a fever or sign of infection on your arm, you let me know right away."

"You'll make a house call?"

He smiled, a bit of the devil in his expression.

"Thanks for saving me, by the way," she said. "Anyone could have had a boat capsize out there. I'm just glad the boat didn't knock you out too, or we might not be here talking to each other right now."

"You're welcome and so right about that, but you saved me too. So thanks for that. I'm sorry for the fishhook. I'll buy you a new suit."

"We're all good. There's no need. Sometime I might tell you about my mishaps with fishing." She hoped that would make him feel better.

Someone knocked lightly on the door, and Robert quickly climbed under the sheets. Maisie wrapped the pieces of fishhook in several tissues and stuffed them in her pocket. "For show-and-tell," she explained. "I have to let my sister know what took me so long while taking marine life pictures today."

He smiled again. "Come in."

Edeen opened the door. "I'm sorry for the interruption, but I brought you some clothes to wear, Robert."

"Thanks."

Eden turned to Maisie. "If you're feeling alright, I'll take you home, but Colleen asked if you would both like some hot tea first in the sitting room."

"Sure, that would be nice. After we have some tea, I'll need a ride to the car park."

"I'll take you." Edeen smiled and then left them alone.

"Oh, I'll come with you," Maisie said as an afterthought. She really didn't need to see the hunky Scotsman dress. She grabbed her wet suit and left the room in a hurry to catch up to Edeen.

Edeen smiled at her. "I'm glad to meet another female wolf. There's always so much testosterone in the place that it's good to see some more she-wolves."

"Oh, I agree," Maisie said.

They reached the sitting room, which was filled with books. Large windows showed off views of the gardens of green hedges and red, white, and pink roses. Lachlan and Robert soon joined them, and Colleen brought in their tea.

"So you were swimming near my brother's boat when it capsized and you swam in together?" Edeen asked.

"Aye. Robert said that the MacQuarries' beach was closest to where we were. He wasn't dressed for the cold water."

"Thank you for saving my brother's life," Edeen said.

"We were really there for each other," Maisie said.

They drank some of their tea, and Maisie knew Robert's

sister was dying to know just why they had to have privacy
and a first aid kit and other tools in the room.

"When you're ready to go home, I can drive you," Lachlan
said to Maisie.

"Oh, thanks, Lachlan, but Edeen is taking Robert home
and she said she'll drop me off too. I would like to peek in
on Conan before I leave if it doesn't disturb his training too
much." Maisie sipped some more of her tea.

"Sure, I'll take you to see him," Lachlan said.

When they finished their tea and Maisie, Lachlan,
Robert, and Edeen got ready to leave, everyone thanked
Colleen. She was thrilled that they had dropped in to see her,
as if this was just a totally unexpected, pleasurable visit and
not a crazy misadventure in the ocean.

Lachlan walked Maisie to the dog kennels while Robert
and Edeen grabbed Maisie's dive gear and put it in Edeen's
car. Maisie peeked into the room where Conan was staying,
and he was sound asleep on a big dog bed. She smiled. She
was glad he wasn't pacing the floor, looking bored or unhappy.

When they left the kennel, she asked Lachlan, "Did
someone get Robert's boat out of the water?"

"They're working on it as we speak. The water's still
rough, but they'll get it done."

"Good. It seemed like a nice little boat. Um, I thought
Edeen was Robert's mate or girlfriend when I first met her.
When she first saw me, she appeared a bit...suspicious."

Lachlan laughed. "She's worried about a she-wolf break-
ing her brother's heart. But she seemed relaxed and happy to
be with you when we were having tea."

"Oh, sure. Once she learned I had one of your dogs from the same litter as hers, we hit it off."

"When they were first born and until everyone picked up their pups and took them home, Edeen loved on all of them. So she remembers Conan. Plus, she has been teaching her terriers to mind her, so she comes to watch Conan's training to get some more tips. If you're free tomorrow, why don't you come over and have lunch with us and Edeen can show you some of the training we're doing with Conan and begin the transition with you?"

"Yes, I would love that."

"Come at eleven, then."

She was glad she would be able to see Conan and hug him and get some honest-to-goodness training in with him. She'd been having nightmares that she would undo all the good training he'd gone through as soon as she and her sister took him home.

Lachlan escorted Maisie to Edeen's car and kissed his mate. "I'll see you later. I've got to take care of some business."

As Edeen drove, she asked, "How was Conan?"

"Oh"—Maisie laughed—"he was sound asleep in his comfortable little room."

"They train them on and off all day and everyone takes turns so they get used to different people giving them the same commands," Edeen said. "I'm sure the dogs that are in training are worn out by day's end. I've been there watching how they do it and have been training Ruby too. My fox terriers are finally really listening to me when we're outside. When I lived in Edinburgh, they had a fenced-in yard, but here, they can run all over, so it took me a while to train them to stay home and not run off."

"Oh, I bet. Everyone at the inn adores Conan. He has really been an added feature at the lodging," Maisie said.

"That's great. Have you eaten at Ye Olde Highland Pie Shoppe?"

"Heather's shop? I picked up takeout from there for my sister and me when we were just moving in. Heather has the best pies. We always recommend her shop to guests for the afternoon and evening meals. We only serve breakfast. Then everyone's off exploring to their heart's content." Maisie snapped her fingers. "I bet you designed some of the gowns for her and her workers since they're wolves too. They were wearing these beautiful new ancient-style tartan gowns, and I told them how much I admired them. They were so busy that Heather and the other ladies didn't have a chance to tell me who created them."

"Aye, it was me. I've been having a lot of fun making them for the locals, and I get orders from all over the world."

"That's terrific. On special occasions at the inn, we dress up," Maisie said. "My sister and I will have to check out your website."

"I'll give you my business card when we drop Robert off at the manor house."

"I would go with the two of you, but I want to check on the installation of all the appliances," Robert said.

"I'll drop by after I leave Maisie at her car. I want to see how they look," Edeen said as she pulled up at Robert's house. It was a beautiful home covered in ancient-looking stone, and

THE WOLF OF MY EYE 25

right next door, a vet clinic had been built that had the same period look with large windows, a door with a sign overhead that said, "Cat Entrance," and on the other side of the building, "Dog Entrance." She thought that was cute, though maybe also necessary.

"It was nice meeting you, Maisie, though it would have been nicer if we'd met under better circumstances," Robert said.

"Oh, our meeting that way was remarkable and memorable."

He smiled at her, looking appreciative that she didn't think being around him had been a complete disaster. Then he frowned. "Remember what I said about you having any trouble at all from the boat hitting you in the head."

"Right. I'll call you." But of course Maisie didn't have his number.

"I'll write his number down for you on my business card so you can put it on your phone, but since he lost his phone in the ocean, you can call me if you need to see him," Edeen said.

"He says he makes house calls," Maisie said.

Edeen looked at her brother, and from Edeen's expression, Maisie assumed that he was making an exception in Maisie's case. Though she figured in cases of livestock, Robert would have to visit the farms.

Robert smiled, then said goodbye to Maisie and headed into his house.

As soon as they drove off the property, Edeen asked Maisie, "So what *really* happened between the two of you on the water? I know you said you were swimming and his boat capsized, but—"

When Maisie just smiled at her, Edeen laughed. "Okay, you don't have to tell on my brother, but I can guess: he hooked you with his fishhook. That's why he needed the first aid kit and other tools. Then the rogue wave hit, the boat flipped, and your fate and his were sealed. You were doomed to make the trip together, swimming to the shore around the cliffs."

"I didn't tell you any of this." Maisie was surprised at how his sister had guessed exactly what had happened.

"You didn't need to. My brother won't care if anyone knows the truth, but I'm sure he didn't want to say anything about it in case *you* were bothered by what had happened and didn't want to tell the whole story. Don't worry. I won't be telling anyone, though I'm sure I'll say something to my brother about it."

Maisie laughed. "All right. Yes. That's what happened. I just didn't want him to feel any more guilty about it than he already did. The thing of it is, anyone, someone who has been fishing for years even, can hook themselves or someone else. I, um, caught my sister once. She wasn't happy about it. I had to take her to the doctor because I didn't have a clue how to proceed at the time."

"Och, I bet she was upset."

"Aye, but we're still best of friends."

They finally reached Maisie's car, and she loaded her diving gear into it. Edeen fished out a business card from her purse and handed it to Maisie. Then they said goodbye.

Maisie got into her car and immediately put Robert's and Edeen's phone number in her phone and drove home to the inn.

"Hey, you're home. That took you a while." Anne started making some tea for her as Maisie headed to the bedroom to change her clothes.

"Yeah, you don't know the half of it."

Anne set the mugs on the table. "Everyone who was staying at the inn has left to explore the area. So you can sit and tell me just what happened."

"Sitting down is a very good idea."

Then Maisie and her sister had tea at the dining table, and Maisie proceeded to tell her sister just what had happened.

Chapter 3

BECAUSE ROBERT WANTED HIS PLACE TO BE IN KEEPING with the period of Edeen and Lachlan's manor house, he had his home constructed in a similar design on the outside—same kind of old stone, same kind of roofing materials, but he had a double front door with large iron knockers. His house didn't have two separate living areas like Edeen's, but its four bedrooms had en suite bathrooms, so if he ever did want to rent out the rooms, he could without jeopardizing privacy too much. He didn't plan to rent them out though. He figured that, instead, someday he would mate with a she-wolf and fill the house with their children. He was glad Edeen was having her children first so he would have time to practice babysitting hers. Which made him think of the beautiful she-wolf in the ocean.

He kept thinking about catching Maisie with his hook. He had been trying to figure out a way to make it up to her. Once she'd removed her wet suit hood, her dark-brown hair had cascaded down to her shoulders. Beautiful hair to match her beautiful blue eyes.

He walked into his house and found all the appliances had been installed.

He heard Edeen's car pull up. He was so pleased that everything was done, he was beaming when he joined her outside.

"You must be thrilled with the way they finished things up—you're smiling." Edeen gave him a hug.

"I am. And it is beautiful. I'll move in this afternoon and have lunch and dinner with you and Lachlan."

"Absolutely. Lachlan will be busy buying some more cows, so it will be just the two of us. I don't have any pressing garment orders, so I can help you move over here too. Are you sure you're alright after being so chilled with the swim in the ocean earlier?"

"Aye, I am, like it didn't even happen." As wolves, they all recovered much more quickly from illness and injuries. "I worry about Maisie though." He led Edeen into the house.

"You'll need to call and check on her. You can borrow my phone anytime." She looked over the kitchen. "The appliances are beautiful. I love the stainless-steel ones. You do realize you'll have to make us meals now too."

He smiled. "I'll be glad to." He had a big, covered patio so he could grill for the family even on days with inclement weather.

"You know we'll have to have an open house so everyone can see the place now that it is completely finished. Since we'll have so many of the wolf pack members there, Chef Maynard will order all the food items, and he'll bring his portable grills to make the grilled foods."

Robert laughed. "I'm not used to being part of a pack yet."

"I know. Right? You'll have to invite Maisie and her sister to the party. You know, because of her using your vet services. It doesn't hurt to encourage business."

"You're not trying to matchmake, per chance, are you?"

Edeen laughed. "Whatever made you think that? It's just good for business. Maybe even for mine too. You never know. Both sisters might end up needing a kilt or something else I can make for them. I looked up their inn and photos featured them wearing kilts on occasion."

"True. I had an established business in Edinburgh. I'm not used to, uh, reeling in vet patients."

She smiled. "I knew you had. I love you. You're not the only person who has ever hooked someone with a fishhook. Remember my good friend, Tilda? Her boyfriend hooked her in the arm, and she had to go to the hospital to have it removed. At least you were able to remove it without any trouble, right?"

"Aye. I was more concerned about the boat hitting her in the head."

"I hope she doesn't feel bad from that, but if she does, she can get ahold of you. Speaking of which, when are you going to replace your phone?"

"I really need to do that right after lunch. I'll pick up some groceries then too."

"But you're still having dinner with us. Lachlan will want to know the details about what happened to you."

"Did Maisie tell you what happened?" Robert was certain Edeen would have gotten the details out of Maisie one way or another.

"She didn't tell me. I guessed, and she said I was right." Edeen let out her breath. "As to the business of the sword fighting—which I know you're somewhat fretting about—Lachlan said he would mentor you any time you're free, so you can get some private lessons."

Private was more Robert's style until he got the hang of it. On the other hand, if everyone was busy fighting each other, maybe no one would notice how inept he was. He guessed the reason he was worried about it was because he'd always been so studious, never really involved much in sports, except for archery, and he'd been ribbed about it when he was younger.

"Oh, and don't worry about getting everything ready for your house party. Colleen and I will help you get it all set up. Or, hmm, maybe not Colleen because those babies are due any day, but someone will step in to help us. Lachlan for sure. I know you're not used to having big parties. Well, neither you nor I were, but the MacQuarries will all help."

"I guess we could do it on Saturday."

"Perfect. Once you open your vet doors, you're going to be busy." Edeen walked through the house looking at all the details. "I like how you have a modern, open plan yet kept a lot of the warm country-estate vibes with the oak-wood floors and tapestries, the soft couches and chairs, and the beautifully hand-carved oak-wood coffee table."

"After working long hours, I want to relax in style."

"I agree."

They walked into his bedroom, and she smiled. "I love your black-and-white decor. A king-size bed is perfect for when you have a mate. You need a picture over your bed though."

"I haven't found the right one yet."

Edeen peered into his closet and chuckled. "Wow, now this is perfect. His and her spaces, and you actually didn't even use 'her' space up."

"If I did and I found the right she-wolf for me, then she would think I didn't have enough room for her. Besides, everything I wear fits perfectly fine in one-half of the closet. If I began shopping just to fill up the other side, I wouldn't ever have time to wear all those clothes." He was totally pragmatic about it. If he didn't wear something that wasn't used only for special occasions after a year, he would find a new home for it.

Edeen peered into his bathroom. "Ooh, I love your bathroom. Nice big whirlpool bathtub with jets for two."

"Um, for getting the kinks out when I have to pull a calf during a difficult delivery and my back needs some extra loving care."

"I sure love it. I've told Lachlan several times about your tub, though seeing it when it's installed and surrounded by tile is really beautiful." She laughed. "I'm hoping we do a bathroom remodel so we can put one in also. After a day of hauling babies around, I could see relaxing in a tub like that."

"Yeah, I agree. If you want me to help convince Lachlan you need one, just let me know."

"I'm sure when he sees yours, he'll feel the same way as me. Do you want me to go with you when you buy your new phone?"

"Sure, if you need to pick up some groceries also, I would welcome the company. I need to buy a lot of staples."

"Absolutely." She looked over the other bedrooms, though only one other had been furnished as a bedroom. One had been turned into an office, and the other he would furnish when he knew what he needed it for. "Everything is so homey and just lovely."

"Thanks. I'm really pleased with it. I never thought you would end up buying the property from our great uncle, mate a wolf next door, and I would end up opening a practice here."

"Are you ready for lunch?" she asked.

"Yeah. I'm starving." They got into her car and parked it at her place, then they went inside to make lunch. They were greeted by a menagerie of pets. "Mittens is going to miss all the company she has had for the last couple of weeks." Robert joined Edeen in the kitchen to help his sister make lunch.

"You can always take the other animals with you, and they would be happy to keep you and Mittens company," Edeen said.

"If you need me to take the three dogs for a while to help simplify your life a bit once the twins are born, I can do that."

"Sure, that would be good for a couple of weeks. I can see all the dogs getting underfoot while we're trying to manage two babies at the same time." She began making cheese toasties while Robert fixed a salad. "I kept thinking you were going to get together with Lana more often."

Lana Cameron was Heather's baker at the pie shop and

really sweet, but they just hadn't really connected in a way that said he wanted to have more of a relationship with her.

"We had a great time at last year's Christmas party. But I think she and I just don't have what it takes to make it for a long-term relationship."

"What about Veronica?" Edeen asked.

Robert was amused. His sister had asked him repeatedly why he wasn't dating either of the women. "Even though Veronica is with the MacQuarrie pack, she is always running off to England to visit her friends. I think she might be seeing someone there."

"Hmm, that may be so."

After lunch, they went shopping and Robert purchased a replacement phone. Even though he wasn't taking calls for new pet patients yet, if the MacQuarrie or MacNeill clans needed his help, they would call on him to take care of them, which meant he really needed a phone.

His contacts were all added, and Edeen made sure to add Maisie's phone number too. He called her as Edeen drove them to the grocery store.

Immediately, she answered. "Robert," she said as a greeting. "You have a new phone already."

"Yeah. I wanted to make sure you knew you could call me now, in case you were feeling bad."

"I'm fine. I don't have any headaches, nausea, or blurring vision. And my arm is already healing up nicely, courtesy of our faster healing abilities."

"You don't know how glad I am to hear it. Uh, I'll be having an open house on Saturday once I can coordinate it with the MacQuarries. Everyone who wants to can check out the vet clinic also. I would love to have both you and your sister come to it too."

"Sure, that will be lovely. We'll have to make arrangements for someone to watch the inn while we're both there, but we look forward to it. How are you feeling?"

"Great, thanks. About your wet suit—"

"Don't worry about it. Anne and I already fixed it. Are you going to the castle for lunch tomorrow?" Maisie asked.

"Aye, and weapons training. I'm not really that great at it."

"My sister and I have done some Highland demonstrations at our inn. If you ever need any tips, let me know."

"Certainly." He wasn't too proud to accept tips from anyone who knew how to fight properly, though he did worry he might hurt her accidentally if they practiced together.

"Well, save me a seat at lunch, then. I'm going to be there to start training Conan."

"Yeah, sure." He was so thrilled she would be there.

"Well, I've to go. I'll see you tomorrow," Maisie said.

"I look forward to it." Then Robert and she said goodbye. Despite the wild turn of events they'd already shared, he was delighted to be having lunch with Maisie tomorrow. Maybe fishing had brought him real luck—not in catching a fish, but something much more important. Only time would tell.

Chapter 4

Maisie was so glad that Robert had a new phone and that he'd invited her and her sister to his open house. When she got off the phone with Robert, she turned to Anne. "Hey, we have a party to go to."

"Oh?" Anne was helping Maisie clean up the kitchen.

Maisie and Anne lived at the inn in their own three-bedroom private quarters; the wing of six bedrooms, complete with en suite bathrooms, was for guests. The inn had two separate living rooms, one private and the other for guests, and the main dining room was off the guests' living area and had views of both the ocean and the gardens. The other living room was in Anne and Maisie's private living quarters, and they had their own smaller dining room with an oak table and chairs that sat eight. The kitchen served both their meals in their private dining room and the breakfasts for their guests in the main dining hall.

Each guest bedroom had a double bed, and a couple of the rooms had pullout couches for additional guests, mostly used by families. Guests could also use the laundry room, which had two washing machines and two dryers. The main dining area had enough seating for thirty. Maisie and Anne picked flowers daily from their garden to put in vases on the tables, along with the white tablecloths that adorned them all. They had also decorated each of the guest rooms and the main inn with Maisie's photos of the castles, lochs, and wildflowers of Scotland.

The inn was always booked. Everyone loved their breakfasts, accommodations, and the location, as it was easy to explore the surrounding area from there.

"Aye. Robert's having a party at his new home and his vet clinic—an open house—to show them off."

"Wow, how neat. Surely he doesn't want me to come." Anne wiped off the kitchen counters.

"No, he said he wanted the both of us to come. Lots of wolves should be there—bachelor males—and we haven't had time to meet any of them much really. Not to mention it would be nice to meet other she-wolves too."

Anne was stuck on the topic of Robert though. "What if he likes me more than you?"

Maisie smiled at her. If Robert found Anne more appealing, it would all have to do with their wolf genetics and finding the one who would be the right forever mate. She wouldn't begrudge them their happiness. Maisie could very well find a mate among the other bachelor males if Robert wasn't the one for her. At least that's what she was telling herself, but then she teased her sister. "I'll be sure to wear a shirt where he can see my bandaged arm."

Anne glanced at it. "You already removed the bandage."

"I could put another one on."

Her sister laughed. "You're too funny. But I look forward to it. Where is his house located?"

"Right next door to the MacQuarrie castle. It's on the same property that Edeen Campbell's manor house is located. Edeen is Lachlan MacQuarrie's mate."

"Oh, how cool. That's not that far from us, and it would be so much fun to live right next to the MacQuarries' wolf pack. So I guess Robert Campbell now belongs to the MacQuarrie pack?"

"Aye. So tomorrow I'm doing transitional training with Conan. I guess he is doing so well, I can start it now. Then I'll swap with you, and you can train with him next week, so we'll be on track with Conan minding both of us."

"I'm sure he will if we learn the commands."

"I can't imagine him behaving. I can't wait to see him during training. I snuck a peek at him at the kennel. He was sound asleep."

Anne laughed. "Great. They're giving him a good workout, then."

"I agree." Between Conan jumping on them and biting their hands in greeting and barking at everyone, Maisie and Anne had to do something.

"So what do you think of Robert?"

Ohmigod, he was hot, hot, hot. Maisie had been surprised when he'd gotten up from the bed and he was completely naked. It wasn't a total shock, as *lupus garous* stripped off their clothes and shifted into their wolves, so she was used to it. She just hadn't expected it in that moment.

"He's, um, sweet," Maisie said.

Anne studied her and chuckled. "You are blushing to high heaven. Did you kiss him?"

"Of course not." Not yet anyway. Maisie wondered if that was a mistake, if maybe she should have kissed him so he would know she was interested. That she was even having these thoughts was a surprise to her. She did want to mate and have kids one of these years, but it had been ages since she'd dated a wolf or had even thought of it.

"But you're going to kiss him soon, eh?"

Maisie frowned at her.

Anne shook her head. "You're definitely more interested in him than you're attempting to let on."

The sisters had moved into the area to take over the inn, and they hadn't really gotten to know many of the wolves nearby yet. They'd been busy remodeling the place, then getting the word out that they had rooms available and booking them, and finally taking care of their guests. But when they'd seen the announcement that the MacQuarries at Farraige Castle had new Irish wolfhound puppies for sale before Christmas—the breed they'd grown up with—they'd gone right over to inquire about them. Little had they known, the MacQuarries were wolves like them, but that had just made the experience even more worthwhile.

Maisie and Anne wanted more of a cushion of income until the inn really paid for itself and more, so Anne had been running the business while Maisie had been taking on freelance photography jobs—since she loved being a photographer—to help pay some of their bills until the inn was making a bit more money consistently. Not only had they wanted to see the puppies for sale, but Maisie had also thought she might be able to offer her photography services to the MacQuarries to help showcase the mother and father dog and their brood. Being that she was a wolf like them, the MacQuarries hadn't even looked at her website before they agreed.

Of course, she and her sister had put a down payment on one of the male pups right away too.

"Hey, when the boat hit you, it didn't hurt your camera, did it?" Anne asked as they sat down to have a lunch of Cullen skink—smoked halibut, potatoes, and onions in a thick soup. "I know that's not as major a concern as the boat hitting you, but I just wondered if it came out unscathed."

"It did, thankfully."

"Did you get enough underwater photos for the magazine article?"

"Aye. Before disaster struck, I was about ready to swim back to the car park, but then fate intervened. Oh, I forgot to tell you. Robert's sister, Edeen, has one of Conan's littermates. A little female. Her name is Ruby."

"Aww, she was the tiniest one of the lot. The only red female too."

"Right. Oh, and another thing. I said I would photograph all of Edeen's pets, including her Highland cows."

"Really? That's wonderful. You're getting booked to do all kinds of photography assignments. That should really help keep us in the black."

"Yeah. It's great. By the way, Edeen makes Celtic period clothes and other kinds of garments." Maisie left the table and got her laptop, then returned. "This is her shop. Edeen's Celtic Fashions."

"She does beautiful work." Anne was looking at several dresses, and Maisie knew she wanted one because Maisie wanted one herself. "You do realize that if we keep buying dogs and now Celtic period gowns, we'll spend all your photography income, don't you?"

Maisie smiled. "I imagine I can also offer my services to the pet owners who go to see Robert. Oh, maybe I can take some photos for his clinic walls if he hasn't already decorated them. Anyway, I thought you and I could order some new gowns for next Christmas since we planned to do a medieval theme for the guests staying here for the holidays."

"I love the idea. I want this one." Anne pointed to one of the prettiest gowns on Edeen's website. "The shimmering, olive-green medieval gown."

"Me too."

Anne laughed. "We always want the same clothes."

"I told Colleen that I would take their baby pictures for her. Also, her sister-in-law is due any day. So we'll have quite a lot of money coming in from all the photography work I'll be doing. I hope that's not putting you in a bind though, leaving you here alone."

"Not at all. You can help me when I need you and then go off to do your photography work. This is working out really well. We want Mom and Dad to know that we can do financially well here so they'll leave Glasgow and join us. Um, about the accident—"

"I don't want them to worry about it because I feel fine.

You know them, and no matter how much we assure them I'm fine, they'll make the trip out here right away."

"Okay, but if you start feeling bad, I'm telling them."

"That's fine with me."

"Are you going to work on the garden?" Anne asked.

"I sure am." Maisie loved being out of doors. So did her sister, so they took turns gardening.

"Then I'm going to clean the guest living area before everyone gets back here tonight," Anne said.

The living area had games, books, puzzles, several couches and chairs, and a place to make tea. A large fireplace made it perfect for cold, wet nights also.

"All right. See you in a little bit." Maisie grabbed her garden gloves and her bucket of garden tools. She loved the flower gardens, and she would often see their guests taking pictures of them, which encouraged her to plant even more flowers. Old stones bordered the gardens, and stone walkways encouraged visitors to stay on the paths and not step on the plants. They also had benches for visitors to sit and enjoy the view.

She was weeding around the bluebells, foxgloves, and carpets of purple saxifrage when she saw man-sized footprints in the soil. She frowned. Who in the world was walking through their garden when they had perfectly good walkways for that purpose? Then she saw one of the garden stones was gone. What the…? Her eyes detected something else half-hidden under the flowering purple Scots oregano. She leaned over to grab what turned out to be a driver's license. The driver's license belonged to Gus Anderson. He was the guest she had gone to dinner with last night.

Then she noticed teeth marks in the plastic and smelled that they were made by a dog—the size of the marks indicating a small dog. A little way from where she found the driver's license, a small pink pet collar underneath some petunias caught her eye. Her heart skipped a beat at the thought of a small dog lost out here. "Och, no."

She lifted the collar off the bark mulch and examined it, finding a little white fur had stuck to the collar. *Lady*, a heart-shaped pink-metal tag said. The collar didn't have a tag with the owner's name, address, and telephone number though. She smelled that the dog belonging to the collar had been the same one that had bitten the driver's license. Worried for her, Maisie hoped she could find the dog and that it was microchipped so she could find her owners. An inspection of the back of the rabies tag attached to the collar showed the dog had received its last rabies vaccination at a vet clinic in Edinburgh. She wondered if Robert, who'd worked at a clinic there, might be able to learn who Lady's owners were.

Near where the collar had been, the sun glinted off something else. "What in the world…" Maisie moved some flowers aside to find a phone. She grabbed it and pushed a button, the screen coming to life. The battery was charged, and—she frowned.

Ohmigod. It was Jude Springer's phone. He had been one of her former boyfriends, the guy she'd dated exclusively back in Glasgow until she caught him on a date with another she-wolf. He hadn't stayed here, so why was his phone in their garden? She recognized his scent on the phone and the picture of him fishing with a friend as his wallpaper. The friend was a good buddy of Jude's, and she had always wondered if he would have been a nicer wolf to date than Jude.

She hurried back into the inn and asked Anne, "Have you seen a little dog running loose around here?" Maisie held up the collar.

Anne frowned. "Och, no."

"I'm worried about her. She's not going to be very big, and if she's lost—well, it's not good. Her name is Lady. Her rabies tag has a vet clinic listed on it in Edinburgh. I came in to call Robert about it in case he can discover whom she belongs to. I found Gus Anderson's driver's license also." Maisie handed it to Anne.

"Oh, he'll probably be missing that. We can call him."

Then Maisie showed her Jude's phone.

"It smells like that bastard you dated, Jude Springer? But he didn't stay here at the inn. I would have turned him down for a room and said we were booked to eternity if he'd tried to make a reservation." Anne turned it on and stared at the guy's smug face, red curly hair framing his face, bright-blue eyes and a smirky grin as he stood next to his fishing buddy. "Jerk."

"But we would need to unlock it. I agree about not getting ahold of him to give it back. I feel like the Good Samaritan in me would let him know I found it. The vengeful part of me says it's finders keepers, and he's out of luck. I'm going to call Robert about the dog now."

"I can't believe you found so many things in the garden!"

"Not only that, but a garden stone is missing!"

"No," Anne said.

"Yeah. I mean, they're beautiful garden stones, but would someone steal just one for their garden?"

"Sounds strange. I'll go search around the area for Lady while you call Robert." Anne set the driver's license and Jude's phone on the dining room table and pulled up Gus's phone number from his registration on their computer. "I'll call Gus about his driver's license while I'm searching for the dog." She left the inn with her phone in hand.

Maisie could have called the clinic in Edinburgh to try to learn who the dog's owners were, but Robert might have more success getting the information as a vet who had worked in the city. Maybe it was even from the one he'd worked at, which would be a real boon. If the dog liked him, he might even be able to coax her to come to him when she might not go to anybody else. Was her owner just visiting the area, or had they moved here? She pulled out her phone and called Robert.

"Hey, Maisie, what's up?" he asked, sounding concerned, maybe worried her head was bothering her.

She hurried to explain. "I found a dog's collar in our flower bed. The rabies tag said it was from True Companions in Edinburgh."

"That's the clinic I worked for."

"Oh, great. Do you remember seeing a dog named Lady when you worked there? I'm really worried about her."

"A West Highland Terrier? I'll get right back with you." Robert hung up.

Maisie hurried outside to help her sister find the lost dog. Maybe Lady had returned to her owner and her collar had just been left behind—that would be the best-case scenario.

Chapter 5

ROBERT HAD TO GET AHOLD OF LADY'S OWNERS TO TELL them that Maisie had found her collar and learn if they actually had her in hand or not. He called the clinic. "Hi, this is Dr. Robert Campbell, calling about a patient."

"Hey, Doctor, we miss you already," his former vet tech said. "What do you need?"

"A friend found Lady's collar. She's a West Highland terrier. I believe Abercromby is her owner. Can you check? I need to try and reach them and see if she's missing out here or she just lost her collar and they have her."

"Sure. Let me pull their record up. Here it is. Bruce and Mary Abercromby are Lady's owners." Allan gave Robert their phone number and address in Edinburgh. "Unless they moved without telling us, they still live here. Maybe they were just visiting your neck of the woods."

"Thanks, Allan. I'll give them a call." The Abercrombys were wolves, and he thought they could probably find Lady alright on their own, so that gave him a little bit of relief.

"You're welcome. If you ever get tired of being out there and want to enjoy city life again, we would love to have you back."

"Sure thing." But Robert loved being here with the wolves. He hadn't realized how much of a difference it would make in his world until his sister moved out here and mated Lachlan and they invited Robert to all the pack functions. He used to be known to just work and chill while watching some TV at night. Everything was different for him now.

After they said goodbye, Robert called Bruce Abercromby. "Hi, this is Dr. Robert Campbell, formerly with the Edinburgh Animal Hospital. I'm living in the Highlands now, and a friend of mine found Lady's collar. Did you lose her or just her collar?"

"Och, Doc, she has run off. We've been in the area, staying at a bed-and-breakfast for the last two nights. We took one last hike before we returned home, and she tore off after a rabbit. We ran after her, but you know when a dog runs like that, it's impossible to keep up with her. We couldn't shift and chase her down as wolves. Way too many hikers were about. Where was her collar found?"

"At the MacTavish Inn. I'm going out there now to see if I can find her. How far are you from that location?"

"About a mile. We've been hiking all over, looking for her. We'll head there now."

"Maisie and Anne MacTavish are searching for her also. They're the owners of the inn. And they're wolves."

"That's great news. Thank them for me. We'll see you soon."

Robert grabbed a box of doggy treats, a leash, and a dog collar and drove off to Maisie and Anne's place. He didn't want to call Lachlan and have more of their clan's members help him quite yet because they might just scare Lady off. On the way to the inn, Robert called Maisie. "I'm on my way over. Lady's owners are going to your inn. She got lost while they were on a hike. Have you made any headway?"

"We've found some paw prints in the garden, and she left some muddy prints on the back walkway, but we're still searching for her," Maisie said.

"Okay, I've got treats for her."

"Oh, good idea. We should have thought of it."

"I'll be there shortly, and so will the Abercrombys. They're wolves, by the way."

"Oh, great. That should help. See you soon."

Not too long after that, Robert parked at the inn and headed for the gardens. He soon smelled Maisie's scent and another she-wolf's and figured it was Anne's.

He began calling out for Lady and shook the box of treats. It always worked to get a dog's attention at the clinic.

Way off in the distance, he heard a howl. He assumed it was one of the sisters, howling to him in her human form to let him know where they were. He howled back and hurried in the direction her howl had come from.

He smelled Lady's scent this way too, so the sisters appeared to be on her trail. He saw some paw prints too. But when he reached Anne—she had the same pretty blue eyes, but her hair was lighter than Maisie's—he was surprised to see she was alone. "Where's Maisie?"

"She ran after the dog. She told me to wait here for you."

Which confused him. He would have been able to find them even if Anne had continued on with her sister.

"The River Shiel is flowing into Loch Moidart," Anne explained. "The tide was out, but it's coming in fast, and the dog went to the island. Maisie followed her. Maybe you can rescue them before it's too late. There was no sense in me getting stuck there too. I'm going to return to the inn and see if I can meet up with the Abercrombys to let them know what's going on."

"Okay, I'll go after Maisie and Lady." Robert took off running for the sandy causeway before it was under water. If they were lucky, he could make it in time, entice Lady to go with him, and then he and Maisie would have to run as fast as they could to cross the causeway before it was impassable.

Before he reached the causeway, he didn't see any sign of either the dog or Maisie, but higher up on the island, the bracken reached six feet and higher, so they could have already been moving through the bracken or even be on the other side of the island and he wouldn't be able to see them. Situated way up above on the granite summit of the Island of Eilean Tioram—Tioram pronounced *Chee-rum*, meaning "the dry island"—the thirteenth-century Castle Tioram was formidable, thirty-three feet high, although in ruins. The island itself was about 200,000 square feet, so it wouldn't be hard to find someone on it.

He shouted for Maisie and Lady, shaking the box of treats and running full out.

When he crossed the sandbar, the water was up to his calves, the tide already beginning to come in. He raced across the disappearing causeway as fast as he could, the water ice cold, and he was reminded of hypothermia and was, again, not dressed for being in the water. He made his way through the rocks and the network of paths interwoven through the bracken, heather, and brambles up to the castle. He was getting closer to the southwestern, pentagonal curtain wall when he saw strands of the terrier's white fur on some brambles. Part of the northwestern wall had collapsed, which made walking the beach on that side risky.

Then he heard Maisie calling for the dog on the other side of the castle.

"Do you want some treats, Lady?" Robert asked, shaking the box and trying to make his way safely around the castle.

"Robert, we're over here!" Maisie called.

"Have you got her?"

"No. She's sitting down, panting, not moving, *finally*, but she's afraid to come to me, probably because I've been chasing her all this time. But she's listening to the box of treats you're shaking and your voice and warily watching me. Oh, she's circling again, digging at the ground, restless, panting more. She's worn out so she's not running any longer, but I think she's thirsty and hungry."

"Is she okay otherwise?"

"Tired, and her parents are going to be shocked when they see what a mess she is. She desperately needs a bath. She's wearing pieces of bracken and brambles. She's way overweight, so all this running has to have been hard on her. How are we doing on the tide?" Maisie asked.

"We have to hurry. It was already up to my calves."

"Tell me about it." She sounded so defeated, he worried she'd injured herself.

"Are you okay?"

"No."

"What's wrong?"

"I twisted my ankle. I was trying so hard to keep up with the dog and not lose her, I was moving too fast for the terrain. I don't think running for the causeway is going to work for me," Maisie said.

He'd figured he would carry the dog, and he and Maisie would run together once they reached the beach, but he couldn't carry her and the dog and make it back down the hill and to the causeway in time before the water was too deep. At high tide, the loch would be nearly fourteen feet deep.

He finally reached Maisie, who was sitting on a rock, Lady sitting nearby. Her ears perked up when she saw him, and she stood, her tail wagging like crazy. She was dirty, just like Maisie had said, but man, she had really gained weight since the last time he'd seen her. He brought out a treat for Lady. She came over for it, and he greeted her, at the same time putting on the collar and leash he'd brought with him. She sniffed at the dog biscuit but didn't take it.

"Either she has been overeating since I last saw her, or—"

"Don't tell me she's going to have pups." Maisie sounded worried, her brow furrowed. "I have her collar." Maisie pulled it out of her pocket. "I just couldn't put it on her."

He handed Maisie the lead and crouched down to check her ankle and saw the bruising and swelling. "It's swollen, alright."

"Can we make it down to the causeway?" she asked.

"We'll try. You hold on to Lady's leash, and I'll carry you down the hill."

"No way. It's too slippery and dangerous. We're likely to fall and hurt ourselves more."

"We've got to try." Though he seriously doubted they would make it in time, he wasn't one to give up that easily. The water would be so cold, he couldn't risk trying to get the dog and Maisie across the causeway if the tide was high enough to force them to swim. "Just easy does it."

He checked over Lady next. Her belly was swollen, and her nipples were distended. She was very affectionate with him. Other conditions could cause weight gain, a swollen tummy, and changes in appetite, but he knew she was having pups. He was surprised Bruce hadn't told him.

"Worst-case scenario, we can build a fire down below. I saw a firepit, probably built by someone who got stuck on the island exploring and didn't leave fast enough." He lifted Maisie into his arms.

"Like us. What time does the tide go back out?"

"Eighteen hours from full tide to low tide."

"No way."

"Yeah. I hope Grant can figure out a way to come and rescue us, but it'll probably take them a couple of hours at least," Robert warned, trying to inch his way down one of the paths, holding her against his chest while she held on tight to Lady's leash, the dog following behind them.

"I can't believe you and I are in another mess like this together." She sighed.

"I'm sorry."

"Oh, it's not your fault. It's Lady's. Normally, dogs will come to me with some coaxing, but she was just too wary, and I wasn't smart about bringing treats. You didn't bring anything to cook over a fire, did you?"

"No, I'm afraid all we've got is the box of dog biscuits."

"Well, Lady is all set then, though she didn't eat the other one you tried to give her."

Robert kept making the slow, tedious journey down the rocky, treacherous bracken trail, slipping a couple of times, Maisie tensing and letting out a soft cry when he did. It was a lot harder to do while carrying someone. Every once in a while, Lady pulled at the leash as if she'd decided to take a different trail, which had Maisie calling out, "Lady, come."

But since they were also worried about Lady now that he knew she was pregnant, they were taking it slow for her too.

When they finally reached the base of the granite hill, he set Maisie down and looked at the water that now separated them from the mainland. Then he got on his phone and called Grant, glad he could get reception. "Hey, are you up for a rescue mission?"

Grant asked, "Aye, always. What's wrong?"

"I'm with Maisie, and we're stranded on the rocky Eilean Tioram Island."

Grant didn't say anything for a moment, then he stifled a chuckle. "A date gone wrong?"

Robert smiled. "Nay. It's a long story. We had to capture an escaped dog. She went straight to the island. Maisie was chasing her and sprained her ankle, and the tide was already coming in when I reached them. So now—"

"You're stuck on the island. Gotcha. We'll bring an inflatable, but it'll take some time to get it ready and there."

"I figured about two hours."

"Aye, or a little longer. Can you keep each other warm until then?" Grant asked.

"Yeah. Someone built a firepit here, so we'll start a fire and cuddle with each other and the dog. One other thing: Can you bring a whelping box and water for all of us?"

"A birthing box?" Grant sounded worried this time.

"Lady, the dog we captured, is full of puppies and is going into labor," Robert said.

Grant laughed this time. "It's a good thing you're there and not me. Okay, we're on it. See you when we get there."

"Thanks."

Maisie smiled at Robert. "Did Grant laugh too hard?"

"He was trying not to until I mentioned Lady is having puppies."

Maisie nodded. "I texted my sister. She said the Abercrombys arrived so she gave them a room for the night. Anne will let them know we have Lady, that she's safe, but we're stuck here until we get rescued. She told us she would have dinner waiting when we get back. And she said you weren't sweet at all. You're hot."

"Oh?" Robert smiled, amused her sister would say that.

"Yeah, she asked me what I thought of you earlier, and I told her you were sweet, which you are. You saved me from drowning and gently removed the fishhook from my arm."

"How are your head and your arm?"

"My arm is already healed. No bandage." She showed

him. "And my head is fine. Now, if my ankle would heal just as quickly, I'll be good as new."

He removed his shirt and then bunched it up under her ankle to elevate it. "I'm going to get a fire going."

"I didn't tell my sister you were hot."

He arched a brow.

"You are, but I didn't want her to know that. She'll give me grief about it later."

He chuckled. He was glad Maisie thought he was hot. He sure felt the same way about her.

Then Maisie called Anne to let her know what was going on.

Lady was lying on the ground next to the rock. She looked exhausted but appeared happy and comfortable to be with them.

The sun was quickly going down, and so was the temperature. He wanted to get the fire started right away, but if they got too cold, they could shift and wear their wolf coats. Maisie was still holding the leash so the dog wouldn't dash off again.

Before long, Robert had started a fire.

"I thought you were going to have to try to light the fire in some more primitive way," Maisie said. "I never expected you to have a lighter on you."

"I always have one in case I have to sterilize a knife to use in an emergency. I always carry a pocketknife also. I had the tools in the first aid kit to take the hook out of your arm before the boat overturned too."

"You're certainly handy to have around in an emergency."

She took a deep breath and let it out. "You know we haven't really had one yet, but do...you think we might...go on a date sometime? Like just a nice lunch out for two?"

He laughed. "I would sure be all for it. How about I take you to the Ye Olde Highland Pie Shoppe, Heather's place? Heather is Enrick MacQuarrie's mate, if you haven't met her. Have you ever been there?"

"I have. The food is great. Tomorrow is out though. We're supposed to be at Farraige Castle, that is if we make it out of here tonight."

"We'll be rescued before then. We could do it the day after tomorrow then."

"You have a date."

"Good." Once he added more driftwood to the fire, he called his sister. "Hey, Edeen, I'm kind of stuck on Eilean Tioram, so I won't be home for dinner tonight."

"Grant called Lachlan about it and said they're still getting a boat loaded and they'll be on their way within the hour. Are the two of you and the dog okay?" Edeen sounded concerned. "He said the dog might be giving birth before they get there."

"Yeah. We've got a fire started, but we can shift if we need to get warm. Unless Lady begins to have her puppies and then I need to help her with that."

"And Maisie's ankle?"

"It's just sprained. She'll be right as rain before we know it."

"Okay. But no dinner for you tonight?"

"Her sister is fixing us dinner for when we get to their place."

"That's wonderful. We'll see you later then. Let us know if we can do anything for Maisie while she's incapacitated." Then they ended the call.

That reminded him that Maisie probably wasn't going to be able to do the training she planned to do with Conan tomorrow. They would have to see how her ankle was doing in the morning.

"You probably have already decorated your vet clinic, but if you don't have enough pictures for the walls, I could have a photo shoot of some animals. Yours, I'll already be doing Edeen's, and the MacQuarries'. That would make it more personalized."

"I would like that. Cats, dogs, Highland cows, sheep, horses, perfect." Then he lifted her off the rock, and she tilted her chin up for a kiss. He thought. He smiled down at her, his gaze navigating to her lips.

She raised her brows as if waiting for him to make the first move. But then she stated just what she wanted. "Kiss me to make it feel better."

He was sure ready to make her feel better any way that he could. He pressed his lips against hers and started slowly, but she jumped right in and became his partner in passion. She licked his lips, stimulating them in such a sexy way. He gently bit her lower lip, and she reciprocated, making him instantly hard with need. She affected him like no other she-wolf ever had.

They touched their tongues and stroked each other, deepening the connection. When they parted, he brought her to the fire and set her down before she got too cold. "I'll be right back." He grabbed his shirt and put it on.

Then he sat down behind her, his legs surrounding her, propping up her leg over his so that it elevated her sprained ankle. He pulled Lady onto her lap and the three of them snuggled together, waiting for their rescue. He'd never had such a nice campfire experience with such a kissable she-wolf. She was a delight to be with. He wrapped his arms around her, and she shivered.

"Are you too cold?"

"No. I'm getting warmer by the minute, in the nicest way possible."

Chapter 6

FROM ONE CRAZY ADVENTURE TO THE NEXT, MAISIE couldn't believe she and Robert were stuck on an island with Lady, all cuddling together in the cold beside a fire. This was so romantic despite her ankle throbbing, but the doctor was taking care of her properly, and she loved the way he was so gentle and caring. She was definitely rethinking her position of being alright about it if her sister became interested in dating Robert too.

Maisie rested her back against Robert's chest, and he leaned around her and kissed her cheek. But she turned her head to have mouth-to-mouth contact with him again. She loved the way he kissed her, loved his lips on hers, alternating between slow and deliberate, gentle and hot and heavy, lots of energy, working her up good, making her feel total happiness. Oh God, yes, he was truly a consummate kisser. She really felt comfortable with him, something that usually didn't happen right away when she met a wolf who appealed to her physically. With him, there was so much more.

And hot? Forget about being chilled by the ocean breeze. He was heating her blood right up.

Here, she'd thought she would be counting the minutes before they got picked up, but instead, she was really enjoying this time with Robert. She was even glad she'd gotten stuck with him here so that they'd have this alone time together.

"So did you ever...um, have a long-term relationship with anyone when you were back in Edinburgh?" She figured it was important to know more about him.

"Not long-term. Edeen says I wouldn't allow it because I was so busy getting my education and working to build a practice. But really, it wasn't that. I just never had a connection with a she-wolf who intrigued me enough. Now you... hell, that's a whole different story." He leaned over and petted Lady on her lap. "My sister always said I was more comfortable with animals than people. But that was just my excuse since I didn't have any interest in a she-wolf long-term. What about you with guys?"

This was why Maisie had brought the topic up, truthfully. She wanted to know if he had any lingering feelings for another she-wolf he'd dated, but she also wanted to talk to him about *her* past relationships so he knew more about her.

"I've dated three wolves."

"Three?" He chuckled and kissed her ear with a whisper-soft kiss, like it didn't matter to him, and she was glad for it.

"Aye. In the first case, the wolf I had dated was way too controlling. He smothered me, and once we started dating each other exclusively, he didn't want me talking to any other male wolves, as if he was afraid I would ditch him as soon as I found someone I liked better. He tried to isolate me from my sister and parents too. We had been seeing each other for three months, but the relationship just didn't progress. I kept pulling away from him when he got amorous. I just didn't feel for him what a she-wolf should for a male wolf that she was interested in mating. He was fun on dates, but beyond that, he just wasn't the one for me. And trying to cut off my ties to my family? That wasn't happening."

"Controlling is not my style."

"Yeah, I didn't believe it would be. You're so sensitive and caring."

"Edeen would say I'm forgetful. I don't know how many times I've forgotten a date with a she-wolf or even an outing with Edeen."

Maisie laughed. "Because of work?"

"Aye. I mean, sometimes it was because of that. But sometimes, I would go home or grab groceries and then suddenly realize I'd forgotten a date. I would always feel genuinely terrible about it, but it proved that I wasn't really into the girlfriend that much. Edeen was just used to it."

Smiling, Maisie shook her head. "You'd better not do that to me unless you have a very good reason."

He laughed. "Like rescuing a dog and getting stuck on an island?"

"You only get to do that with me." She kissed him again. "Anyway, with that guy, I called it quits with him three years ago. So then I dated a wolf for two months, not as long as the other guy I had dated, but he was so jealous. He kept asking me if I was seeing other guys behind his back. It just seemed bizarre to me that he was so distrusting of me when

I never gave him a reason to doubt me. Until I saw him with another she-wolf, having dinner at a restaurant where Anne and I went to celebrate my getting a really good-paying photography job. I could have pretended that I hadn't seen him, but then they were kissing. That was the end of it for me.

"I fought with myself over whether I should confront him at the restaurant or talk to him later. I realized that he had been projecting his own deceitfulness on me. Sure, that was the first time I'd caught him at it, but how many other times had he been with another woman that I didn't know about? Since he'd been thinking that I'd been with another man a month before that, I suspected that he had been doing it for a while."

"Did you confront him at the restaurant?"

She smiled. "Yeah. At first, when I rose from my seat, Anne grabbed my arm and asked if I was sure. But I was. It was the easiest way for me to break up with him. He couldn't deny he had been with another woman then. I joined them at their table and kissed him on the cheek. He looked horrified that I'd caught him at it, and the woman looked just as shocked that I would show up and kiss him. She immediately asked who I was."

Robert laughed. "I'm glad you confronted him."

"I had to. When I can't trust the guy I'm dating, there's no sense in dating him further."

"I agree."

"I haven't been thinking about him, since we broke up six months ago, but when I found Lady's collar in the flower bed, I also found Jude's cell phone."

"Oh?"

"Aye. He hasn't stayed at the inn. Neither Anne nor I would have allowed him to make a reservation there."

"That sounds...odd." Robert sounded a little worried about it.

She had been too, but then searching for Lady had taken over any concern she had about Jude having been in their garden. "Yeah, I know. That's what I was thinking. He never came into the office to talk to either of us. It's a conundrum. The only reason I can think of is that he was visiting a guest. Yet he was from Glasgow, so what would be the likelihood that he would end up at the inn that Anne and I own to visit a guest who just happened to be staying there?" Then she paused. "You...wouldn't happen to know how to hack into a cell phone, would you?"

Robert laughed.

"I'll take that as a no," she said, laughing. "I have to admit, I would love to know why he was at the inn, if I should be worried that he is stalking me."

"Aye, I see where you're coming from. I don't know how to do it, but maybe someone in the pack can."

She sighed. She was glad that Robert hadn't just dismissed her concern. "I could call him at his work and ask him if he was at the inn, not mentioning that we had his phone, just seeing if he would be honest with me about it."

"That could work."

"I don't want to give up his phone though."

Robert chuckled.

"Because I really want to know what he was up to. He has

lied to me before, and that's just the one time I know about. I wouldn't be surprised if he lies about coming by the inn. If I can break into his phone, I might be able to learn the truth." She had to explain her reasoning. She didn't want Robert to think badly of her.

"I totally understand."

Did he? She hoped so. She let out her breath. "So the third guy was nice enough. I thought that three was the charm, but there really wasn't any physical attraction between us. I think he didn't want to find anyone else, so he just kept asking me to go out with him. He didn't feel anything more for me than I did for him. We were just comfortable with each other. When Anne and I bought the inn, I called it quits with him. We had only been seeing each other for a month. He wasn't unhappy when I told him I was leaving. There just wasn't anything between us more than a nice friendship."

"That makes sense. So back to the situation with the phone you found in the garden. Do you think Jude learned you were here and was trying to discover if you're going out with someone else?" Robert still seemed concerned about her former boyfriend.

She was so glad she had met Robert. "I think that might be dangerous for his health if he returns again."

"Oh?"

"I believe there would be a whole MacQuarrie wolf pack that would chase them off."

Robert kissed her again. "Me leading the pack, not Grant this time. Believe me, I'll find someone who can get into his phone, and maybe we can learn what he was up to. I don't want you to have to worry about some guy stalking you."

She kissed him back and sighed, glad he would be willing to help her out if she needed him to. "I'm so glad Anne and I made the move here."

"I'm glad you did too, and that I did also, or I might never have met you."

"Which would have been a real shame. So I know you have a twin sister, but what about any other family?" Maisie asked.

"A cousin, but he's in America and we don't expect to see him again."

"Is there bad blood between you?" she asked.

"There is. He tried to take Edeen's property away from her, claiming it was his inheritance. It wasn't, and he didn't have any right to it."

"Oh no. I'm glad it was cleared up then."

"Aye. What about you?" Robert asked.

"Our parents are in Glasgow still, but they plan to move here once they know we're staying for good. They are afraid they would move, our business would go under, and we would return to Glasgow and then they would have relocated here for no reason."

"I understand that. Did you tell them about our fishing incident?"

"No. I know if I had, they would have been here in a hurry to make sure I was okay, when I'm fine and I didn't want to worry them for nothing."

"How is your ankle?"

"It still hurts."

"Okay, hold on." Robert stood and pulled off his shirt.

She smiled to see his beautiful abs again. Robert was truly sexy. She watched him as he walked over to the water and dunked his shirt in, then wrung it out and brought it back to her. He wrapped it around her ankle like it was an ice pack. She shivered. "Cold."

"Yeah, it might help with the swelling and bruising. I should have thought of it earlier." Then he worked on the fire again to keep it burning warmly. "So what do you like to do for fun?"

"Just about anything outdoorsy—snorkeling, scuba diving, boating, fishing, hiking, running as a wolf. What about you?"

"I also love the outdoors, and I love archery."

"You'll have to teach me archery. Oh, and I sword fight. My sister and I love to do that. Our guests love it when we don kilts and fight each other. They share videos on social media, and then we end up getting more guests."

"That's a great marketing ploy."

"It is. We didn't know how successful it would be."

Robert finally returned to his spot on the ground, Maisie leaning back against him, between his legs. His shirt around her ankle was wet but no longer ice-cold. The dog was sleeping across her lap, perfectly happy to snuggle with them for warmth as if they were her packmates. At least she wasn't searching for a nesting spot, and she seemed perfectly comfortable where she was.

But Robert was shirtless, and Maisie was afraid he was cold. She wanted to warm him more. "I need to turn over.

Are you okay? I haven't cut off your circulation anywhere, have I?"

"No. Let me help you."

They both sat up, and he moved Lady off Maisie. The dog didn't look happy about it.

"Okay, lie back down and I'm going to lie on top of you, where I can hug you to keep you warm," Maisie said to Robert.

He smiled. She laughed. She loved that he was enjoying this too. Then she laid down on top of him and snuggled against his chest. This was way better. Lady made a nest between their legs and got comfortable. The sun was setting, and it was beautiful, with pink paint spread across the blue sky and orange, blue, and pink coloring the loch, mixing and creating purples. The castle was silhouetted by the sky. Maisie wished she had her camera. She had never imagined being on a castle island at sunset, hugging a half-naked wolf. Anne and Maisie had talked about coming here when they had free time, but neither of them had taken the time to do it.

This was surreal and Maisie loved it, and she couldn't think of any other wolf she would rather be with there.

———

Robert and his companions had been sound asleep for an hour when he woke to hear Lady scratching and panting.

Aw, nuts.

He had been dreaming about fighting off Jude, Maisie's

stalker, as a wolf, tearing into him so he wouldn't harass her any further.

Maisie tried to sit up in a hurry, but she cried out. "Ouch, darn it! I forgot all about my ankle."

"We'll get you home and get it elevated with some ice, but for now, it looks like Lady's getting ready to have a pup," Robert said.

"Oh," Maisie groaned. "Take your shirt, mine too, to use as a bed for her."

"Mine is big enough." He didn't want Maisie getting cold. He carefully removed his shirt from Maisie's ankle, and he heard her suck in her breath. "I'm so sorry."

"Nay, don't be. Lady needs it for her and her pups."

The heat from the fire had dried his shirt, and between that and the warmth of Maisie's leg, it was warm when he laid it on the ground for Lady. She scratched and scratched at it, circling around and around, looking just for the right spot.

"She's going to have the first pup before she lies down," Maisie said.

Robert smiled. "I know. They have to find just the right spot."

Then Lady finally settled down and began moaning and groaning.

"How many pups do West Highland terriers normally have?" Maisie asked.

"About three."

The water sac came out, and he knew a puppy was in the birth canal. "The first puppy is coming." He looked at Maisie, and she was watching, looking on in awe. He was glad for it. He sure wished he was at the clinic delivering Lady, in case she had any real difficulties though. As far as he recalled from having taken care of her at the clinic, she'd never had puppies before.

The puppy finally delivered fifteen minutes later. Lady was being a good mother and licking the puppy vigorously, tearing off the membrane. Lady cleaned the little male pup up and severed the umbilical cord. The pup cried, which was a good sign that the puppy was going to be fine. Robert wanted to wipe the puppy's tummy with iodine to prevent infection, but he would have to do that at Maisie's house. "Do you have iodine at home?"

"Yes, in our first aid supplies."

"Good." He took a corner of his shirt and cut it with his knife without disturbing Lady, then made some tiny strips of cloth. He tied off the umbilical cord an inch away from the first pup's belly.

"Two more, right?" Maisie asked.

He placed the puppy next to Lady's belly so he could nurse. When he began suckling, Robert was relieved. "Or just another or maybe three more. It depends. We'll just have to wait and see. Sometimes it can be hours, or it can happen really quickly. You never can—"

Then the next pup arrived, and Lady did her duty with him. Once she had cut the umbilical cord and cleaned him up, Robert tied off the cord and placed the second male next to his brother to begin nursing.

"Her owner didn't say anything about her having puppies, did he?" Maisie asked.

"No. This was a real surprise."

"Could he possibly not have known?"

"Yeah. Some pet parents can be in denial that their dog ended up getting impregnated." Robert smiled at her.

"Boy, will this be a shock to him if that's the case."

"Yes, they might not have taken her in to see the other vet after I left and thought she was just overeating. I've had a couple of cases like that."

Maisie watched the pups nursing. "You can't tell what they are, can you? I mean, if she got mixed up with another breed."

"No. Not yet. DNA would tell me. Or if Lady had been around a male dog that they know of and they didn't realize she could end up with pups."

Another pup suddenly came.

"They are so adorable," Maisie said. "It's a little miracle."

"It truly is."

Lady worked to take care of the first little female. She wasn't having any more contractions, and he had three placentas for the three puppies, so he hoped that was the last one. The female snuggled against her brothers and began nursing. That was a good sign for all three of them, though she had some catching up to do.

About an hour later, they heard voices on the mainland nearby—Grant, Lachlan, and Enrick—and a splashing sound. Lady woofed, alert, concerned, though he could tell she was tired from delivering her pups.

Lachlan and Enrick were coming to their rescue in a rubber dingy, motoring to the island. Grant was waiting on the mainland shore for them to return.

Robert was relieved and gave Maisie a hug. "We've been saved."

She kissed his mouth. "We survived with a kaboodle of pups."

Robert chuckled. "Totally unexpected when I first followed the two of you onto the island."

"Sorry it took us so long to get here." Enrick pulled a plastic storage bin lined with newspaper and rags to serve as a temporary whelping box out of the boat. He carried it to them, then smiled to see the pups, as Lachlan joined them. "Hell, we have little pups. Well done, you three. We didn't realize she would have them before we got here."

"I was just watching how this was all done," Maisie said. "Lady and Robert did all the work. It truly is amazing."

"It is." Lachlan handed bottled waters to Maisie and Robert and another one for Lady. "They're adorable. I wonder what they are."

"A DNA test will tell," Robert said.

"Well, no matter what they are, they're cute." Enrick pulled a water dish out of the box and handed it to Robert. "We realized we had to patch the boat and wait for it to dry before we could bring it here. Plus, Edeen was trying to put together a temporary whelping box in a hurry. She said the pet owners could keep it."

Lachlan raised his brows when he noticed Robert was shirtless, then he saw the shirt underneath Lady and her litter of pups. "Talk about an emergency delivery."

"It sure was." Maisie drank from her bottle of water. "Lady was so lucky to have Robert."

"How are *you* doing?" Lachlan asked Maisie.

"My ankle hurts, but I'm sure it will heal up soon. Thanks for asking."

Robert gave Lady some water in the dish, and she lapped it up. Then Robert drank from his own bottle of water. "I'm going to put Lady's puppies in the box because her fur is standing on end. She's worried about you guys around her puppies, and I don't want her to bite anyone. She's used to Maisie and me now." Robert took one pup and set him in the box, and naturally he began to cry. He'd lost his nipple as well as his siblings' and his mother's warmth. Lady was already standing up, frantic, wanting to get her pup out of the box but not wanting to leave her other pups behind. Then Robert set the others in with the first. Lady was jumping at the box to get to them. He lifted her up and set her inside with them, and she quickly inspected them, making sure they were all there, then quietly settled down with them. Robert put his shirt in the box behind her so she would feel she hadn't lost her nest.

"I'll get Maisie," Lachlan said.

"Okay, thanks." Robert carried the whelping box to the boat.

Lachlan smiled at Robert. "Any excuse to remove your shirt in front of the lassie."

Robert laughed. "Well, if it hadn't been for her ankle and then Lady having her pups—"

"You would have removed your shirt so that Maisie could have worn it to keep her warmer." Enrick continued to put out the campfire.

Maisie chuckled. "He is *so* my hero."

The MacQuarrie brothers laughed.

Smiling, Robert shook his head at them and climbed into the boat.

"You've got your car there, right?" Lachlan joined him in the boat. "You don't need us to drive you home after we take Maisie and Lady to the inn, do you, Robert?"

"No. Thanks. I've got my car there and I'm having dinner with the ladies before I return home." Robert was looking forward to it.

As soon as they reached the mainland, Grant leaned over to help Robert climb out of the boat as he held on to the whelping box. Enrick climbed out of the boat and Lachlan lifted Maisie and handed her to Enrick while Grant steadied the boat.

Enrick and Lachlan followed them, carrying the boat to the truck.

"We'll drive you back to the inn," Grant said.

"Thank you," Maisie said. "If you hadn't, I was afraid Robert would have to carry me all the way back there."

Lachlan laughed. "No. We'll get there so much faster this way, and you can return Lady to her owner."

Lachlan and Enrick loaded the boat into the back of the truck and secured it.

Maisie peered over Robert's lap to look into the whelping box. "They are so adorable. She seems to be happy enough about the whelping box and the transportation. Poor worn-out momma."

"She is. I'm glad it turned out so well. I'll clean the pups up a bit at your place, use some iodine on their tummies, and if you've got some unwaxed dental floss, I'll retie their umbilical cords." Robert put his hand on Maisie's knee. "Can you put your leg up on my knees and elevate your injured ankle?"

"I'll try." Maisie and Robert moved around in their seats until she could rest her leg over his.

He wasn't sure that was helping her any, but he wanted to keep her ankle elevated. "I should have made a list of stuff that I needed," Robert told the MacQuarrie brothers as they climbed into the truck. "I really didn't expect Lady to deliver. A dog that is that close to delivering isn't usually that active. She could have ended up having pups on the way."

"Did her owner tell you she was ready to have pups?" Grant started the engine and drove his truck down the one-lane road. At least at this time of night, no one else was out here.

"No."

"They're lucky the two of you found her. She could have had her puppies anywhere," Lachlan said.

"That's for sure. And she could have been in trouble herself." Robert pulled out his phone and called Bruce Abercromby. "We're bringing Lady and her three puppies to the inn."

"She had puppies?" Bruce sounded shocked.

Robert smiled. So her pet parents didn't know it. "Yes, you're the proud owner of two male puppies and a female pup. We'll be there in a few minutes."

"Thanks so much, Doc."

Robert knew Bruce was glad to get his dog back safe and sound, but he wasn't sure he was as excited about the prospect of having puppies he hadn't been planning.

Chapter 7

MAISIE'S ANKLE WAS KILLING HER. THOUGH SHE HAD HER leg elevated on top of Robert's lap as Grant MacQuarrie drove to her inn, her ankle was just throbbing. That's when she remembered what she was supposed to do tomorrow. "Oh, Lachlan, I guess I'll have to cancel the transitional training tomorrow with Conan. I'll have to wait until my ankle feels better in a couple of days. But I still want to have lunch at the castle."

"Yeah, that will be fine. I figured that could be the case once we learned you had sprained your ankle," Lachlan said. "That will give us more time to work with Conan before you start transitional training. We normally wouldn't start that until next week anyway."

"I'll pick you up from your inn and take you to the castle for lunch." Robert moved around to try and help Maisie feel more comfortable. Then he gently massaged her ankle to help reduce the pain and swelling, and she smiled at him.

She swore his touch was sensuous, his small smile telling her he was enjoying taking care of her as much as she was enjoying the intimacy between them.

"Thanks. Then I guess I'll sit and watch you in weapons training instead," she said.

She swore she heard Robert groan a little bit under his breath.

When they arrived at the inn, the Abercrombys came out of their room and Anne hurried to greet the MacQuarries, Robert, and Maisie. Bruce and Mary were smiling broadly.

Lady's owners and Lady were so excited to see each other, though they still looked astounded to see she'd delivered three healthy pups. They were so grateful to everyone for bringing her back.

"I told you she was pregnant," the wife said, frowning at her mate.

Maisie wanted to laugh. She was sitting on the back seat of the truck with her legs hanging out, the door open, glad to watch the heartwarming reunion. Anne came over to check on Maisie and squeezed her hand. "Sprained ankle, not a break," Maisie assured her sister.

"I'm so glad for that," Anne said.

"I know, I know. I thought she was just overeating," Bruce said to his wife. "We couldn't be more grateful to all of you. Now that we know wolves own the inn, we'll be staying here every time we want to visit the area. But the next time, we'll make sure Lady stays home with friends. And if she begins gaining weight again like this, we're taking her straight to see the vet."

Everyone laughed.

"You must have been walking her daily and that's how she managed to cover that much distance even so close to giving birth," Robert said.

"We have been. We walk or run five miles a day," Bruce said. "She loves her walks. We thought she needed them too."

"That was good for her. It probably made it easier for her to deliver. I need to clean the puppies up a bit and retie their umbilical cords. Lady will need to relieve herself also, but she's not going to want to leave them for long," Robert said. "We might as well try and let her out of the box now to do it."

Even though Maisie and her sister did not normally allow a pet in a room, they allowed it for Lady and her pups this time.

Bruce said to the dog, "You, young lady, need a bath."

"That will have to be a little later. If you can carry the whelping box after Lady relieves herself, I'll carry Maisie inside. She sprained her ankle when she was chasing down Lady."

"Oh no, I'm so sorry for all the trouble our dog caused you," Mary said to Maisie.

"It was my fault. I should have heeded how slippery the rocks could be. I was just glad Lady finally stopped running and *she* hadn't been injured," Maisie said.

Robert lifted Lady out onto the grass. She sniffed a little grassy area, hurried to relieve herself, probably the fastest she had ever done, and wanted right back into the box.

"She's a really good momma dog." Robert helped her into the box. "Not all dogs are. She hasn't had a litter before, has she?"

Bruce and Mary shook their heads. Bruce lifted the whelping box.

"Sometimes first deliveries are confusing for a new

momma dog, but she did really well." Robert leaned over and lifted Maisie out of the truck and into his arms.

"If you are all set, we'll head home," Grant said, as he, Lachlan, and Enrick waited to make sure they weren't needed for anything further.

"We're good. And thanks for coming to our rescue. We'll see you tomorrow," Robert said, and then carried Maisie into the inn.

She hated that she needed to be helped like that.

Anne followed them inside. "I've got everything Maisie said you needed to take care of the pups. Where do you want to do it?"

"In the living room if you have good lighting in there. I'll take care of them and then Bruce can take them to their room. The plastic container and my shirt are my gifts to you." Robert set Maisie on a couch.

Bruce and Mary laughed as Bruce set the whelping box on the floor next to the coffee table.

Anne turned on all the lights in the private living room and brought in the supplies and set them on the coffee table.

In the living room, Robert removed a tie off one of the males, disinfected his belly with iodine, then retied the cord with dental floss. With each puppy, he did the same procedure and placed them back with their mom. "Do you have some human nail clippers?"

"Yes, I'll go get them." Anne hurried off and returned with them and handed them to Robert. He clipped the tips off the puppies' sharp, little nails with the clippers so they didn't scratch Lady while she nursed them. "If you see their nails are getting too long, just clip them like that." Once he was done, he went over dietary requirements for a nursing mother and said, "Watch that all the pups are staying warm and nursing. They'll gravitate toward the heat of their mother's body, so if you have extra heat on them to keep them warm, it can confuse them about where the food is coming from, so keep that in mind. Don't handle them unnecessarily for the first couple of weeks. Between two and three weeks, deworming can be done. Paper training and chew toys can be introduced at three weeks. By three to four weeks, weaning can be started. They'll open their eyes between ten to fourteen days, and they'll open their ears between ten and twenty days after birth."

"When can we wash her?" Mary asked.

"Two to five days from now. But don't keep her away from her pups for too long. Do you know who the daddy might be?" Robert asked.

"A couple of friends of ours visited us from Glasgow, and one, Stuart Michaelson, brought his dog with him—also a Westie—and they all stayed for a few days. Gus and his twin brother, Ike, weren't big on being around the rambunctious dogs, so we kept the two dogs outside a lot in the fenced-in backyard since the weather was so nice. The dogs ran in the yard, playing with each other," Bruce said.

Robert smiled. "Well, it looks like they might have been doing something more than just playing with one another, if no other dog has been with Lady. The two of you might be the proud owners of a litter of purebred Westies."

"That would be totally unexpected but happy news.

What do we owe you for the emergency delivery, Doc?" Bruce asked.

"Nothing. It was my Good Samaritan deed for the day."

"Let me at least give you a brand-new T-shirt that I picked up to replace yours." Without waiting for a response, Bruce took Lady and her puppies to their guest room. Mary went with them and then returned, carrying a blue shirt with the imprint of the Scottish lion in white and gold.

"This is really nice. I can ship it back to you later," Robert said.

"No way. It's our small token of thanks."

"Okay, thanks. Just another tip: if Lady normally wants to stay with the two of you—some dogs shadow their owners—keep her and her puppies nearby so she doesn't leave her pups alone for long just to be close to you. They need to nurse, and they require her body heat to keep them warm."

"Thanks so much, Dr. Campbell. We'll have to let our friend, Stuart, know that his dog is a daddy. McKie is just as sweet as Lady. We'll give Stuart one of the pups if he wants one. And you too. If you hadn't found her and helped her with the delivery, she most likely would have lost her pups, and we might have lost her too," Mary said.

Robert pulled on the shirt. "I would be happy to give one of the pups a home if you can't find someone to take all of them in. Tell Bruce thanks for the shirt."

"I will. It's the least we can do after all the trouble you had to go through." Then Mary returned to her room, and Robert checked on Maisie.

"Maisie and I had started a beef stew in the slow cooker earlier today, and it's ready to eat. I already ate shortly before you and she returned, since I didn't know when you would get in," Anne said.

"I don't blame you, and that sounds great. It smells delicious too." Robert placed a decorative pillow from the couch on the coffee table, then elevated Maisie's foot on top of it. "Do you have an ice pack I can use on Maisie's ankle, Anne?"

"Yes, in the freezer."

He walked into the kitchen to get the ice pack.

"Sorry I'm so much trouble," Maisie said when he returned. She really wished she hadn't sprained her ankle.

"Nonsense. It could have been *me* who sprained my ankle and then you would have had to carry me down those slippery rocks," Robert said.

Anne and Maisie laughed.

"If you had to rely on me to do that, we wouldn't have made it." Maisie moved her leg a little to make it more comfortable. "We would have had to tell the MacQuarries to pick you up near where Castle Tioram was, and I would have had to do all that you did for Lady and her puppies while you guided me."

"I have every faith in you that you would have taken care of Lady and her puppies just fine." Robert placed the little felt pack of ice featuring a polar bear on her ankle.

"Thanks. I'm glad we didn't have to put me to the test. I like your new shirt." Maisie reached out to touch it.

"Yeah, a perfect gift for me. Otherwise, you poor lassies would have had to see me bare-chested through dinner." Robert flexed his muscles.

"We weren't about to complain," Anne said, smiling.

Maisie agreed with her sister. "I can't believe you told them that you would give one of the puppies a home only if no one wanted one of them. You should have said for sure you wanted one. They will all find homes otherwise."

He chuckled.

"You should know this about Maisie: she's always ready to take home all the puppies in the world and care for them," Anne said.

"That sounds like Edeen. She wanted the little red Irish wolfhound puppy the MacQuarries had because they couldn't find her a home right away, like they'd been able to for all the brindle males," Robert said.

"Well, Ruby is adorable, and I bet she is cute with Edeen's fox terriers," Maisie said.

Anne began dishing up the stew for them, then brought in glasses of water. She'd set them on the dining room table, but then glanced at Maisie. "Do you both want to sit in the living room and eat so Maisie can keep her foot elevated?"

"Yeah, that works for me." Maisie didn't want to have to hop to the dining room table or have Robert carry her.

"Sure, that's fine," Robert said. "Whatever is easiest for Maisie."

Anne carried their glasses of water into the living room while Robert moved their bowls of stew in there.

"I can leave you two alone, if you would like." Anne smiled.

Maisie shook her head and spooned up some of her stew. "No. I'm sure you want to hear all about our nearly three hours on the island." She didn't want her sister to feel like she was being left out or had to leave.

"Aye. We're glad for your company," Robert said to Anne.

"Okay. Oh, and I called Gus's cell phone to tell him that we have his driver's license but could only leave a message. I tried about four times, but I just kept getting his voicemail," Anne said.

"I can call him later too, though if you left a message for him, that should be enough," Maisie said.

"I agree."

"Gus?" Robert said. "It's probably a stretch, but Bruce was telling us that a man named Gus and his twin brother, Ike, were at his house and were from Glasgow."

"This Gus *is* from Glasgow. Did Bruce tell you what his last name was?" Anne asked.

Robert took a spoonful of the stew. "No, it didn't seem important at the time."

"If it's the same Gus, maybe Bruce and Mary know another way of getting in touch with him. I'll call Bruce and ask what Gus's last name was to make sure it wasn't just a coincidence." Maisie got on her phone. "Hi, Bruce, I hate to disturb you and Mary, but we found a driver's license in the flower garden belonging to a Gus Anderson of Glasgow, and we wondered if he was the same person that you knew." She put it on speakerphone so her sister and Robert could listen in. "We wanted to let him know we have it here. We haven't been able to get in touch with him."

"Yeah, that's our friend, Gus. He lives near Stuart, the owner of the male Westie. We've known each other since we were kids. They both used to live in Edinburgh," Bruce said, "and they're wolves like us. But now Gus and Ike live in Glasgow."

"Oh, great. Do you have another way to get in touch with him? Maybe his twin brother's phone number?" Maisie asked. "We can just send his driver's license to his address, but if he is still in this area, he probably would want to drop by and pick it up."

"All I have is his cell phone number. If you have the same one, that's all I can say. But I can give Ike, his twin brother, a call, and I can check with Stuart and see if he knows where Gus went to, but we don't talk to each other all that much. We get together once a year is all," Bruce said.

"Okay, thanks. We'll continue to try and get in touch with him, but if you have any luck, just let us know," Maisie said.

"I will. Thanks."

Then they ended the call.

Maisie then told her sister about their experiences on the island. "Another thing. Robert said he would check to see if someone in the pack could unlock Jude's phone and discover if there are any messages that indicate why he was at our inn."

Anne frowned at Maisie. "Do you think he's stalking you now? That he learned that you were here?"

"It's possible, and that bothers me. We need to really watch for any sign of him." Maisie finished her stew, and Anne took her bowl from her. "That's why I would love to know why he was here."

"Me too," Anne said. "You know, I was wondering, if you had shifted into your wolves on the island, how poor Lady would have reacted to seeing you."

Maisie drank some of her water. "She could have smelled we were the same people, but she might have been worried about her puppies around us. I forget about that because the family dog we had when we were young and Conan were both raised around wolves, but having puppies can change the whole dynamic between animals."

Robert carried his bowl into the kitchen, and Anne quickly asked, "Would you like some more stew?"

"Uh…" He eyed the slow cooker still filled with bubbling stew.

"Yes, give him some more," Maisie said. "He had all that extra work getting a fire started and carrying me around, then delivering pups."

"Of course." Anne served up some more stew for him.

"Thanks." He took the bowl.

"I'll be back in a minute. I'm just going to put the rest of the stew away for later," Anne said and returned to the kitchen.

When he finished his stew, he took the bowl into the kitchen, then said to Maisie, "I need to get out of your hair and let you get some rest. Keep your foot elevated." He paused. "Do you want me to carry you to your bed?"

Maisie blushed. His question was so innocent, but immediately she thought of him carrying her to her bedroom for other business. The look on her sister's face said she was thinking the same thing.

Maisie smiled. "Thanks for the offer, but I think I'll stay up a little while longer. Anne can help me get to bed later." If push came to shove and she really couldn't manage, which she could, she could sleep on the foldout sofa. Or she could remove her clothes and shift into her wolf and walk three-legged to her bedroom. That might be the best idea actually. Three legs were better than one.

Anne had returned to the kitchen to clean it up a little more.

Robert smiled at Maisie. "I'll see you a little bit before eleven tomorrow."

"That sounds good."

When he leaned over and kissed her, Maisie was so glad. He didn't give her just a peck on the mouth or the cheek. The kiss built up to the same passion they'd experienced on the island.

Maisie parted her lips for him, and he stroked her tongue with his and she did the same thing with him. Kissing him was like experiencing a slice of heaven.

When he pulled away from her, they saw her sister watching them from the kitchen, her mouth agape. Anne smiled.

"Thanks again," Robert said, "uh, for dinner."

"Thanks for staying with my sister and taking care of her on the island," Anne said.

Robert glanced back at Maisie. "It was my pleasure."

"Mine too," Maisie said.

"I can tell," Anne said, still smiling. "Oh, here's Jude's phone if you can find someone to access it."

"I'll sure try." Then Robert left.

Anne eyed Maisie. "That didn't look like it was your first kiss."

Maisie felt her cheeks blushing profusely.

"And here you said he was just sweet. You neglected to tell me *just* how hot he is."

Maisie smiled. Yeah, she did. On purpose.

Chapter 8

As soon as Robert arrived home, he headed over to the vet clinic. He needed to remove the pictures from the walls so Maisie could adorn them with her own animal photography, and he didn't want her to know that he'd already decorated the clinic. Edeen had actually picked out the pictures and helped him hang them. He hoped he wouldn't disappoint his sister when she saw the changes he was making. Though he suspected Maisie couldn't take the photos right away because of her sprained ankle.

To his surprise, he heard Edeen say, "Knock, knock!" at the door of the clinic.

He left one of the exam rooms, carrying some of the pictures, and she frowned. "You're redecorating the clinic at this hour? Are you planning to paint the walls a new color? I thought they were perfect—a light beige that isn't as glaring as all white."

Now he felt really guilty that Edeen had done all of this for him. "No, you picked out the perfect paint for the place. Maisie asked if I wanted her to photograph some of the animals that we take care of to put them up on the walls. What you did was great, though, and if she hadn't offered to do the photos for the clinic, I wouldn't have changed a thing."

Edeen smiled. "Aww. That's a wonderful idea, instead of using the generic pictures we bought online. She probably could use the extra money and you have plenty."

Both Edeen and Robert had inherited quite a bit of money from family, and with his income from his vet business also, he was doing well. He always tried to support wolf businesses whenever he could. "Yeah, between the MacQuarries, the MacNeill pack, and us, I already have a lot of animals I'll be working with. Having photos of different breeds of dogs would be nice."

"Veronica could frame them," Edeen said. "You don't think Veronica will mind that you spent time dancing with her at Christmastime and now you are spending time with Maisie, do you?"

"Veronica and I have never indicated to each other that we want to date. Though with Maisie, that's another story." He removed some of the pictures in the lobby.

"Oh?" Edeen took down the last of them in there.

"We decided we needed to do something that wasn't so dangerous on our next get-together, so we are going to Heather's shop for pies the day after tomorrow for lunch." He moved into another exam room.

Edeen laughed and followed him in there. "That sounds good. How are Lady's puppies doing? When Lachlan came home for dinner, he told me all about them."

"They are all perfectly healthy, and so is Lady."

"That's good. I guess you met Maisie's sister, Anne?"

Edeen took down the last picture in an exam room, and they carried them out to the lobby.

"Aye. She seems really nice. I had a great dinner with them. Are you going to have lunch at the castle and watch Lachlan spar tomorrow?" Robert asked.

"I wouldn't miss it. I'm going to be there to make sure that Lachlan doesn't get too caught up in the fight and forget you're just in training."

Robert loved how his sister was always looking after him, just like he did with her. "I'm sure he'll be really easy on me, or Colleen would have words with him since she needs me to deliver her babies. If you get to the castle before me for lunch, save Maisie and me seats together, will you? She was supposed to go there by herself and be working with Conan, but because she has a sprained ankle, I'm picking her up and taking her."

"Good, and I sure will. She and I, and probably Colleen, if she's not too uncomfortable, will watch you spar then."

He really wished he wouldn't have an audience, though he knew it was inevitable. "Of course." Everyone would want to know how the newest male member of the clan could sword fight.

"Oh, I realized that I haven't invited the sisters to the wedding. I need to do that." Edeen set the picture she had removed on the floor next to the others.

"I'm sure they would love to come," Robert said.

"I'll be sure to invite them then. So...how is it going between you and Maisie?" his sister asked.

After the kiss they shared? No way was he going to pursue

any other she-wolf unless things didn't work out between them. "Great. We just sync on so many levels."

"Like Lachlan and me."

He chuckled. "Yeah, and in disastrous situations, she's a gem. She was eager to rescue a wolf in need—that's me—and a dog giving birth. She's a rugged individual with a heart of gold."

"I knew you liked her the way you were all in with wanting to do more things with her."

"On another note, I'm worried that she might have a stalker situation with her ex."

"No. Did you tell Grant and Colleen?"

"Yeah, on the way home, I called them to let them know." Then he told her about them finding the driver's license in the garden.

"Hmm, that all sounds mysterious. Keep me posted on it."

"I will."

Edeen glanced around at the walls. "They look so barren now. I hope Maisie takes some photos that will go up soon."

"I have three weeks before I'm open, so I'm sure they'll be done by then."

Edeen gave Robert a hug. "Well, it's so nice of you to hire her for some photography work." She looked at the pictures leaning against the wall. "Do you want to put them in one of my storage buildings until we can find a new home for them?"

He smiled. "Yeah, that would be great."

"You've had a wild day of it. I'm sure you want to get some rest. I definitely need to. I'll see you tomorrow."

"Thanks. It has been that." Ever since Maisie had come into his life. He hugged his sister, then left the clinic with her, carrying the photos to her storage building.

Then he returned home, and Mittens greeted him, purring while winding her body around his legs. "Time for bed, little one." Robert took a shower before he went to bed. All he could think of was snuggling with Maisie on Eilean Tioram by the campfire with Lady. He smiled. He was sure their date at Heather's shop would be uneventful and really nice. But before that, he would enjoy having lunch with her up at Farraige Castle and hope he didn't look too inept while he sparred with Lachlan.

The next morning, Robert was up early, still unpacking his stuff at the house—though twice when he went to break down a box, he found Mittens had climbed into one and curled up to sleep—and needing to get everything ready for the open house party that weekend. Chef was eager to make the food for the celebration, and Robert was happy to let him be in charge of the whole thing.

Robert called Colleen to check on her after breakfast. "Hey, how are you doing?" he asked when she answered. He hoped he wasn't making a nuisance of himself, checking on her and Heather all the time, but they were both first-time mothers and he didn't want to miss delivering them or learning if either of them was having any kind of distress. Both Heather and Colleen were alphas and tended to believe they could handle things on their own.

"I'm good. I've just been having those false labor pains. No big deal. They've been going on for the last week, but just on and off, you know. Nothing steady or long-term," Colleen said.

"Okay, well, let me know if anything changes as soon as it does." He thought she sounded fine.

"I sure will. Thanks, Robert." Her voice was warm and welcoming.

He could tell she was glad he was checking on her, and he was relieved about that.

When they ended the call, he checked in with Heather, who was due about the same time, only a couple of days after Colleen.

"I'm fine," Heather said, and he could hear customers in the background ordering meals.

Then he heard Oran say, "Who is that? Enrick?"

"No, it's Robert." Heather sounded annoyed with her brother.

"Let me have the phone," Oran said.

"No, go away, Oran. I'm fine." Heather said to Robert, "I'm not having any contractions."

"Hey, Doc," Oran said, "tell Heather she needs to get off her feet. Callum, Ethan, and I are filling in for her so she can get some rest, but she insists that she doesn't need to rest. That if she keeps working up until the time she goes into labor, it will happen more quickly than if she just lies around at home. But we're all feeling like we're dangling from a cliff here. We don't know how Enrick can be so calm about it, except he's not here to see her working so hard."

Robert smiled. "If she feels fine, she's okay to work. But if she is having a lot of swelling in her legs, ankles, and feet, then she needs to get off her feet. Let me talk to Heather."

Heather said to Robert, "Sheesh, you're lucky you don't have a bunch of annoying brothers."

Oran said, "We heard that." Then the brothers laughed.

"Are you having any swelling in your legs?" Robert asked, glad her brothers were watching out for her while her mate was working up at the castle.

"No. I put my feet up at night. Enrick insists upon it, but really, I'm good."

"Okay, well, if you feel any discomfort at all, let me know."

"Thanks, Robert. Colleen and I are just really glad you're here to help us through it. I'm sure the rest of our families are also."

"I'm glad to be here. I just wanted to check in with you."

"Thanks, Doc. I'm glad you're doing so. If my brothers had had their way, I would have stopped working a month ago. As it is, all three are in here constantly, trying to help out or take over, and are driving me nuts. The thing of it is, once the babies are born, they'll have to work in here, so they really should leave me to my work until then."

Robert suspected she was saying that more to her brothers than to him. "They just worry about you."

"They're worried they're going to have to deliver the twins at the shop."

Robert chuckled. "I don't blame them. I wouldn't want to have to deliver your babies there either, even as your doctor."

Heather laughed.

Then they ended the call, and he checked in with Maisie. "Hey, how's your ankle?"

"Much better. It helps to be a wolf."

"Yeah, it sure does. Can you walk on it?"

"Nay."

"I've got some crutches. Would you like to use them?" He had that and wheelchairs just in case anyone needed some assistance if they were injured.

"Aye! Thanks. I don't want you to have to carry me everywhere, so that would be perfect." Maisie sounded grateful, and he was glad he had them for her to use.

"Okay, I'll bring them with me when I come to get you."

"The Abercrombys had breakfast with us and our other guests. They couldn't get ahold of Gus's brother, Ike, but they did reach Stuart, and he said that all he knew was that Gus was going to be in our area for a couple of days. They gave me Ike's phone number. They are returning home, but they wanted to thank you again for helping to locate Lady and delivering her pups."

"They were so welcome. I'll be over about a quarter of eleven."

"Super. See you soon."

Then he went back to work on organizing his kitchen. He was thinking once he got his house in order—no packing boxes all over the place any longer—he would invite both Maisie and Anne over for dinner to reciprocate for the lovely dinner he'd had at their place. He needed to get some more groceries also.

With all the unpacking he was doing, it didn't take long

before he needed to leave. He donned his kilt, shirt, and boots, grabbing his sword and dirk for the sparring activities after lunch, and then drove out to the inn to pick up Maisie.

Anne opened the door and greeted him. "Oh, Maisie didn't tell me you would be all dressed up in your kilt." She looked impressed.

Maisie waved to him from the dining room where she was seated, having a cup of tea. "The MacQuarries are battling it out after lunch. You know, warriors will be warriors."

"Aww. Then you're watching them?" Anne asked Maisie.

"Yeah. I'll pick up tips while I do, and we can use them in our own demonstrations," Maisie said.

"Well, you're looking mighty fine in your kilt, that's for sure," Anne said.

Maisie laughed. "I agree, but I was going to tell Robert that once we got into the car."

"Thanks," Robert said, glad he at least had the kilt and rest of the wardrobe for the affair. He had the sword his grandfather had passed down to him, though he hadn't used it in a good long while. Actually about twenty years ago, sparring with his da.

He checked over Maisie's ankle. "The swelling is really going down, and the bruising is starting to fade. Have you tried to step on it?"

"Yeah, it still hurts. Not really bad, but enough that I don't want to put a lot of weight on it yet."

"Maybe by tomorrow you will be able to." He lifted her off the dining room chair and carried her to his car.

THE WOLF OF MY EYE

"Thank you. But at the castle, I'm strictly using your crutches."

Anne walked outside with them. "Enjoy lunch and the rest, you two."

"You know you could join us." Robert didn't want Anne to believe she wasn't just as welcome as Maisie.

"I figured that, but I need to work on the rooms and monitor the reservations," Anne said. "It really is better if one of us is here, though we would like to train someone else to fill in so both of us can be away if there's something important for both of us to go to."

"Check with Grant and Colleen. You might be able to find a wolf or two who could use some extra income and a job away from the castle," Robert said.

"I'll do that today while I'm up there," Maisie said.

She and Robert said goodbye to her sister, and then he drove off to the castle.

"Okay, so you look super-hot in your kilt," she said.

He laughed. "Thank you."

"I wasn't sure that you would be dressed for the occasion."

"I might not be a master swordsman, but I've got the wardrobe to make it look like I am."

She smiled. "You sure do, and you have the body to make it work."

He reached over and squeezed her hand. "You say all the right words."

Once they reached the castle, she used the crutches. When they walked inside the great hall, the Irish wolfhounds all greeted them. Edeen and Lachlan welcomed Maisie and Robert to the high table, where she'd saved seats for them like she promised she would.

Maisie sat in the seat saved for her, and Grant and Colleen both came over to check on her. "How are you doing?" Colleen asked, looking concerned.

"I'm good. I'm going to sit and watch everyone sparring instead of training Conan today. Maybe in a couple of days I'll be able to work with him." Maisie loved how genuinely caring everyone in the wolf pack was.

"There's no rush. He's a good dog, and whenever you're ready to do it, he'll be ready for you," Grant said.

"On another topic, we need a phone hacker, if anyone in the pack can do it," Robert said, bringing out Jude's phone. "I don't know if anyone can or not."

She was relieved he had brought it up because she had been concerned about it.

Grant raised a brow in question. Colleen looked just as interested in learning what that was all about.

Maisie instantly worried they would think that hacking into the phone was an invasion of someone's privacy and not a wolf's way. Before she could explain the situation, Robert did.

"He is an ex-boyfriend of Maisie's from Glasgow and lost his phone in her garden. He wasn't a guest, and he didn't go to see her, so we need to know what he was up to," Robert said. "Hopefully he's not stalking her, but we need to be sure about his intentions."

"Ah, I see your point." Grant took the phone from him and

turned it on. "We'll have to find someone who has a charger that fits this phone and get it charged up too before it dies. I'll see who might be able to deal with it."

"Thanks," Robert said.

Maisie echoed his comment, so glad Grant would look into it for them.

Despite having an injured ankle, Maisie was having a grand time. All the guys eating in the great hall looked like they were getting ready to battle it out in a movie. She knew a movie had been filmed here before. If she and Anne had lived at the inn at the time and had known the MacQuarries were *lupus garous* also, they might have been able to take part in the movie. If nothing else, they could have watched it being filmed. That would have been fun. Even though the movie had featured wolves, she and Anne had never guessed they were shifters and not just real trained wolves.

Once they finished their delightful lunch, she, Edeen, and Colleen had front-row seats outside, in the inner bailey, to watch the battle. It was a warm, sunny day, just perfect for the practice session.

Maisie had walked out on the crutches, wishing she could ditch them tomorrow, when she and Robert would go to Heather's shop for lunch. She glanced at Colleen, who was so big with her twins, she looked like she could have them at any minute. The guys had even erected a sun umbrella for them so they would stay cooler. They were served refreshments, which Colleen definitely needed, but Maisie thought the guys working out would need them a lot more than

Maisie did. Men and women on staff were setting up a table filled with refreshments for the warriors. That was good.

This was so cool. The men were stripping off their shirts, looking hot and muscular, but Robert had all Maisie's attention. Now that Robert was shirtless—again—it made her think of the comment Lachlan had made about Robert removing his shirt in front of her, which had tickled her. She would never tire of seeing Robert's hot abs on full display.

The men started to fight, Grant and Enrick sparring with each other while Lachlan was working with Robert. Despite Robert saying he didn't know how to fight, Maisie was impressed with his skills as she watched him attacking, parrying, and holding his own. Maybe Lachlan was holding back a little, but Maisie didn't think he was doing a whole lot to ease Robert into the training. Here she thought she would have to take Robert in hand and show him all the moves she knew when he could definitely teach her a trick or two.

"Robert is really good at this," Colleen said, rubbing her belly.

"Yeah, he has really surprised me. I thought the way Robert was so worried about fighting the guys that he would lose his sword or have to take it really easy to begin with," Edeen said.

"He is amazing," Maisie said, so impressed.

Edeen suddenly grabbed Maisie's arm, startling her. "I keep forgetting to tell you about our wedding. Lachlan and I are getting married in a week. We would love to have you and your sister both come to it. We were so undecided about the time of the wedding that we only just finally firmed it up.

We'll have it a week from Saturday at ten at the castle for the wedding and reception."

"We would love to come. We'll have to make arrangements to have everything covered at the inn, but I'm sure we'll be there. Do you have a registry set up anywhere?" Maisie was delighted that meeting the members of the wolf pack had opened their world up to all kinds of celebrations with more shifters. It was really fun, and she wanted their parents to move here and be able to enjoy all the happenings.

"If you want to take the photos at the wedding, we don't have an official photographer. That would be wonderful."

"Oh, sure, I can do that. I would be honored. Are you going somewhere for your honeymoon?"

"Bali, Indonesia. Robert will be taking care of all the animals."

Maisie laughed. "I'm sure he'll love it." She continued to watch Robert battle it out with Lachlan and hoped he wasn't trying to show off in front of her. Though being a wolf, he was probably trying to prove his worth to everyone, guys and ladies both.

A dark-haired woman with the prettiest brown eyes joined the group of women. "Hi, I'm Veronica Daniels," she said, introducing herself to Maisie. "I do all the picture framing for the pack as well as creating other wood-crafted items. Robert said once you take photos for his clinic, he wants me to frame them."

"Oh, that's wonderful. As soon as I'm off these crutches, I'll take the photos and you can work your magic."

Veronica nodded. "Colleen said you and he got stuck on Eilean Tioram for a few hours yesterday. It must have been romantic."

While Veronica was talking to her, Maisie was watching Robert, not wanting to miss any of the action. Robert glanced their way, and Lachlan whacked his sword hard and sent it flying. Poor Robert. But truly, he needed to focus fully on fighting and ignore everyone else around him.

Robert smiled at Maisie, and she smiled back. He quickly retrieved his sword and began fighting Lachlan again. Maisie cheered him on. She probably shouldn't have. Several of the men fighting smiled, though they kept their eyes on their targets.

She was amazed to see all the fighters' footwork, sword skill, and general cheerfulness as they sparred with each other. They were getting a workout, but they appeared to be having a blast doing it. Verbal banter between the guys made her smile.

"Hey, brother," Grant said. "You do so much better when you and Enrick are both ganging up on me."

Lachlan laughed. "I hate to admit it, but Robert's making me work for it instead of you, Grant."

As the oldest triplet and the pack leader, Grant always had to prove he was the most powerful of the brothers.

When Grant called a break, they all went to get drinks. Grant got a cup of water and walked over to see Colleen. "How are you doing?"

"I'm great. You're doing fine as usual," Colleen said, squeezing his hand.

Veronica smiled at Robert. "I told Maisie I would frame her animal photos when she has them done for you."

"That's wonderful," Robert said. "You do a superb job."

"I bet," Maisie said. Watching the two interact, she suspected that Veronica's speaking with her earlier was the reason for Robert's distraction. Had Veronica dated Robert? Women's and wolf's intuition made Maisie suspect so and that's why Veronica had said that getting stuck on Eilean Tioram with Robert was romantic.

Now Maisie wondered if Veronica was still interested in Robert or if it had been a short-lived thing.

"How's your ankle, Maisie?" Robert asked.

"It's fine, really, Robert."

"Good." He turned to Colleen then. "And how are you feeling?"

Colleen smiled. "Ready to deliver these babies. But otherwise, I'm good."

"I bet," Maisie said. "At least you're not having triplets like Lachlan and his brothers' mother had."

"That's for sure," Colleen said. "I know Heather feels the same way as me about it. She has three brothers, so she was worried she might end up with quadruplets even because of our wolf heritage."

"Oh no," Maisie said. "I can just imagine. Oh, Colleen, I meant to ask if you have anyone who works here who might want to work part-time at the inn. Sometimes my sister and I need some additional coverage, like when we go to Robert's open house or like with me injuring my ankle."

"I can put out the word," Colleen said.

"Perfect. Thanks."

After another hour of sparring and another beverage break, Robert took Maisie to the kennels to see Conan. He was so excited to see her, but Robert immediately made him sit before he knocked her over.

"I truly need to do the transitional training with him." She sat down on a bench, and he came over to greet her. "I miss you so much." She hugged her dog, and he wagged his tail like crazy. She was glad he hadn't forgotten her in the two and a half weeks he'd been here for training. She couldn't wait for him to come home with her.

After that, Lachlan had to take him back to training.

"Would you like to have dinner with me?" Robert asked. "Or do you need to help at the inn?"

"Let me call my sister and see if she needs me. Otherwise, I would love to." They got into his car, and Maisie called Anne. "Hey, Robert invited me for dinner. Are you going to be alright, or do you need my help?"

Anne laughed. "You know I can't say you're needed here when you have an all-important date with Robert. So how did it go?"

"Robert was amazing. He could teach us a thing or two about how to sword fight. Tomorrow, I need to sort through the marine life photos and then send them to the magazine. But if you need me to do anything at all, I'll do it."

"You can take care of online reservations if you want. Otherwise, we're covered. You can't do a whole lot with your bum ankle. We're good."

"Okay, thanks, Anne." Maisie felt a little guilty that she was eating out with Robert and Anne was on her own, but she knew if the roles had been reversed, she would have been just as happy for Anne.

Chapter 9

THAT EVENING, ROBERT TOOK MAISIE TO HIS PLACE TO have dinner, and she looked refreshed and happy as he set her up on the couch and smiled when his tuxedo kitten came out to greet her.

"Oh, she's so adorable." Maisie picked her up and cuddled with her.

"That's Mittens, and she is the sweetest little cat." He smiled to see Maisie rub her cheek against Mittens in a friendly nuzzle and Mittens began to purr. The moment was precious. "Would you like a cocktail, glass of wine, or glass of water before I make dinner?"

"A glass of water would be great."

"Okay, you've got it." He got her a glass of water, then he gently set her foot on a pillow on the coffee table to elevate it before he started dinner.

She smiled. "Thanks. I will leave a review for you on your clinic website saying you're an excellent doctor."

He laughed. "I will need all the reviews I can get once I open the clinic, but I suspect I'll have a ton from pack members, since I've been seeing their animals after I moved into the manor house with Edeen and Lachlan. Now we have to decide what we want to eat. Red meat? Fish? Or chicken?"

"Haddock appeals, if you've got some."

"Coming right up. Chips?"

"Aye! So I want to tell you that I was so impressed with your swordsmanship. You were great. Now you're going to have to give me some tips instead of the other way around."

"It's been so long since I even held a sword that I didn't think I would be able to do well at it at all."

"I guess it's like riding a bike. Except of course when you got distracted on the battlefield."

"Uh, yeah," he said, as he prepared the haddock to cook. "Veronica and I danced at Christmastime up at the castle. We haven't done anything together since then. She is constantly taking off for England to see friends, and I suspect she has a male wolf friend there, but that's just speculation. Anyway, we really had a great time, but neither of us have really reached out to see each other further."

Light dawning, Maisie said, "You were afraid she was going to tell me that you'd dated her and worried how I would react."

He smiled at Maisie. "I should have told you about it, though there's not much to say. I also spent an evening dancing with Lana Cameron, Heather's baker. When we have lunch at Heather's shop tomorrow, Lana might say something about it. But again, that was just dancing at a party one night and nothing after that."

Maisie laughed. "Okay, I'm forewarned. Veronica didn't say you two dated. She just said she was the one commissioned to frame the photos I'll take for your clinic. Oh, that reminds me, tomorrow before our date, I need to get those marine life pictures ready to send for the magazine. I found a few that will be suitable, but I need to check out the rest of them to give them a variety."

"At least you can do that even if your ankle is still bothering you," Robert said, hoping that Maisie wasn't concerned about him socializing with Veronica or Lana.

"Yeah. So have you been dating any other wolves while you've been here?" she asked, sounding like a curious wolf.

He served up glasses of sauvignon blanc. "No. I danced with Lana and Veronica only. I didn't have a date with them per se. I just showed up, and they weren't with anyone either. We were single, so we danced."

"Oh, okay." She sounded a little relieved, probably because Veronica lived here and worked with the pack, so Maisie would be seeing her from time to time.

"What about you?" he asked.

"I've been on only one date since we've been here. Gus Anderson, a lone gray wolf, was staying at the inn, and he took me out to Heather's pie shop."

"Gus, the guy who had lost his driver's license in your garden."

"Aye. I think he asked me out because we're both from Glasgow, but I never met him there. He was nice enough but kept glancing at the clock like he had an appointment, and it kind of annoyed me. I finally just had had it and I told him if he had an important meeting to go to, he should drop me off at the inn. He seemed affronted and said he was meeting with someone, but that he had to eat, and he hated eating alone. He said he was enjoying my company, but if I felt that way about it, he would take me home. I felt a little guilty about bringing it up. He told me he was sorry, that he was just making sure he didn't miss meeting the…person.

"In that instant, I felt something was really off. He didn't say who he was meeting, and when he hesitated, he switched from looking at his steak pie to looking at me, as if he had nearly made a slip and he hoped I hadn't caught it. He looked…*guilty*, the tips of his ears turning a little red. I thought maybe he was seeing another woman. After dinner, he took me back to the inn, and I figured he retired to his room. I don't know if he ever met with anyone else afterward or what that was all about. When I told Anne, she said he'd been terribly rude. He checked out early the next morning, and I never heard from him again. So I guess it was like your time spent with Veronica and Lana—nothing came of it, not that I expected anything to since he was living in Glasgow."

"That sounds like an odd situation he had put you in." Robert served up the meal and seemed glad to hear that she wasn't interested in Gus.

———

Maisie dug into her delightful haddock, feeling pleased that they had discussed past relationships with each other. "This is so good." She took another bite of the haddock, which had been breaded and cooked to perfection. "You can cook this for me anytime!"

"Thanks. You made my day. Edeen and I would take turns trying to outdo each other cooking dinner. She taught me how to cook. I would like to have both you and Anne over for dinner some night before I open the clinic to thank you for dinner last night."

"That would be great. You'll have to fix this again. She'll love it. If my ankle wasn't still bothering me, I would have loved going for a wolf run with you."

"As soon as it's all better, let's make a plan of it."

"You're on."

After they finished dinner, Robert took Maisie home, carrying her inside and setting her on the couch. "I'll grab the crutches and be right back." When he returned, he set them next to the couch and leaned over and kissed her. "See you tomorrow. Bye, Anne."

"Bye," they both said.

As soon as he drove off, Anne said, "Well? Spill."

Maisie smiled at her sister. "We had a great time. Everyone was very welcoming. It's going to be really nice being part of the pack."

"That sounds great. What about Jude's phone? Did you have any luck with that?"

"Robert gave it to Grant, and he said he would try and find someone to crack the passcode. I'm sure it's not something that the pack members are often asked to do, so it might take a while," Maisie said. "Did you see any sign of trouble while I was gone?"

"No. Everything was just the same as usual. Guests checked out. Guests checked in. No problem at all. Though, believe me, I was keeping an eye out just in case Jude was sneaking around the inn."

"Good. Maybe we'll get word about the cell phone within a day or two." At least Maisie could hope. Her imagination was truly running wild about it. She was dying to know why he had come to their place, and she was certain it had to do with her, but she couldn't imagine why, after all this time, he would want to hassle her.

The next morning, Maisie's ankle was feeling much better. She was still walking gingerly on it to make sure she didn't sprain it again, but she was glad to ditch the crutches.

Anne frowned at Maisie as they wrapped up cooking their own food. "Are you sure you don't need to be on the crutches still?"

"While we were cooking breakfast for our guests this morning, you never said anything," Maisie reminded her, amused her sister hadn't said anything earlier.

"Aye, but then I saw you wince while we were making our own breakfast—twice."

"I just felt a twinge of pain a couple of times. Really, if it gets worse, I'll use the crutches again. But I'm being really careful," Maisie said. Or she was trying to.

"If you need to just sit down, I can do this."

"We're almost done."

Then they dished up their eggs, bacon, chips, and toast and sat down at the table to eat it.

Once they ate their breakfast, they chatted while cleaning up.

"We need a couple of people to make breakfasts for guests when one of us is incapacitated or you're off on photography jobs. I know you always try to do your shoots in the afternoon or evening so that you're free to help me, but like now, with your ankle giving you trouble, it would be nice to have additional assistance. And we could use a person to manage reservations and the front desk part-time and somebody on standby to clean if we both are unable to get it done," Anne said. "Oh, and don't worry about doing anything at the inn today. I know you need to get the pet pictures for Robert's vet clinic scheduled and done."

"Okay, thanks. I'm going to work on the marine wildlife photos to submit them this morning." If all the other excitement hadn't happened—the lost dog included—Maisie would have already taken care of this, though she had until the weekend to send the photos to the editor. She downloaded her photos onto her laptop and combed through them while Anne headed out to the vacated rooms.

Maisie had gotten perfectly clear shots of several colorful starfish. Beautiful. A school of flounder—great. Seahorses, coral. She viewed them at 100 percent to see how clear they were and used a Photoshop tool to sharpen the images further.

The rock reefs were colonized by starfish, sea anemones, soft corals, hermit crabs, queen scallops, shrimps, squat lobsters, and congers. The eelgrass beds around the rocky outcroppings kept the mud and silt from stirring up, making the water clear to see in. The grass was wavering, beautiful, streams of sunlight penetrating the water, shadows of the plants moving across the sandy and rocky bottom.

Then she saw something odd in the seaweed, something that looked like glass. Was it trash, perhaps? It seemed to be floating. Her dive light had bounced off it, but when she viewed a closer shot of it, she couldn't make it out.

She sent her best photos of marine life to the editor of the magazine, and he came back within the hour and told her he loved them and that he needed her to do a cave dive for some more pictures in a few weeks.

Awesome, she wrote back. She added it to her calendar that was getting booked, which she was truly thankful for. She called up Edeen.

"Hey, Edeen, my ankle is feeling much better, and I wondered if I might be able to take some photos of your animals this afternoon after lunch." Maisie still wanted to do the transitional training with Conan too, but for now, she really needed to get the animal photos done for Robert's clinic.

"Oh, absolutely," Edeen said. "I don't know how well they'll behave, but I can't wait to do this with you. It'll be fun. We'll have tea when you come."

"Alright. Would two o'clock work for you?"

"Perfect. See you then."

Maisie looked back at the photo of the floating glass and blew it up some more. It was too blurry then, and she just couldn't tell what it was. Normally, glass was denser than water, and it shouldn't have been floating, unless it was a small shard of glass and the currents were keeping it afloat.

She couldn't think of what else it would be that would reflect her dive light like that. She couldn't help puzzling over it. Then she realized what was bothering her. If it was a piece of glass, her dive light would have reflected through the back of the glass. The light only reflected off the front. Which meant? It was attached to something solid, she thought.

She sighed and called Colleen next. "Hey, it's Maisie. How are you doing?"

"I'm ready to have these kiddos."

"I bet. I was going to ask you if I could take pictures of your animals later on this afternoon, about four? I'll be taking pictures of Edeen's at two."

"Yeah, sure. I'll let Lachlan know and he can take you around to help you get the best shots you can. I was kind of surprised Veronica came over to talk to you during the weapons training."

Maisie laughed. "I wondered if she and Robert dated."

"They danced at an event, but they haven't seen each other exclusively, as far as I know."

"Well, Robert and I are having our first official date at lunchtime, so as far as I'm concerned, we're dating." Maisie was ready to let the whole pack know that—Veronica included, in the event she was interested in upping her game with Robert.

"I'm so glad for you and Robert."

"Thanks." Of course, they were just getting to know each other, which meant that they might not end up mating each other. Still, he was so hot and so kind to her and protective, it was hard not to envision being mated wolves.

Once Maisie and Colleen ended their call, she got ready for her date with Robert. She was really excited about going out on her first official date with him. If she could handle it, she would love to go running with him as a wolf tonight, after she did her photo sessions with Lachlan and Edeen's pets.

Robert was early to pick her up, and she loved that. One of the guys she'd dated had been late for all their dates—Jude, in fact—and it was great being with someone who cared about being with her enough to show up early. Being late for a date for no good reason made her feel as though the guy hadn't really wanted to be with her, even if that wasn't the case.

What made it even better was that Robert kissed her like this was only the beginning for them, and she certainly felt that way about him.

"Oh, I needed that." She kissed him back, tongues stroking and lips melding. Damn, she wanted to take him to her bedroom and skip lunch!

He separated from her, smiled at her, and kissed her lips again. "Are you ready?"

"Yes. I'm going to take photos of Edeen's and the MacQuarries' animals this afternoon. I could take pictures of your cat also. And we can run as wolves after that?"

He opened the car door for her. "Yeah, that sounds like a great idea, if your ankle can handle it. But dinner before the wolf run?"

"Yeah, perfect. I'll let Anne know I'll be having dinner with you too."

"She can come over also, if you want to have dinner with her, so she doesn't feel left out."

"I'll text her." Maisie didn't want to put Anne on the spot.

Anne texted back: No, you have fun. I'm watching a reality show.

Maisie smiled, knowing her sister better than that. Anne wanted to give Robert and Maisie their time together alone, and Maisie was happy to do that, but she knew Robert would be just as happy to have her sister join them, to show he wanted to include her as family and get to know her better. It was important to Maisie also that if she and Robert ended up together that he and her sister were like family. And her and her sister's parents too.

Maisie texted: If you change your mind, we would love to have you there.

I'll let you know. Have fun on your first real date. Thanks!

Maisie set her phone down on her lap. "Anne wants to watch a TV show."

"She wants us to have more time to ourselves."

"Exactly." Maisie laughed. "But I told her she could change her mind and join us."

"Absolutely."

When they arrived at Heather's pie shop, they found that she'd set up a romantic table for them—candles, a special red tablecloth, and fresh red roses. Maisie smiled. "Was this your idea?"

"I told Heather I wanted a special table for our date, and she went all out," Robert said.

"This is so cute."

Heather was taking a payment for some pies and waved at them, smiling broadly.

They quickly took their seats, and one of Heather's brothers, Oran, came over to take their orders. Maisie got a Scotch pie and Robert ordered the steak pie, both dishes accompanied by baked beans and chips.

Then another of Heather's brothers came out of the kitchen to help take some other orders. Maisie thought how uncomfortable Heather looked, like the babies would come any second.

When Heather came over to their table to check on them, Robert said, "Thanks for doing such a beautiful job of making this the perfect date."

"You won't believe it, but Callum was the one who set it up, though Ethan and Oran kept telling him how to do it right, as if they were the experts. Of course, part of the reason is that my brothers really want me to stay home on bed rest."

Maisie chuckled. "I don't blame them. They're afraid they're going to have to deliver the babies here."

Heather smiled. "Absolutely."

"How are you feeling?" Robert asked.

"Oh, I'm tired. I'm not sleeping all that great. Uncomfortable. Heartburn. I'll be glad when the babies are born, but I know then I won't get any sleep either."

"But you'll have a ton of nannies wanting to take care of the babies," Maisie said.

"Aye, that's true. And Enrick will be there for me and the little ones, so it'll be good."

A customer came in and went to the counter, and Heather excused herself to help her.

Oran delivered the pies to Robert and Maisie's table. "Enjoy." He was smiling.

"Oh, we will. Heather's meals are terrific," Maisie said.

"I totally agree," Robert said.

Then another customer came in and glanced in her and Robert's direction, grabbing Maisie's attention.

"Oh, that's Gus Anderson!" She was relieved she could give him his driver's license. "I'm going to tell him his license is at the inn." She hopped up from her chair and went straight across the shop to see him.

Gus was just paying for a pie, and he looked startled to see her approach.

"You dropped your driver's license in the garden, and I found it," Maisie said, smiling.

He stared at her, appearing as though he didn't comprehend what she was saying. She guessed he hadn't realized he'd even lost his driver's license. She wondered why he hadn't answered his phone messages Anne had left for him about it.

"At the MacTavish Inn." She swore he didn't remember who she was. Talk about being an unremarkable date! Though he had been terribly distracted when they went out. "We still have it there if you would like to pick it up."

"Uh, yeah, sure. Thanks." He got his order, glanced at Robert again, and headed out.

Maybe he was afraid of having a wolf-to-wolf confrontation with Robert.

When she returned to their table, Robert was watching Gus get into a pickup and drive off. Maybe Robert had been giving Gus the evil eye and that's why he was in such a hurry to leave the pie shop. Or maybe Gus had another meeting with someone and was trying to eat before he met up with them. Who knew? Maisie often overthought situations when she just needed to let them go.

"At least now Gus knows where his driver's license is. I swear I must have been the most unremarkable date he has ever gone out with, the way he acted like he didn't even know me," Maisie said to Robert.

Robert waved at their romantic table. "You went out with him a couple of nights ago and now he sees you with another wolf having lunch here with wine, roses, and candles. I'm sure he was worried I might want to punch him out if I learned he'd had dinner with you."

She laughed and took another bite of her pie. "You don't think it had anything to do with the way you were eyeing him with a warlike alpha-wolf stare, do you?"

Robert scoffed. "After the way he treated you on your date, I would say he deserves it."

She smiled. Robert was so sweet. "Well, I agree."

After they finished eating their pies, Maisie ordered Scottish macaroons and Robert asked for Scottish tea cookies because they were just too good to pass up. Then they thanked Callum and his brothers for the beautiful setup. He looked happy to have done it for them.

"Hmm," Maisie said, biting into a macaroon. "These are so good. I'm glad you wanted dessert too."

"Aye, always. When I come here, it's standard fare. A meal with dessert."

They thanked Heather and her brothers for the lovely meal.

"Oh," Heather said, "I want you to do a maternity shoot for me before it's too late. Edeen already made me a beautiful gown for it, but I've been so busy, I forgot about scheduling it. Maybe tomorrow after closing here at the shop?"

"Take the afternoon off," Callum said, "and get it done before the babies come or you'll forever regret it."

"Okay, tomorrow afternoon then?" Heather asked.

"Yes, that will be perfect." Now Maisie wondered if Colleen would want one too. She could imagine her missing out and regretting it, since Heather was getting hers done now. "See you tomorrow. Is there somewhere special that you would like to do it?"

"At the MacQuarries' castle gardens."

"Do you want me to meet you there at noon then?" Maisie was delighted to be able to do this for her.

"Aye, let's do it."

"Good. I'll see you then."

After that, Robert drove Maisie to her home, but on the way there, she asked, "Hey, do you have time to look at one of my underwater photos and see what you think of it?" She wanted to see if Robert could identify what her dive light had reflected off. She needed to ask her sister too.

"Yeah, sure."

They parked at the inn, went inside, and Anne greeted them. "Did you have a good time?"

"Yeah, it was great. Heather's brother Callum set up a really romantic table, with candles and roses and everything," Maisie said.

Anne laughed. "That's so cute."

"It really was," Maisie said. "Oh, and I saw Gus Anderson there and told him that he dropped his driver's license here and he could pick it up. It seemed like he hadn't even realized he'd lost it. Did he make it here?"

"Yes. He came by. I was busy with reservations at the time and put it on the counter for him. When I turned to speak to him, he had taken his ID and was gone."

"He never thanked you for saving it for him?"

"No. I guess he was in a hurry."

"He acted odd at the pie shop, I thought."

"After seeing you with Robert at a romantic table setting? I can see why," Anne said.

"True. Anyway, I was going to show Robert a strange picture I took while scuba diving. I need you to look at it too, and maybe one of you can figure out what we're seeing," Maisie said.

"Sure," Anne said.

As they scanned through the pictures on her laptop, Robert said, "You do a beautiful job."

"Thanks. I was thrilled so many of them had turned out."

"Especially since I thwarted you while you were working."

Maisie chuckled. "Luckily, I had finished taking the pictures."

Then they came to her favorite shot: Robert, the upside-down boat, and the floating ice chest. But only because they had safely made it to shore and gotten help.

Smiling, he shook his head. "Now that is one for posterity's sake."

Anne laughed. "I love it."

Maisie got to the photo in question, and Anne and Robert peered at it while Maisie enlarged it. "That's my dive light reflecting off something."

"Glass?" Anne asked.

Maisie sighed. "Aye, I think so, but glass doesn't normally float unless it's really small and the currents are moving it."

"A watch face," Robert said.

Anne and Maisie stared at the picture a bit longer. "I think you're right," Maisie said, chill bumps dotting her arms. It might not be anything, but she couldn't stop worrying that there was something more to this than just a bit of debris in the water.

"Why is it floating?" Anne asked. "A watch would have sunk to the bottom of the ocean, don't you think? A small shard of glass might have been swept around, but a watch?"

Maisie couldn't stop looking at it, seeing it in a new way.

"I think it's a watch," Robert said.

Maisie didn't want to say why the watch was floating in the ocean among the eelgrass but felt she had to: "What if it's not floating there all by itself? What if it's attached to an arm?"

Chapter 10

ROBERT STARED AT THE PHOTO, THINKING THE SAME thing as Maisie. That someone had drowned in the ocean and her dive light was reflecting off a watch face. They had to check it out at once and learn the truth. He rubbed his forehead, rife with tension. "That's what concerns me," Robert said. "I scuba dive, but I'll need to get someone else to accompany me—especially if we find a dead body. I don't know if anyone besides my sister does. I'll contact Grant and see."

"I can go down with you," Maisie said. "Not that I want to see a dead body"—she shivered—"but I can find the location where I took the picture."

"I'm dive certified also, so if you need me, I can help," Anne said, squinching up her nose and giving a little shudder. "But if you don't, I'm fine with that."

"Let me call Grant first." Robert really didn't want the sisters down there, checking out a dead body, if there was one. His sister couldn't either because she was pregnant, but even if she hadn't been, he wouldn't have wanted her to witness a body either. "Hey, Grant, we kind of have a situation. When

Maisie was taking the marine life photos before I hooked her and the boat overturned, she snapped a shot of something that we're not quite sure about."

"Oh, yeah? Like what?"

"It looks like a watch floating among some eelgrass."

"Hell. Like it's on a body?" Grant asked.

"Yeah, that's what I'm afraid of. We might be completely wrong about it, but we need to investigate it just to make sure there's nothing to it. Anne and Maisie both are scuba certified. So am I. Do we have any other divers in the pack?" Robert asked.

He had done autopsies before while he was in medical training, so he was more used to dealing with something like this.

"We have seven wolves who are scuba certified," Grant said. "In addition to yourself and Edeen, but since she's pregnant, that leaves her out. Lachlan wants to know what you need a scuba diver for. Let me tell him."

Robert heard Grant telling Lachlan in the background about their concern.

"Okay, Lachlan wants to go with you," Grant said.

"Anne and Maisie want to also."

"Anne only wants to if nobody else is available," Anne said.

Robert smiled. "We've got it covered."

"We'll get a boat ready. Meet us here and you can leave via our beach," Grant said.

"Okay, we'll collect our scuba gear and meet you there. Lachlan's going with us."

A couple of guests came in to get the keys for their rooms, and Anne said, "Good. I really need to be here."

Robert looked at Maisie, but she said, "I'm getting my gear and dressing for it."

When she finally came out of her bedroom dressed in a dry suit this time, she said, "I'm so glad my ankle healed up so I could do this with you."

"I'm glad your ankle feels good." But he didn't want her to go hunting for a body, if that's what it was.

"Good luck," Anne said to Maisie and Robert. "Let me know what you discover. Hopefully, it's just a watch or maybe a bit of glass."

"I hope that's all it is," Maisie said, Robert agreeing.

They got into his car and drove to his house so he could get his gear.

"I know you don't want me to go with you, but I just can't stop thinking about this, and I want to see what it is," Maisie said. "Not to mention, I know where I took the photos."

"I understand. I just don't want it to upset you. But I know you have to do what you have to do, and I support you all the way."

After getting home, he dressed in his dry suit, then loaded his dive gear into the car while Maisie called Edeen to let her know that she might be late for taking photos of her pets.

―――――――

"Och, Lachlan told me what you're all doing. Are you sure

you want to go too and do the dive? You and your sister?" Edeen asked Maisie.

"Anne is managing the inn, so she's staying behind, but yeah, I've got to find out what is going on," Maisie said.

"Okay. If it is a deceased person, you won't be able to unsee it."

"Yeah, I know. But I think my imagination will get the best of me otherwise."

"Well, the animals and I will be here whenever you are ready. Even if you decide that you need more time, we can do it another day. I'm always at the house working on garments," Edeen said.

"Sure, thanks. Hopefully, I'll get them done today. It's good weather and Robert needs them framed and hung up before his place is open," Maisie said.

"True. Okay, well, Lachlan will tell me what you find. Be safe."

"We will be." As long as Robert was in the water with Maisie and not fishing from his boat this time.

Once they arrived at the castle, Lachlan and Iverson went down to the beach with them. Iverson was going to stay in the boat. Iverson was a former cop, and he had a body bag that was a blend of nylon-reinforced vinyl and heavy-duty woven polyester mesh that allowed for rapid draining that would keep forensics intact just in case they found a body. They'd had a couple of their own people drown while fishing, and the bags were a necessity. Though if the body was human, they would call the police and say they were diving and found it and wouldn't remove it from the water.

They climbed into the boat and then motored it to where Maisie thought she took the picture. Iverson cut the engine and tossed the anchor into the water. The waves were rocking the boat and she felt a little uneasy, just remembering the way Robert's boat had capsized and knocked her out briefly.

Then Lachlan, Maisie, and Robert entered the water, Lachlan carrying the body bag just in case they needed it. She hoped they would find just a watch or piece of glass, but it might even be gone by now if that was the case. She really hoped they wouldn't see a body.

They stayed near each other, searching for any sign of what Maisie's dive light had reflected off, and then Robert, who was swimming to her right, motioned to some of the eelgrass. Lachlan and Maisie joined him to see what he'd found.

That's when she saw the watch and, yes, it was on a man's arm. But what horrified her the most was his bearded face. It was Gus Anderson. The guy who had been looking at the clock at Heather's pie shop so much, like he had another date or meeting planned after dinner. She wondered if he had met with the man who had killed him. A rope was tied to his ankle, and it was secured around a paving stone. It looked just like the missing stone from their garden! Had the killer removed Gus's bags from the room too, to make it appear that he'd checked out? God, that's why they couldn't reach him by phone when she had found the driver's license. He'd been dead!

Maisie felt sick to her stomach. The salt water had bleached out Gus's skin so it was really white. Salt water preserved dead animals better than freshwater, and if he'd been here since that night she and Gus had their date, that had been only three days.

Then she indicated she was going up to the boat, pointing to its looming presence on the water. She couldn't look at the body any longer.

Robert, being the kind person he was, pulled her into his arms and hugged her to reassure her, and she thought the world of him for doing that. Then he released her, and she swam for the boat.

After doing her dive checks, she made it to the boat that was rocking in the waves, pulled out her regulator, and took off her mask. She probably looked as drained as she felt as Iverson helped her with her tanks and assisted her in climbing into the boat. She was nauseous but managed to keep from upchucking her lunch. "We found the body of a man who had been a guest at the inn, Gus Anderson. I told Robert about him already. He's a wolf."

"Hell, are you okay?" Iverson pulled out his cell phone and squeezed her arm in a comforting way.

She really loved the wolves in the MacQuarrie pack. Even though she wasn't a member of it, they treated her and her sister like they were. "Aye. I mean, sure, I'm shaken up. A million different scenarios are coming to mind."

"Okay, we'll figure it out." Iverson called Grant.

The wolves would have to handle it. She was glad they hadn't alerted the police in case a wolf had murdered the victim. If a wolf was responsible and got life in prison, he might shift anytime anyone aggravated him. Just the fact he would be incarcerated for any length of time, he would have difficulty keeping his wolf at bay at some point. And if he wasn't a royal, one whose roots had been strictly wolf shifters for generations, he would not be able to avoid shifting during the phase of the full moon.

She suspected Robert would do an autopsy to learn how Gus had died.

"Aye," Iverson said to Grant. "Maisie recognized him."

"He's from Glasgow, but I'd never met him before he stayed at the inn," she said.

Iverson relayed the information to Grant.

She was glad she'd returned to the boat so they could let the pack leaders know what was going on. She wished she'd had the stomach to help Robert and Lachlan, but Edeen had been right: she would forever remember the look of horror on Gus's face. Having actually met him before made it worse.

Chapter 11

Robert took his dive knife to cut the rope tied to the man's leg that was secured to a stone. Then he and Lachlan carefully pulled the body bag over the man. They had planned to leave him there for the police to recover him until he realized it was Gus. And that meant Robert would be doing an autopsy on the body to determine what had killed him. They already knew it was murder, unless Gus had tied a stone to his own leg and jumped into the water, but he suspected it wasn't a suicide. Robert had wanted to go up with Maisie to the boat to make sure she was okay, but he had to help Lachlan retrieve the body. He hoped Iverson was taking good care of her in the meantime.

Once they secured the man's body in the bag, Robert gave the signal to Lachlan to take the body to the boat. Robert headed back down for the rest of the rope and the stone it was secured to. That's when his dive light reflected off glass down below and he went to the bottom and found his cell phone. He was shocked to find it so close to where Gus's body was. Robert put the phone in his pouch, then grabbed the stone and pulled it up with him. It was heavy, but not so heavy that he couldn't lift it in the buoyant seawater.

As soon as he reached the boat, he realized Grant had sent another boat, and Lachlan and Enrick had put the body in that boat. *Good.* Robert didn't want Maisie to have to be near the body any further. He took the rope and stone to the other boat, and Lachlan and Enrick heaved it in. Then Lachlan rode back with Enrick and two other men—both Colleen's cousins, Edward and William Playfair.

Robert climbed into the boat with Iverson and Maisie. They followed the other boat back to the beach.

"Anne and I thought Gus had checked out the next morning, like people often do without saying anything. They just leave the key in the room and their charges on their credit card stand."

"You said he was looking at the clock at Heather's pie shop the whole time when he went out to dinner with you," Robert said.

"Aye, like he had a meeting with someone. He was really anxious. I think the stone you collected is the one missing from the garden. I saw that it was gone when I went to the garden to weed and found a man's boot prints, a driver's license, the cell phone, and Lady's collar. With finding everything else, I forgot about the stone going missing."

"What about the rope? It sounds like the murderer was an opportunist, just grabbing things that were handy, and hadn't planned this out," Robert said.

"I...I don't know. We have some rope in a shed, but I

never looked to see if any of it was missing. What…what happened to him?"

"I'll have to do an autopsy to know for sure. I'm glad the clinic isn't open yet. I have a walk-in refrigerator unit, so we can keep him until I conduct the autopsy. We need to notify next of kin so they can bury him properly." Robert put his arm around her and kissed her cheek. "Are you alright?"

"No, but I'm glad I was able to help you find him."

"Aye. Finding Gus means that the man we saw at Heather's pie shop wasn't him."

"What if the dead man isn't Gus, but his brother, Ike, and the man we saw at Heather's shop was Gus?" she asked.

"Except that he didn't act like he recognized you, you thought. To me that sounds more like it could have been his twin who didn't know you."

"True."

"Do you have video security around your place?" Robert asked.

"We do."

"We'll need to see what it captured that night," Robert said.

"I'll tell Anne when we get in. I still want to do the pet photos for Edeen and Colleen, and I guess I can do the photos of the dead man."

Robert shook his head. "I'll take care of it."

"Are you sure?"

"Yeah." He really didn't want her to have to look at the body again. She'd seen enough of him already.

When they reached the shore, Enrick and Lachlan were

carrying the body up the steps. Other men had come down to help with their scuba gear. He was glad they were unencumbered so he could hold Maisie's hand. Iverson was carrying the stone with the rope on it. He was wearing gloves, though Robert didn't think they would get any forensics off them, considering how long they had been in the seawater.

"Oh," Maisie said, "it hasn't rained since I found Lady's collar and the missing garden stone."

Robert glanced at her and raised his brows.

"Someone left big boot prints in the garden bed."

"We need to get a cast of them."

"I need to tell Anne not to walk in the garden." Once they had made it up to the castle, Colleen hurried as much as she could to come to see Maisie and guided her inside.

"You must have been horribly shocked to see his body."

"I was," Maisie said.

"Come in and you can have some tea or water. We'll skip the photography session this afternoon."

"Oh, no way. I need to get it done, and the weather is perfect for it. Besides, it'll get my mind off what happened. I just need to go home and change and get my camera. I'll be by after I take photos of Edeen's animals."

"If you're sure," Colleen said, getting her some tea and taking her into the sitting room.

"I'm going with the men to put the body in refrigeration, and then I'll come back for you," Robert said.

"Someone else can take me home," Maisie said.

"No, I'll do it." He had brought her here; he needed to return her home.

"We need to take the garden stone back to my place and prove it's the one missing," Maisie said.

"Yes, that's a good idea," Robert agreed.

She called Anne and explained what they'd discovered.

"Och, not one of our guests. Don't you think that whoever was meeting Gus must have done him in?" Anne said.

"Maybe." But Maisie was thinking that if he had been seeing a woman, it had to have been someone else who had killed him. "Hey, whatever you do, don't walk into the garden."

"Wait, so who came to the inn to pick up his driver's license?" Anne sounded spooked.

"We assume it was his twin brother, Ike."

"Do we have to be worried?" Anne asked.

"I hope not. Someone will come and take a cast of the boot prints, and I'll be home to shower, change clothes, and grab my camera equipment," Maisie said to her sister.

"Do you feel alright about it?" Anne asked. "I'm not sure I could do anything the rest of the day after what you went through."

"Yes, it'll get my mind off it."

"Okay. I'll see you in a little bit," Anne said.

"Alright."

By the time Maisie finished her tea, Robert had returned for her. He had already changed into jeans and a T-shirt and pulled her into a warm embrace. "I want you and Anne to be safe."

"You're worried about the murderer returning to the inn? I doubt he would unless he left evidence behind that he wants to destroy," she said.

"It does concern me."

"Me too," Colleen said. "Any number of males would be willing to stay at your place to provide some extra protection."

Maisie smiled at her. "Bachelor males?"

"Or married, if you would feel more comfortable with that," Colleen said.

"I'll stay with you," Robert said.

Maisie let out her breath. "You need to be there for Colleen and Heather if they suddenly have their babies."

"They are close by, and I'll be there in a flash. But if there's someone else you want to have stay with you…"

"Maybe…both you and someone else? That way, if you have to rush off, we'll still have someone else there to watch over us," Maisie said.

"Would you like anyone in particular besides Robert to stay with the two of you?" Colleen asked.

"Let me touch base with Anne on that." Maisie felt her sister should have a say about it too.

"Okay, well, let me know. Whoever you choose will be happy to do this for you," Colleen said.

Robert took Maisie home. When she got there, she thought Anne looked haggard. Maisie gave her a hug.

Someone drove up in a truck, and Robert checked to see who it was. It was Iverson. "I'm going to go out and help Iverson with casting the boot prints while you get changed and grab your camera."

"Okay." Maisie gave him a quick kiss, but he hugged her soundly, telling her he was going to be there for her to help her and Anne through this.

When he left the inn, Anne gave her a hug too. "God, how do you really feel?"

"It was awful. I know why Robert didn't want me to see the body, but I had to have closure, to know what it was I saw, to be able to guide them to the location. I'll shower and change and be out in a minute." Maisie called out from the bedroom as she dressed, "Robert's going to stay with us for safety's sake. Because he'll have to leave for Colleen's and Heather's deliveries, we're going to have another male stay with us. Who else do you want to be here besides Robert? Colleen said bachelor males or married males would be happy to stay with us to watch over us—our choice."

"Do you think we really need another guy here?" Anne asked.

"Well, it would make us feel more secure. I mean, you didn't see the dead guy. And the fact that he possibly was killed here at our inn…"

"Okay, I agree."

"So who do you want to stay with us?"

"Oh, I don't know. I guess just tell Colleen whoever wants to join us here. I don't know anyone else by name all that well," Anne said.

Maisie came out of the bedroom dressed and with her camera equipment in hand. "We're likely to have a whole bunch of bachelor males vying for the position."

Anne laughed. "Let the fighting begin."

Chapter 12

MAISIE HAD HOPED HER SISTER MIGHT HAVE LIKED ONE of the bachelor males she'd seen up at the castle and wanted him to come, though all that really mattered was that the wolves who stayed with her protected her.

"Okay, I'll be home later tonight. I'll probably still have dinner with Robert after the photo shoots and go running. I suspect Iverson might stay here until another wolf shows up to watch over you."

"That sounds good to me. About the sleeping arrangements, the guys can share the guest room on this side of the inn, I guess," Anne said. "Or one of the guys can use the fold-out sofa bed in the living room. We do have the trundle bed that can be pulled out from underneath the guest room bed also."

"Sure." But Maisie was already thinking she wouldn't mind sharing her bed with Robert. She would see how things went though.

Then she walked outside and joined Robert and Iverson. "We're going to let Colleen decide who will come to stay with us. Are you going to be here until someone else shows up?"

"Yeah," Iverson said. "And I'm the one who has Jude's phone. I've been trying to hack into it. Hopefully I can do that soon."

"I hope so." Robert turned to Maisie. "If you have all you need, let's go see Edeen. We did check the marks on the stone that had been tied to Gus and your missing garden stone. It is the same one. We looked in your storage cabinet for rope and found some that matches the one used to tie the stone to Gus's leg. I'll be performing the autopsy on him while you see Edeen and take your pictures. Then I'll drive you to the castle."

"Or Edeen can if you're too busy." Maisie didn't want Robert to think that he had to take care of her all day.

"Okay," Robert said.

They loaded her camera equipment in his car, and he drove to the manor house. She had to get her mind on photographing animals and off seeing a dead man in the ocean.

As Robert helped her with her camera equipment, Edeen came out with her two fox terriers, Jinx and Rogue. "I thought we could take the pictures in the garden since the flowers are all blooming right now," Edeen said.

"Unless you need me for anything else, I'm off to the clinic," Robert said.

"Go. We've got this." Maisie really wanted to know what Gus had died from. But she was soon having a ball with the terriers, Edeen holding up a treat for them so they would look up and focus. They were doing so well sitting and behaving for photos. Some dogs wouldn't look at the camera. Some wouldn't sit still or would lie down and go to sleep. Edeen's dogs were being really good.

"Okay, I'm getting Ruby now, and we can take some of the three of them together," Edeen said.

Before long, a large male Irish wolfhound came running down the hill from the castle, and Edeen laughed. "You know who that is, don't you?"

"Conan and Ruby's daddy."

"Yeah, Hercules has made a home with us here too. He loves the other dogs."

Maisie had Hercules sit next to Ruby, the two fox terriers serving as bookends. Perfect. Once she was done taking pictures of them, she took a photo of Edeen's Scottish fold cat sitting on the windowsill, then her two Highland calves out in their corral. "Do you want pictures of anyone else?"

Edeen shook her head, rubbing her belly. "Just the babies when they come."

"I should do a maternity shoot with you and Lachlan too," Maisie said.

"Yes, that would be grand. I'll talk to Lachlan about it so we can make some time for it." Edeen ushered all the pets back into the house, even Hercules.

"I'm off to take some photos of Colleen's animals. Then I'll take pictures of Mittens afterward."

"I'll drive you up there. We have a great walk path and gate through the ancient stonewall dike, but since you have all that camera equipment, it's better if we drive." Edeen got her car out of the garage, and they loaded Maisie's equipment into it, taking Hercules with them, and then drove up to the castle.

When they parked, they let Hercules out, and Lachlan

met up with the ladies. "Here, let me help you with your equipment. What were you doing at our house, Hercules?" The dog wagged his tail vigorously. Lachlan gave Edeen a kiss and hug first, then rubbed her back.

"Hmm, that feels good. We're going to do a maternity shoot in a couple of months, so we'll have to schedule you some time off from work," Edeen said to Lachlan.

He smiled. "Sure thing."

Maisie thought they were such a cute couple.

Lachlan led both of them into the kennels so Maisie could take pictures of all the Irish wolfhounds. She even took some photos of Conan while she was there and loved how well behaved he was for it. "I still want to do the transitional training with Conan, but it will have to wait until after the open house because of doing all these photo shoots. They're a priority."

"Certainly. Transitional training isn't usually started until the fourth week, and we're nearly at the end of week three, so there's no problem at all with waiting. He's doing so well that you can do it whenever you're ready. Also, who do you want to stay with you and Anne?" Lachlan asked. "Colleen told me you were going to get back with her on it, but she's taking a much-needed nap."

"Oh, just tell her that we'll let her decide." Maisie snapped some shots of their two Scottish fold cats with folded ears— Rapscallion, a blue, and Tinker, a white—as they roamed into the kennel.

Lachlan laughed. "We'll have to have a lottery then."

Edeen chuckled. "That's for sure."

"What about a maternity shoot for Colleen and Grant?" Maisie asked.

"I'm sure she would love it. She's so close to giving birth that it does need to be done quickly though," Lachlan said.

They went to the horse stables, and Lachlan brought out a couple of horses for her to photograph. After that, they walked into the field to capture some shots of their Highland cows and Scottish blackface sheep. Maisie was so glad she was getting this done as she'd planned. Setting goals and deadlines for herself was important, especially reaching them in time.

Once they were done, Lachlan texted someone and said to Maisie, "We'll be sending someone in half an hour to the inn. I take it Iverson is still there with Anne."

"He is. And Robert's doing the autopsy at the clinic," Maisie said.

"Good. Colleen said she would love to do a maternity shoot in the gardens right now since you've got the camera equipment here and you're done with the animals, if you have time. After her nap, she felt rejuvenated."

"Absolutely."

Lachlan carried Maisie's camera equipment to the gardens, and they met Grant and Colleen there. She looked lovely. The garden was bathed in light as the sun began setting. Maisie chose the red rose garden, Colleen's red hair and green eyes complemented by a soft green, medieval-style dress, the ancient stone walls behind them fitting with the style. She also had a MacQuarrie tartan throw draped over her shoulders. She was beautiful. Grant was wearing a kilt and shirt, his sword hanging at his waist as if he were protecting his ladylove. It was just perfect. Maisie hoped that Heather and Enrick had a similar setup.

"Now that's what I want too when we do ours," Edeen said to Lachlan. "Just like that."

"Heather wants to come here to have her photo shoot with Enrick tomorrow. She said you made her a beautiful gown," Maisie said.

"Yes," Colleen said, before Edeen could respond. "Edeen made mine also."

"It's just lovely," Maisie said. The whole experience was beautiful. They were truly wolves in love. When Maisie finished up with them, she smiled to see Lachlan's arms around Edeen, both of them smiling.

"Thanks for doing the photo shoot for me on such short notice," Colleen said. "I can't wait to see the photos. And we'll want baby pictures too."

"Of course."

Lachlan helped carry Maisie's camera equipment back to the car, and Edeen hugged Lachlan again. "See you tonight, honey."

"I'll see you later, and be sure to rest," Lachlan said to his mate.

"I will." Edeen drove Maisie to Robert's house so she could take pictures of Mittens. "I'm so sorry you had to go through what you had to on the dive today. If you need me for anything, just call me."

"Thanks. It truly was a shock, but it helped to take photographs of everyone's animals, and the maternity shoot was so beautiful, which totally got my mind off it."

"I know. I want one just like that when it's time for me. I'll see you later."

"See you."

Maisie took her camera equipment out of Edeen's car and walked to the front door of Robert's home as Edeen drove off. Before Maisie could knock, Robert threw it open. He was standing there with a towel around his waist, his hair wet and water droplets clinging all over his gorgeous body—chest, arms, legs. She laughed. He was so hot. And definitely sexy. She'd never envisioned this, but truly, he was a welcome sight.

He smiled, taking her camera bag from her. "I heard Edeen's car as I was getting out of the shower. I didn't want you to have to carry all that camera equipment in by yourself."

"I'm used to it. Not that I mind you coming to my rescue like this at all." She ran her finger over some of the water drops on his chest, and he smiled, took her hand, and kissed it. "Where's Mittens?" she asked.

"She's around here somewhere." The cat came out as if summoned using her name and wound around his legs and then Maisie's.

"You are adorable." She crouched down to pet Mittens. "Did you know that it's rumored that the first cat to reach Mount Everest was a tuxedo cat?"

"I'm surprised the cat could make it up to that altitude. Mittens is really playful. I'm going to dress, and I'll help you set her up for pictures." He settled his hands on Maisie's shoulders, leaned down, and kissed her lips briefly. "I'll be right back." Then he hurried off to his bedroom to get dressed.

They'd avoided talking about Gus's body, but after photographing Mittens, if Robert didn't mention it, Maisie would ask him how he thought Gus had died.

She found the right place to set up her camera, the perfect natural light coming through the windows, and added some additional artificial light. Now she just needed to get kitty to sit still.

When Robert came out of his bedroom, fully dressed, Mittens ran straight for him.

"She's so cute. Just like a little puppy dog." Maisie had never had a cat, so she was surprised that Mittens was so affectionate and not aloof, like she thought she would be.

"She is." He scooped her up and cuddled her. Maisie felt warm all over seeing him loving on his cat.

"Okay, Mittens, you have a job to do." He set her on a black-and-white polka-dot pillow, and she looked up at him. "What do you want me to do to help her show her best side, Maisie?"

"Do you have a cat toy? You could dangle it over her head, and I'll take pictures of her looking up at it or trying to catch it."

"That would be cute." He retrieved a stuffed pink mouse on a string, Mittens observing him, her tail twitching.

Then he dangled the mouse above Mitten's head and her big green eyes were focusing on it first, and then she began trying to grab it with her claws while Maisie was taking pictures of her. "These are so cute." She'd even taken pictures of Mittens watching Robert before he reached her with the toy mouse.

After she took several photos, Maisie said, "Those should be good. When we're making dinner, I can take a couple of photos of her when she's just sleeping or resting." Mittens hopped off the pillow and onto a windowsill, where she sat to watch the birds outside. Maisie snapped some more pictures of her.

"How does pizza sound for dinner?" Robert asked, peering into the freezer.

"Ooh, that would be good."

"What kind of toppings do you want? These are mini cheese pizzas, but I add extras. Mushrooms, black olives, green olives, onions, pepperoni, ham, bell peppers, extra cheese?" Robert brought out the pizzas.

"Um, everything but green olives, onions, and ham."

"You got it."

"What can I do to help?"

"Do you want to cut up the mushrooms?" he asked, bringing out all the ingredients and then turning on the oven.

"Yeah. Do you want them too?"

"I sure do. All the same ingredients as you."

"You're okay about staying with us for a little bit, right?" She really wanted to make sure he was alright with it when he might need to be home doing other stuff. She cut up the mushrooms.

"Hell yeah. I'm just so lucky that I won the lottery without having to put my name into the pot." Robert brought out a pizza pan and covered it in aluminum foil.

She laughed.

"Believe me, every bachelor male will want to put in for the job."

She realized that was a real perk to being in a wolf pack—lots more bachelor males to choose from. She began to cut up the bell peppers while he added extra shredded cheese to the pizzas.

Then he sighed. "Do you want to learn about the autopsy?"

"I do."

"Okay. Gus was manually strangled. The U-shaped bone of the neck, called the hyoid, was fractured. The murderer had to have been a male, his hands large enough and strong enough to do the job. Gus had to have been murdered before he was dropped into the ocean. There was no water in his lungs."

"Och, no. Strangled where? At the inn?" God, how awful. Every time she went into the garden, she would be reminded of the horrible deed that had been done.

"It's hard to say. We would need to go over the room he stayed in and look for any evidence. Since the garden stone was taken from your place, I would say it's a distinct possibility that he was murdered on your property. Unless he was murdered elsewhere and the murderer returned to grab his bags from the room and took the garden stone and the rope at that time."

"So Gus was in the murderer's vehicle at the time."

"Or his own vehicle. We'll have to see if there was a vehicle there other than Gus's. Or your other guests' vehicles. Because he was in the water, I couldn't find any carpet fibers on his clothes or body."

"They were the same clothes that he had on when he

went out with me that night. So it had to have happened after our date, before he went to bed." Chills raced down her skin, and she involuntarily shivered.

"Do you know if he was with a wolf pack or had family other than Ike?"

"No. We really were just talking about places we'd eaten at when we both lived in Glasgow. I didn't even realize he had a twin brother until later. Likewise, I didn't mention my twin sister."

"We'll need to look up his guest registration and see if we can locate any other family or friends who knew him and might know what he was doing in this area. We might be able to learn who might have wanted him dead. Stuart and Bruce didn't seem to know what he was doing here." Robert helped cut up the rest of the vegetables. He added the rest of the toppings on the pizzas and slid the pizza pan into the oven.

Maisie saw Mittens sleeping on her pillow, and she took some pictures of her. She looked so angelic. "I'll call Anne and see if she can get us the registration details for Gus's vehicle so we can look into this further. Do you have anyone in the pack who does investigative work?"

"Yes. Three wolves have worked in law enforcement— Colleen's cousins, William and Edward Playfair, who are from Texas and moved here when Colleen mated Grant and joined the pack. Iverson was a homicide detective and has a degree in criminology and forensics. But they all just work for the pack now, so they're free to do whatever needs to be done. Iverson has contacts at his old jobs too."

"Oh, good. We'll do everything we can to help them with

the investigation since our inn was part of the crime scene," Maisie said, feeling awful that anything like that could have happened there. "Oh, another thing. We need to learn where Gus's vehicle went to."

"Once we have the registration information that he filled out at the inn, we should be able to do a search for his vehicle." A few minutes later, the oven beeped and Robert pulled out the pizzas.

"Hmm, those look and smell great." Her stomach growled, and Robert smiled at her. "So tonight, when you stay with us, you can sleep with the other wolf in the guest room or on the foldout couch, or you can join me in my bedroom." She hoped she wasn't being way too forward and putting him off.

Robert smiled even bigger as he poured glasses of zinfandel. "I would be lying if I said I wanted to stay with some other wolf in the guest room. As long as you're fine with it, I'll join you in your bed."

Her body flushed with warmth and intrigue as she thought about being with him tonight.

They sat down to eat at the dining room table. She took a bite of her first slice of pizza and moaned. "This is delightful. I never thought of adding fresh ingredients on top of a frozen pizza. This makes it so much better."

"Edeen was the one who showed me how to do this. I never learned how to cook until Edeen taught me. She would come over to my apartment to have a meal on occasion, instead of me eating at her place, and scoff at what I had in my fridge. So one time, she just took me to the grocery store and showed me the staples I needed and taught me how to make some meals. Then later we began competing with each other."

"That sounds like fun. You seem to be very close to your sister."

"We are best friends. Like you and Anne seem to be."

"Oh, absolutely."

"You don't think Anne will be…uncomfortable with me staying with you in your bedroom, do you?"

"No. I'm sure she would tell you to stay in *her* bedroom with *her* if I rejected you."

Robert chuckled.

"Well, this is delicious," Maisie said. "My compliments to the chef."

"Thanks. I'm glad we could do this together." They finished eating and cleaned up the dishes. Then he said, "Are you ready to run as a wolf?"

"I sure am." Before he could tell her where she could undress and shift more discretely, she started pulling off her clothes. She was going to sleep with him tonight at the inn. She wasn't going to be shy with him now.

He began to remove his clothes, signaling he was comfortable with her like this too. They were used to shifting in front of others, but sometimes in new wolf relationships, it could be awkward. She had already seen him naked when he took the fishhook out of her arm, and she felt safe and secure with him.

He wasn't watching her, just working on removing his own clothes, but when he glanced at her just before she shifted, he smiled. She smiled too, loving the way he looked

at her, and then they both shifted. He was a beautiful gray
wolf with a distinctive black face mask that made him look
distinguished. Her face was lighter. His belly was lighter
than hers, and he had a black saddle. Her back was more of
a dark tan.

To her surprise, he licked her face, and she loved it.
She nuzzled him and licked his back—a true sign of wolf
affection. He smiled at her, appearing to love her wolf
response too.

Then he barged through his wolf door, and she went after
him. They ran like the wind, letting the breeze blow through
their fur, feeling rejuvenated, one with the land. This was
so much fun. She hadn't run as a wolf since she and Anne
had moved here, but now she figured they could run with
Robert and the other wolves safely on his property on a regular basis. She loved being a wolf.

After he took her around the property for a while, show-
ing her the loch, woods, and a stream, he led her up to the
dike and they went through the wolf door there. Then
they explored the MacQuarries' castle properties, the
woods, and another loch. It was really beautiful out here.
Both properties were. They loved their inn, but that was
one problem they had: a creek ran by their place, so they
didn't have a lot of land. They overlooked the ocean, which
everyone who stayed there loved, and some woods for privacy, but there wasn't enough land to run freely and safely
as wolves.

This was refreshing, and for the moment, she wasn't
thinking about finding the body in the water, just about

having a blast running through the woods with a beautiful bachelor wolf. And later on when they settled down for the night? *That* was to be continued.

Chapter 13

ROBERT WAS SO GLAD THAT HE AND MAISIE GOT TO RUN like this. Edeen's acreage was substantial—a hundred acres in all, of which she had gifted him half because they were family—and they hadn't run all over it yet. He'd used some of the money from his inheritance to build his home and clinic, so his places were clear and free of mortgages. He had taken Maisie to the MacQuarries' property to extend the run, to show her their beautiful surroundings too. She seemed to be having as much fun as he was. He realized he had never run with a she-wolf that he was dating, and the experience was amazing. She kept bumping into him in a playful way, and he loved it. He played with her just as much, nipping at her cheek, bumping her, chasing her tail, and that had her yipping and shooting off to keep ahead of him.

He quickly caught up to her. He couldn't believe Maisie wanted him in her bed with her tonight, but he was all for it. He hoped her sister wouldn't object or that Maisie wouldn't wish she hadn't done it after the fact. The secret would be out soon enough because wolf packs shared these things. It wasn't a bad thing, really, because in the case of relationships, the other wolves in the pack would be hesitant to encroach on a bonding. Wolves outside the pack might still try to cause problems though. Some alpha males just figured they had what it took to get any female they wanted, even if she was seeing another wolf.

Robert and Maisie were headed back to the dike when they heard some wolves howling. They howled back in greeting. He loved her beautiful howl and howled again just with joy at being with her like this. She nipped at him in playfulness, and they continued on their way.

Once they were through the dike, they raced each other back to the house. He was longer legged than her, and he knew he was going to reach the house first, so he was in a quandary. Should he just beat her or let her win? Everyone reacted differently to a situation like that. His sister always wanted to try to win a race on her own. But his mother had always wanted him to hold back when they went running as wolves so she would have a better chance to win. So which would Maisie prefer?

He decided to stick with her and ask her about it later, but he might win by a nose. What he didn't expect was her nipping at him, distracting him right before he reached the house, and her bolting ahead. He loved her for it. She was so cute.

They headed inside the house, and she shifted and laughed. He shifted and pulled her into his arms and kissed her. "You tricked me."

She chuckled, sounding so pleased with herself. "You were being so sweet not to get ahead of me. But I had to beat you. I probably should have told you about my competitive nature."

He laughed. He was having so much fun with her. "Yeah, I wasn't sure if you would want to beat me on your own or if you wanted me to give you more of a head start."

"Oh, I want to beat you on my own, but if you want to make allowances for me, I'll take advantage of them." She was so cute.

Smiling, he kissed her again, loving the way she was so much fun. Okay, so now he knew how she felt about running with him. She wanted to win—in her own way. "I guess we'll get dressed and head over to the inn."

"Absolutely." Maisie started pulling on her clothes.

Robert quickly pulled his on too. He got them some glasses of water, and they drank them. "I'll pack a bag and take your camera equipment out to the car."

"Okay. I'm sure Anne will be glad when we get back. I wonder who the mystery guard wolf is."

"We'll find out soon." He packed enough clothes for several days and rejoined her in the living room. Then they packed up her stuff.

"What about Mittens?" Maisie was cuddling with the cat.

He loved that Mittens loved to be held or sleep on his lap or curl up in bed with him.

"We'll drop her off with Edeen so she can have all the other animals' company while I'm staying with you." He could have left her at the house and Edeen would have dropped by to feed her, but Mittens loved all the other animals and she loved people, so she would be happier at Edeen and Lachlan's house.

"Okay, that will work."

Then he packed up Mittens and her food, toys, and litter box and called his sister to let her know.

When they drove over to Edeen's house, Lachlan came out to get the litter box and food while Edeen took Mittens in her arms.

"See you later," Edeen said.

"Let us know if you need us for anything," Lachlan said, and Robert knew he meant in the event they had trouble with the murderer.

"We will," Robert said.

"'Night," Maisie and Robert said, and then they headed back to the inn.

At the inn, Anne was having tea with William Playfair. He was as dark-haired as Colleen, his eyes hazel. So one of Colleen's Texas cousins was going to stay with them. Robert wondered if William's twin brother, Edward, felt like he'd lost out.

"My bedroom is in there," Maisie said to Robert, making it clear to both her sister and William that Robert was staying with her in her bedroom tonight.

He carried his bag into her bedroom and set it in the corner, out of the way. Then he helped her carry her camera equipment in from the car, and she took out the memory card and put it in her laptop. "I'll edit these in the morning," she said.

"Yeah, that sounds like a good idea. It's getting late," Robert said. "Though I want to know if anyone looked at the security videos for the inn yet."

"Yeah," William said. "Anne, Iverson, and I watched it and saw Gus parking at the inn, getting his key, then leaving his bag in the room. He met Maisie and asked her out to dinner. Then he left with Maisie and returned about an hour and a half later."

"And then?" Maisie asked, all ears, grabbing some water for Robert and her.

"He left again," William said. "After an hour, he returned. But he wasn't alone."

"He was with the killer?" Maisie asked.

"A woman," Anne said. "She had curly, chestnut-brown hair, pretty features."

"Sheesh, I really pick them, don't I?" Maisie said. "Here he asks me out to dinner, then he has a woman stay with him afterward? I kind of assumed he was seeing a woman from the way he hesitated to talk about it when he said he was meeting up with someone."

"He was with her for only about an hour. Then he left again, taking her with him," Anne said, "and aye, they were all lovey-dovey. Which really made me mad, considering he'd asked you out first and never indicated he was seeing someone else."

"Been there before," Maisie said.

"Yeah, I think your luck might just be changing." Anne glanced at Robert and smiled.

"Not all wolves are like that for sure." Robert drank some of his water. "If the guy wasn't already dead, I would have had words with him."

"Then the guy returned to the inn again," William said.

"He was wearing a gray hoodie and a wrist splint and black boots."

"Gus wasn't wearing a wrist splint or a gray hoodie," Maisie said. "That has to be someone else."

"He was driving Gus's car then," Anne said. "If the murderer met up with him and then drove his car back here to the inn, no one would have been the wiser. Then he took Gus's bags from the room, loaded them in the car, and drove off for the final time. Gus's body might have been inside his vehicle. The man on the video was the same size as Gus, but we couldn't see his features that time because of the hoodie."

"Did we get any footage of the garden?" Maisie asked, hopeful.

"No. The cameras don't capture images in that spot. We didn't have any reason to concern ourselves that anyone would steal from the flower garden," Anne said.

Maisie sipped her tea. "That's true."

"Iverson said he was going to put up another couple of security cameras to cover some more areas that we don't have coverage for right now." Then Anne frowned. "Wait. What if the two things are related? Gus's driver's license in the garden and Jude's phone being out there?"

"It seems like too much of a coincidence if they aren't related," Maisie said.

"Speaking of the phone, Iverson left it here for you to look at. He unlocked it and he left a charger for it. He couldn't really find anything on it that would explain what he was doing here, but maybe—since you knew him a little better—you can learn something more from it," William said. "Iverson did say that Jude had a couple of recent calls that he hadn't answered and some text messages he hadn't responded to since he dropped his phone in the garden—which shows he dropped it on the same day that you went out with Gus."

"Well, darn, I had hoped Jude would reveal something more to us, but the timeline helps," Maisie said.

"What about the boot prints?" Robert asked.

William said, "Iverson got some good prints off it. He's running it through a database to determine what the brand of boots is if he can discover it."

"I wish we knew what size Gus's shoes were," Anne said.

"They could have been Jude's," Maisie said. "I have no idea what size shoes he wears. I just know he had big feet. The night we went to dinner, I didn't notice what Gus was wearing on his feet. We also need to find Gus's car."

"Iverson took the information Gus gave you on his registration and is looking into it," William said.

"Where's Mittens?" Anne suddenly asked, sounding concerned she was on her own.

"She's at my sister's place, getting lots of loving." Robert finished his water.

"Okay, good," Anne said. "William, I wanted to tell you about our routine for the inn so you know what we have to do in the morning. Sometimes we make breakfast for ourselves before the guests come in if we get up early enough. Otherwise, we have to wait until they're done eating."

"You can stay in our guest room, William," Maisie said.

Each of the three bedrooms had a bathroom en suite, and another bathroom was accessible to the living room.

"There are spare towels in the bathroom you'll be using, William. If you want anything from the kitchen, feel free to raid it. I'm off to bed. 'Night, everyone," Anne said.

"'Night," Robert and Maisie said, and Maisie took his hand, grabbing Jude's phone off the dining room table, and led Robert to her bedroom.

"'Night," William said.

"I'll take my shower after you," Robert said to Maisie as she closed her bedroom door. "I'm going to talk to William about the case for a few minutes. I'll be right back."

"Okay, sure." She went into the bathroom, stripped off her clothes, and began showering.

Robert went to check on William. He had taken a quick shower and was wearing a pair of boxers and grabbing a cup of water from the kitchen. "Are you going to stay here until we know what we're up against?" Robert asked.

"Yeah." William motioned to Maisie's bedroom. "Looking good."

Robert smiled. "We'll see. You made out alright on the lottery."

"Yeah, my brother wanted to trade places with me in the worst way. He offered to do my chores for a month. Two months even."

Robert laughed. "I bet. Did you learn anything else from the crime scene?"

"We went over the guest room with a fine-tooth comb. It didn't appear that Gus was killed in the room. Neither of the sisters had seen any disturbances—no furniture over-turned, everything was neat and tidy—which would have concerned them. But one thing Anne said was odd was that the bed hadn't been slept in."

"Like he'd been murdered before he had a chance to retire," Robert said. "But he'd been with the woman there, and I had assumed they wouldn't have just been talking. So that doesn't make any sense."

"Right. Anne said the shower had been used."

"Okay, so if he was intimate with the woman, maybe they did so in the shower. Was Anne able to smell any wolves in there?"

"Yeah, the woman who had been there was a wolf too. At the time, Anne hadn't thought anything of it until she saw the security video," William said. "I wonder if he met up with or ran into the guy after seeing the woman and that was the end of him. What about the autopsy? What did it reveal?"

"He was manually strangled and died before he went into the water. He had no identification on him, so it was good that we recognized him from his driver's license. He had a cell phone in his pocket, but because of the corrosive nature of salt water, it was probably destroyed. I have it drying out though, just in case."

"That's a good idea, in case the other guy texted him to have the meeting. Or called him," William said. "Even the identity of the woman might be on it."

"Right."

"Anne gave Iverson and me the information on Gus Anderson. He was here alone. We're looking on social media and searching Glasgow for his family and friends. We haven't located his brother, Ike, either. He's not answering his cell phone, but we assume Ike was the one who picked up the ID. We don't know if Gus had a job in Glasgow or not, so we're still checking. We want to know if he had any known contacts in this area—like the guy who met up with him, if it wasn't his twin brother."

"Okay, so Gus was a wolf. What we need to know is if the guy who murdered him was too," Robert said.

"Well, we'll have to take care of him no matter what, right? I mean, we can't tell humans what happened to Gus, and so we can't let human law enforcement deal with him."

"True. We need to know if anyone else was involved also," Robert said. "But I'm also wondering about this strange business with Maisie's former boyfriend being here and losing his phone in the garden."

"Yeah, it makes me wonder if he lost it when he was grabbing the stone from the garden. If he killed Gus, then maybe he meant to get rid of his driver's license so if anyone did happen to find the body, they wouldn't know who it was. But then Jude lost his phone and Gus's driver's license in the garden. We need to learn if he knew Gus. Though it could have been a random encounter," William said, "and something just torqued Jude off."

"True."

The shower had shut off in Maisie's room a while ago, and Robert glanced in that direction.

"Join her. I know I would if I had the same rapport with her that you do."

Robert smiled. "Good night, William. See you in the morning."

"Night, Robert."

Robert headed for Maisie's bedroom, and when he opened the door, he saw her in bed, under the covers, smiling at him, waiting for him, Jude's cell phone in hand. She had left the reading lamp on for him. He dug a pair of boxer shorts out of his bag. "I'll be quick." Then he was in the shower, soaping off and rinsing off. Once he dried off and put on his boxers, he left the bathroom. He still didn't know if she wanted the intimacy or just wanted him to sleep with her. He was definitely ready for either.

"Did you learn anything from Jude's phone?" he asked.

She pulled the covers aside for him, and he joined her in bed.

"There has been no contact between him and Gus. Jude dated a woman named Chelsea, but I couldn't find any mention of him coming to the inn for any reason or that he was intending to get in touch with me." Maisie put the cell phone on the bedside table.

"Okay, we'll figure this out." As soon as Robert pulled the covers over them, he moved in close, judging her reaction.

She took him in her arms and began kissing him. He was all for the intimacy between them to continue and deepen.

"Tell me if you want me to stop," Robert said, cupping her face and kissing her deeply. He was glad they were in bed together, having thought of being with her in bed like this since they'd snuggled with each other on the beach. This was much more comfortable, private, and enjoyable. She was soft and warm, and her kisses made him want so much more.

"Don't stop," she murmured against his ear.

Already his blood was fired up, his pheromones taking charge, telling her just how much he wanted this with her. Her pheromones were giving him the go-ahead too.

He slid his hands over her pajama shirt, feeling her lovely breasts under the soft cotton fabric. Her nipples grew taut, and he could feel them against his palms, enticing him to go further. He continued to massage her breasts, and she moaned with pleasure. He wondered just how soundproof her walls were or if her sister could hear everything that was going on. Maybe William too.

As if Maisie could read his mind, she broke off their kiss and whispered, "Anne will be listening to music on her headphones. She always does before she goes to sleep."

"Good." He didn't want to disturb her sister, but he really wanted to go as far with Maisie as she wanted to go. He hoped they wouldn't disturb William.

He slid his hands up her shirt and cupped her breasts, massaging them, loving the feel of her warm, soft flesh in his hands.

They were kissing, tongues sliding over each other's, mouths pressed together. He slid her shirt off so he could move his mouth to one of her breasts, licking the nipple and then the other. She ran her hands through his hair and sighed.

She seemed lost in his touching her. He was thinking he would love to have her in his bed at home; then there would be no worry if they got rather noisy. He hoped he wasn't thinking too far ahead of himself here.

His gaze centered on hers, and she smiled. He told himself he hadn't known her long, but what little time they'd been together with all their wild adventures just showed him that he sure wanted to be with her more. Though maybe not on those kinds of adventures in the future. More like running as wolves tonight, preparing and sharing a meal together, fishing, scuba diving—just fun things.

He slid his hand down her belly to her waistband, and she held her breath in anticipation. He slipped his hand under her waistband, his fingers sweeping over her short, curly hairs, until he found the dewy softness between her feminine folds. Her body was definitely ready for him, but he couldn't consummate the relationship or he would be mated to her for life. He ran his finger over her nubbin and began to stroke.

She quickly slid her pajama shorts down her hips, and he removed them the rest of the way. Then he was back to stroking her feminine nub, hoping he was doing it the way she liked best. She arched her back, pressing herself harder against his finger, wanting more. She was tense as he rose up to kiss her mouth again, his finger keeping contact with her, stroking, bringing her to climax.

He could tell she was about to come, and he quickly covered her mouth with his as she cried out against his lips, their tongues stroking hard, her arms wrapping around him tight and holding him there for a long moment. "Oh God," she whispered. "I'm so glad you caught me."

He thought she meant about muffling her cry so William and Anne wouldn't hear her. But then she said, "The fishhook."

He smiled and kissed her nose. "That was the best fishing I ever did. Definitely the catch was a total keeper."

"I'm glad to hear it." She pushed him onto his back and removed his briefs, which was a bit of a struggle because he was fully aroused. She smiled and threw the covers aside. She began stroking him, making him feel as though he'd gone to heaven.

In the worst way, he wanted to enter her and consummate the relationship, mate her with his heart and soul. But he could be impulsive at times, and he wondered if she was too.

Right now, she was stealing every thought he had from him, and all he could do was smell her beautiful she-wolf scent of flowers and sweet wine, of sex and pheromones that were still through the roof, telling them to do it, to mate, to go all the way.

She leaned over to kiss him and continued to stroke him all the way to the end. He was absolutely in ecstasy as he climaxed and pulled her against him, wanting the intimacy to continue between them after what they'd shared.

Then he rolled over with her in his arms and out of bed to avoid messing up the sheets and carried her to the bathroom. Finishing up in the shower only added to the sensual pleasure he'd experienced with her so far.

The next morning, Maisie woke to see Robert smiling at her. He kissed her forehead and then her mouth. "No regrets," she said, "in case you're worrying about it."

"I definitely have no regrets. I'm glad you have none either. You are sure nice to wake up to."

"Hmm, I feel the same. I didn't disturb you by cuddling with you during the night?"

"No, it was really nice."

She sighed. "Same here." Better than nice.

They smelled ham and eggs cooking in the kitchen, and she pushed her covers aside, got up, and began getting dressed. "Anne is up making breakfast for us. I should help her, then after we eat and clean up, we'll make breakfast for our guests."

"Can I help at all?" Robert looked perfectly happy to stay in her bed, which she loved.

"No. Stay in bed and continue to look sexy, but I won't be able to come back to bed with you."

He chuckled and got out of bed.

"Or," she said, eyeing his package, "you can get *out* of bed and look sexy." She gave him a quick hug. "See you in a few minutes."

Before she changed her mind and returned to bed with him, she left the bedroom and joined Anne in the kitchen. "Where's William?"

"He's out looking around the property for any other clues of what had happened." Anne served up their breakfast. "What about you and Robert?"

"Hmm, it was good."

"I heard the guys talking about the case last night." Anne poured cups of tea for them.

"I meant to ask Robert what they had talked about, but we didn't do a whole lot of talking once he joined me in bed."

In truth, Maisie had totally forgotten about it, which was really unusual for her.

Anne smiled. "I'm not surprised. I would have been worried about the two of you if all you'd done was talked about the case. What about Jude's phone?"

"Nothing on it except he was dating a woman named Chelsea. Nothing connecting him to Gus or mentioning coming out to the inn or harassing me."

Anne shook her head. "Figures we wouldn't discover anything."

Chapter 14

BEING WITH MAISIE LAST NIGHT WAS PURE JOY, AND Robert decided that this was the end of his bachelorhood if she was agreeable. He had dated enough she-wolves over the years to know when he had found the right one for him. But he wanted to give her the time to decide and not rush things if she wasn't ready.

He dressed and hurried to join everyone for breakfast, giving Maisie a kiss before they all sat down to eat. William gave him a conspiratorial look as if he knew just what Robert had been thinking. Robert and Maisie's relationship was easy for all to see because of the affection she and he already shared with each other every time they saw one another.

While they ate, they began talking about the security videos.

"I keep thinking about the way that Ike, at least I figure that's who that had to be at Heather's pie shop," Maisie said, "looked so surprised to see me speak with him like I knew him. I'm wondering if he was in the area because he was looking for his brother. What if Ike was acting so strange because he was trying to learn where his brother had disappeared to?"

"But why wouldn't he have talked to you about Gus at the pie shop if that were the case? He didn't talk to me either when he picked up Gus's license," Anne said.

"Maybe he's not very outgoing. Gus was, but maybe his twin is more reserved," Maisie said. "He hasn't been answering his phone, but maybe the charge ran out or something else happened to it. We just don't know. Also, what if Ike suspects that someone had done something to his brother, but he felt confiding in us wouldn't help because we're just a couple of women? Or maybe he even suspected Gus had been up to something bad and no way did he want to share that with other wolves."

"Okay, you could be right on all accounts," William said. "Anne gave me some of the backstory on all this. How about we inform Stuart, the owner of the male dog that is probably the father of Lady's pups, that we're looking for Ike? He lives in Glasgow, and we can tell him we found Gus's body and we're trying to locate Gus's brother or any other family to give them the news. We looked over social media, and Ike isn't on anything. We looked for Gus, and he wasn't either. So except for their friends Stuart and Bruce, we don't have anyone else to contact. Bruce lives in Edinburgh, so I think it would be best to contact Stuart first, since he lives in Glasgow where Gus and Ike lived."

"I agree," Robert said.

"I'll call him," Maisie said, "since Gus and I went out together that night and I found him in the water."

Everyone smiled at her.

Maisie sighed. "Yeah, I know how that sounds. But he

saw another woman after me, and we do have the man in the hoodie."

"And the wrist splint," Edward said.

"Maybe Stuart or Ike knows someone like that." Then she called Stuart's number, and when he answered, she said, "Hi, this is Maisie MacTavish from the MacTavish Inn. I'm trying to reach Ike Anderson. His brother, Gus, stayed here with us, and—"

"Ike is trying to locate his brother. He hasn't heard from him in a few days. He said he got his driver's license from your place, that Lady had chewed on it, but that Gus's car wasn't there. So he has no idea where he went," Stuart said.

"I'm sorry. We found Gus after Ike picked up Gus's license. We're trying to get ahold of Ike to tell him what we discovered, but he's not answering his phone," Maisie said.

"Hell, Gus is dead, isn't he?" Stuart sounded genuinely upset about it.

"We wanted to tell Gus's next of kin first, but yes. Do they have any other family that we can reach out to?" Maisie asked.

"No."

"Okay, do you know anyone who knows Gus and is currently wearing a wrist splint for any reason?" she asked.

Stuart didn't say anything for a minute.

"We're all wolves, by the way. We're keeping all of this under wraps. Wolves need to deal with this if the guy who"— Maisie sighed—"if the person who murdered Gus was a wolf. We need to deal with it ourselves if he was. We don't know if the man we saw wearing a hoodie was the one who harmed

Gus, but he was also wearing a wrist splint, so we need to identify who he is and question him."

"Jack Wolfson. If he's the one you saw," Stuart said. "He broke his wrist six weeks ago. For us, it would have healed in three weeks, half the time it takes humans to heal. He and Gus have been having an ongoing fight over a she-wolf. It's crazy because I don't think Chelsea Bowers is all that interested in either of them for the long term. It's like they're having all these issues with each other and Chelsea's not even a consideration...or shouldn't be. A few weeks back, Jack injured his wrist and was wearing a splint."

"Do you have an address and or phone number for Jack Wolfson?" Maisie asked.

"I've got his phone number. He lives in Glasgow. We all met at a party that Ike and Gus had thrown at a club. Chelsea was there. She'd come with a female friend of Ike's, and Jack and Gus both were interested in her."

"Is... Is Jack on social media?"

"He is."

"Please tell Ike to give us a call." Maisie gave him her phone number. "We're the ones who found Lady, and our friend who is a vet delivered her pups. Your dog's pups too, as far as we know."

"Aye. Bruce called me about that. That sure was a surprise. I'll tell Ike to call you as soon as I can reach him," Stuart said. "I believe he has a new phone number."

"Thanks. What about the woman? Chelsea? Gus saw a woman the night he disappeared. Do you have a picture of her?" Maisie asked.

"No. But Gus might have or Ike even. I'm not sure."

"Okay, thanks."

Anne was already looking up Jack Wolfson of Glasgow on social media sites. "No way."

"What?" Maisie looked at Anne's phone and gave a little gasp. "That's Jude Springer."

"Well, apparently, he's also known as Jack Wolfson," Anne said. "I told you he wasn't to be trusted."

"I know." Maisie shook her head.

Robert friended Bruce and Stuart on Facebook. Once they accepted his friend requests, he friended Jack Wolfson to Anne's and Maisie's surprise.

"What are you doing?" Anne asked, sounding alarmed.

"If he accepts the friend request, we can see his pictures and friends' names, as long as he allows friends to see them. By adding Bruce and Stuart, Jack will know some of his friends are my friends." It wasn't long before Robert's friend request was accepted.

They looked through Jack's friend list and photographs. "Chelsea Bowers is one of his friends. She's not listed as his girlfriend though. The same one who Gus and he were fighting over?" Maisie asked.

"Probably," Anne said.

They saw a photo of Chelsea at a club and one of Bruce and Stuart at the same club. Ike and Gus could be seen in the background, Gus smiling and talking to Chelsea.

"There are no pictures of Jack or mentions of him wearing a splint. These were taken a week before Gus's death." Maisie frowned. "If Jude—*Jack* murdered Gus, he would have smelled that I'd been with Gus that night. Then if Chelsea was the next woman Gus saw—"

"That would give Jack motivation to do something about it," Robert said. "We need to find Chelsea and make sure Jack isn't coming after you, since you were also with Gus that night."

———————

After breakfast, Robert and William cleaned up the kitchen, and then Anne and Maisie began taking orders from their guests for breakfast.

When they returned from the main dining room to start preparing breakfast for the guests, Robert said, "If you don't need our help, we're going to review the security videos, since I haven't actually seen them yet."

"Aye, and if you would like, you can look at the animal photos I took and pick out your favorites so I can order the prints." Maisie set up her laptop on the coffee table in her and Anne's living room. "If you need anything else, just let me know. If you want anything from the kitchen, feel free to help yourselves."

"Thanks," Robert said.

They started looking at the security videos first. "The guy with the hoodie has one of those drugstore splints on his wrist," Robert said. "They're easy to remove and put back on."

William looked at the video. "You're right. Go back to where we first see Gus."

Robert backed up the video. Gus didn't have a splint on. "Okay, the guy wearing the charcoal-gray hoodie is definitely a different guy. But if he's our murderer, how could he strangle Gus if he had an injured wrist?"

"What if it was a ruse? Like Ted Bundy, the American serial killer, who wore a cast on his arm, pretending to be hurt," William said. "He was one of the cases we studied when we were going through the police academy training in Texas."

"Yeah, he made the news all over the world. So this guy's wearing a wrist splint and size-ten boots." Robert paused the security video. "Look, those are Derby black safety boots."

"Okay, go back and look at Gus's shoes and we'll see if we can recognize what he's wearing."

"There. Gus is wearing brown hiking boots and blue jeans. The other guy is wearing black trousers." Of course, Gus could have changed his pants and shoes, but the wrist splint the one man was wearing made Robert believe they were two different individuals.

They looked at the videos several more times but didn't see anything new. Then Robert pulled up the animal photos Maisie had taken. He laughed when he saw the ones of Mittens trying to catch the toy mouse. Those were his favorites.

William laughed too. "Maisie takes great photos. I love these of Mittens."

"She does." Robert and William picked all the ones they liked the best, writing down the numbers.

When they were finished with the photographs, the

ladies were clearing the tables, so Robert and William got to work cleaning the dishes, which made Anne and Maisie smile.

"You don't have to do that," Maisie said.

"Don't discourage them. This is really nice," Anne said. "I'm going to clean up a couple of the rooms."

Anne and Maisie didn't offer daily cleaning service unless guests paid extra for it. Guests usually only stayed the night or two and then were off to another spot, exploring their surroundings from another lodging.

"I'll be at the reservation desk," Maisie said, "and after lunch, I have a photo shoot with Heather at the castle gardens."

"For her maternity shoot?" Anne asked.

"Yeah."

Anne said, "When I need a maternity photo shoot, I want you to do them too."

Maisie laughed. "Oh, and I was thinking we should order our medieval Christmas gowns so that Edeen has time to make them."

"Yeah, sure. You know which one I want. Just order two of them."

Maisie smiled. "I'll do that."

When Anne went out to the guest rooms, Robert asked Maisie, "Do you often dress alike?"

"Sometimes. It's not because we want to look like twins. We just really like the same things. But I might select something else because I really like everything that Edeen makes." Maisie glanced at her laptop. "Oh, you already picked out the pictures you wanted?"

"Yeah. I wrote down the numbers here."

"Okay, I'll order the prints, and they should be here tomorrow through their expedited service."

"Great."

After Maisie ordered the prints, she began taking guest reservations, while Robert and William went back over the video.

"What about the vehicles? Let's look at the earlier ones and see if we can locate anyone leaving in a vehicle who is wearing a wrist splint," Robert said. As they were looking them over, he thought back to seeing the man they thought was Gus in the pie shop. He had been wearing a jacket, not a hoodie, gray trousers, and black boots. He couldn't remember what kind. Maybe Heather would have security video that would show more of the man's details than he recalled.

He got on his phone and called the shop. Heather answered. "Hey, it's Robert. We're looking into this matter with—" He wondered if she even knew about the dead body.

"I know about it. Enrick told me. What do you need to know?"

"When Maisie and I had lunch at your place, a man came in and ordered a pie. Maisie went to tell him that he'd left his driver's license at the inn, and then after lunch we saw the man she thought she'd spoken to dead in the ocean."

"Okay. So you want me to pull up security video to see what we can of him?" Heather asked.

"I'll do it," Callum said, butting in on Heather's conversation.

"Do you see what I have to put up with?" Heather asked Robert.

Robert smiled. "Okay, Callum, if you can find any footage of the man Maisie had spoken to, send it to me, will you?"

"Is he the one who murdered the guy you found in the water?" Callum asked.

"We believe he's Gus's twin brother, Ike, but we need to know what he was wearing and if he had a wrist splint on his left arm." They had to discount his own brother if they could. What if he had only said he was looking for his brother, but in truth, he had been the one who had murdered him? Or what if they were mistaken about Gus's identity, the body was Ike's, and Gus had been the murderer?

"I'll send what I can find on it," Callum said.

"Thanks."

Heather said, "Okay, that keeps Callum out of my hair for a bit."

Robert laughed. "Thanks for helping us with this."

"Of course."

"Maisie is eager to do your maternity photo shoot this afternoon."

"Oh, me too, before it's too late," Heather said.

Robert frowned. "Are you going into labor?"

"Nay. I mean, I'm experiencing the same as Colleen has been. Intermittent contractions, nothing lasting any time at all. I keep hoping this is it, and then they stop."

"Okay, well, keep me posted."

"I will. Believe me."

After a while, Callum sent the video of the man in the

shop. He wasn't wearing a wrist splint, and he was wearing blue jeans and sneakers. So no match there.

Then Iverson called. "I found Gus's car. It was left near a petrol station about ten miles from here."

"What are you doing with it?" Robert asked.

"Hauling it to the castle and going over it with a fine-tooth comb for forensics. I'll swap out with one of the brothers so William, Edward, and I can all look over it. Since we're all former homicide detectives, it would be good if all three of us look for clues. I did check with the petrol station to see their security videos. They showed Gus dropping off that woman he was with at the inn. Then he left. The car smells like it's been wiped down with a bleach cleaner. It's really pungent. I think it was to get rid of any fingerprints but maybe also to disguise the murderer's scent in the event a wolf was investigating this."

"Can you tell if Gus's scent was there?"

"Aye. And another male wolf's, but I don't know who it is. Also, a female's scent, which might be Chelsea's. The bleach couldn't cover all the scents."

"Okay, good job. Let us know what else you discover."

"I sure will."

Robert sure wished they could get somewhere with this faster than they were. He thought of himself as patient, but when it came to Maisie's and Anne's safety, he realized he was really impatient, and for good reason.

Chapter 15

THAT EVENING, MAISIE WANTED TO RETIRE EARLY WITH Robert, which made her want to go to his place for some solitude and loving. She was tired after the wild night making love to Robert last eve, and she was eager to make love to him again before they went to sleep. Finally, when it seemed like a decent time to go to bed, William gave them an out and said he was ready to call it a night.

Yes!

Then they all said good night and headed to their beds.

This time, Maisie and Robert made love before showering together, and it truly was as good as the first time. In the shower, they were smiling as they soaped each other and washed each other's hair, which felt amazing. She could really get used to this routine.

They climbed into bed naked, pulled their covers up, and snuggled as if this was just the way it should always be. She already didn't want Robert to return to his home once they didn't need him for security any longer. She never thought she would feel so strongly about a wolf after all her failures with other wolves she had dated.

Man, Robert could really get used to being with Maisie like this—the loving, the showers, the intimacy, sleeping with her. He hadn't known what to expect when he slept with her, but they fit like two peas in a pod, complementing each other. He hadn't slept this well in forever. She soothed him and made him forget anything else other than being with her. He loved his new home, but returning to it meant leaving her once he wasn't needed for security, and that was already making him think of changing that arrangement in a hurry. They didn't know when the sisters would no longer need him and William, but he hoped the arrangement would give them time to get to know each other better, and by the time he moved back home, maybe Maisie would want to move in with him—permanently, of course. A mating, definitely. But he would give it a while to make sure she was of the same mind. He sure hoped so because he already didn't want to give her up for anything.

She was sleeping securely in his arms. This was the life, he thought, as he finally dropped off to sleep.

In the morning, Maisie remembered the animal photos for Robert's clinic should be in the mail and Robert could give them to Veronica to frame. She hopped out of bed, got dressed, and said, "Mail time!"

He smiled. "I've never seen anyone who is that eager to get the mail."

"Your photos should be in the mailbox."

"Oh, great." He climbed out of bed and began getting dressed.

"I'll be right back."

William's guest room and Anne's bedroom were quiet and dark, and Maisie envisioned them both sound asleep under their covers. She headed outside the inn to get the mail, and when she returned, Robert was dressed and starting the coffee in the kitchen.

Maisie handed the package of animal photos to Robert. He looked through the photos and smiled. "These are great."

She glanced at them. "They turned out beautifully." She started making breakfast.

Robert said, "I'll take the photos to the castle to give them to Veronica to frame after we have breakfast, and then I'll be right back. William will stay with you ladies in the meantime."

"You don't have to be in any rush to return. We're fine for now, and if you need to get anything else done while you're away, go for it. I just need to be at the castle at two this afternoon to do the photo shoot for Heather and Enrick. We could…meet at your place maybe for lunch?" Maisie didn't want Robert to feel like she was planning his life for him if he had other things to do, but she really craved spending more private time with him. She was thinking about their time on the island and how nice it had been to be together alone for those hours. "In the meantime, I'm going to look over Colleen's photos and then get them ready for her to choose which ones she wants also."

"Absolutely, I would love to have lunch with you. Does noon sound good?" Robert asked without hesitation, sounding just as eager to enjoy some more time with her.

"Yeah. I'll just drive over to your place, we can have lunch, and then I'll run over to the castle to do the shoot. I need to go early so I can show Colleen the proofs of her photo shoot also."

"That will be perfect. I'm going to work on the house a little more before the open house Saturday."

"If you need any help with anything, just let me know."

"Sure thing."

Anne came out of her bedroom dressed, rubbing her eyes. "You two are up early."

William came out of the guest room and yawned. "I guess it's morning."

Anne laughed. "Yes, how can you tell?"

William motioned to the kitchen, where Robert and Maisie were dishing up omelets and bacon. "They're making breakfast."

Anne began getting them mugs of tea, coffee for William, and glasses of orange juice. Then they sat down to have their breakfast.

After breakfast, Anne and William took over cleaning the kitchen so Robert could get out of there.

Robert kissed Maisie, giving her one of his wonderfully long and delicious kisses, then they hugged, and he smiled down at her. "I'll see you at lunch."

Already looking forward to seeing him at lunch, Maisie waved goodbye, then went back inside, and while Anne took breakfast orders from guests, Maisie began cooking the meals. Even though William had offered to help with preparing breakfast for guests the last two days, they hadn't needed him to yet. His job was to be there for protection, to watch and make sure that someone who didn't belong there didn't show up and threaten Anne or her.

"Lunch with Robert, eh?" Anne said, coming into the kitchen to give her more of the guests' orders and to start making omelets. "I don't blame you. I would want to spend every waking hour with him alone and not with a couple of other people within earshot all the time."

"I love you," Maisie said, giving her sister a hug.

"I know you do. And I love you right back."

Once they finished serving breakfast and cleaning up after their guests, Anne went out to take care of the rooms that needed cleaning, William going with her.

Maisie began going over the photos of Colleen and Grant while manning the front desk.

William and Anne returned a lot sooner than Maisie thought they would. She wondered if William had actually helped Anne change the linens on the beds because they'd returned so quickly. Anne put the used bed linens in the washing machine and started it. By the time she arrived at the check-in counter, it was time for lunch.

"I'll make lunch for us," William said to Anne.

"Oh, great. Thanks."

"I'm out of here." Maisie grabbed her photography gear and her laptop.

"Have fun with the photo shoot. I can't wait to see Heather's gown," Anne said.

"Me either."

"And have a nice lunch with Robert," Anne said.

"I'm sure I will. He's an amazing cook." Maisie left and drove over to Robert's place.

When she arrived, she knocked on the door and Robert hurried to open it, Mittens greeting her too. "Aww, you came back." She crouched down and petted her.

"Yeah, I brought her home while I was doing some laundry and other chores. You and I didn't talk about what we wanted to eat. Do Scottish salmon sandwiches appeal?"

"Oh, aye, I haven't had one in ages. What can I do to help?"

They soon were adding the cheese, avocado, mayonnaise, tomatoes, and cooked salmon to slices of sourdough. Then they sat down to eat.

"Ohmigosh, this is so good," Maisie said, tomato juice running down her chin. She laughed, and he wiped her chin with his napkin before she could grab her own.

Then, and she didn't even know how or why or exactly when it happened, they were kissing. She was on her feet, and she guessed he'd pulled her from her chair. It was just so amazing, spontaneous, fun-loving, and he tasted so delicious. "You make everything even more special," she said. "Meals, the island adventure, sword fighting, nighttime fun, all of it."

"I swear, Maisie, when I caught you in the sea, our stars had to have been aligned." Robert kissed her again. "I feel like when I'm with you, I'm standing in sunshine, no clouds in sight, though if they come, we'll chase them away."

"You're all that I want in a wolf," she admitted. "I know we don't want to rush into anything, but I've never been this close to a male wolf before, to be ready to mate. I feel so comfortable with you, like I've known you forever. You're so easy to love."

He smiled. "I feel the same way about you. It feels so nice being with you no matter the wild situations we've been in. You're an amazing woman."

"Let's finish our lunch, and then we've got some time to try out your bed before I have to leave."

"I'm so glad we're on the same page."

She swore they finished their sandwiches in record time, and then he grabbed her up and stalked toward his bedroom. She was glad he did because she wasn't sure which of the rooms was his bedroom. It was beautiful inside with one large picture hanging over his bed of Mittens sleeping on her pillow.

Maisie laughed. "How did you get it framed so fast?" It looked so perfect with his black-and-white bedroom decor—his black comforter and black-and-white pillows, the black lamps on the bedside tables and white lampshades. His furniture was all light oak that complemented the black-and-white furnishings.

"While you were working at the inn, I took the pictures over to Veronica first thing, and she did that one right away so I could bring it home and hang it."

"It's just adorable."

"Yeah, because you did such a beautiful job taking the photo in the first place."

"Thanks. I love the way Mittens is color-coordinated perfectly with your bedroom."

"Exactly." Then Robert and Maisie were kissing, hugging, cherishing each other.

He made her feel so special and so loved.

He started to slip her shirt over her head. He sat her down on his comfortable bed to remove her shoes and socks. "Oooh, I love your bed. Once I'm in it, I'll never want to leave it."

"I would love to keep you there with me," he said, smiling.

He removed his shoes, and she began to kiss him again. She treasured kissing him, enjoying his warm mouth on hers, the tenderness, loving, genuine force while he was pressing his kisses against her lips. Then she was unbuttoning his shirt and dragging it off his shoulders.

He unfastened her pants, and she did the same with his. Her bra was tossed aside, and then his boxer briefs and her panties joined her bra on the floor. They were on the mattress, moving against each other, bodies undulating, pressing against all their most sensitive spots, working up his arousal. He was getting hard with all the friction between them. Together they were amazing. She was so hot and wet for him already.

She was certain he was the one for her, and she would have just said *screw it and mate me already*, but she was afraid she was being way too impulsive, and she needed to slow down. But slowing down wasn't what she had in mind as she gently scratched his back with her nails and he nipped at her bottom lip, telling her how much he loved the feelings between them.

"I don't want to wait," she said in his ear, wanting him to know she needed this with him and making herself vulnerable to rejection. But she was also ready to accept it if he wasn't ready for it.

"I know I'll never feel this way about another wolf." Robert smiled. "You're the only woman I've been with that, when we have plans to be together, I don't forget them."

She smiled at him. "That says a lot."

"It sure does. What about your parents? Do they even know that we've met and have been dating?"

"Aye. They're thrilled. I think Anne's been telling them more details than I have."

He laughed.

"But this is my choice. Our choice," Maisie said.

"I agree."

"Then mate me, Robert Campbell. Put me out of my misery."

He laughed. "You'll be doing the same for me, Maisie MacTavish."

Then they were heating up the bed, kissing and sliding their bodies against each other until they had built up the sexual tension again. He slid his hand over her breast, squeezing it and then tonguing her mouth at the same time.

She loved the way he set her blood on fire. Just from the touch of his stiff arousal against her, she knew she was making him experience the same thing.

She breathed in the male scent of him, his wolfishness and sexiness. She absorbed his warmth as he crushed her to his chest and whispered in her ear, "I love you, Maisie.

Catching you was the best thing that has ever happened in my life."

She smiled and hugged him back tightly. "I love you. Catching me the way you did changed my life forever—in a good way."

They kissed again, pressing their lips together, their tongues colliding and dancing.

She was sure her sister would be shocked to learn that they went this far today, but Maisie had no intention of holding back. She expected Robert to penetrate her sheath with his rigid staff to claim her as his mate right away, but instead, he began to slide his hand down her belly, separating from her and working her feminine bud to bring her pleasure. Ensuring he pleasured her first was another reason she loved him.

He continued to stroke her, kissing her breasts, licking her aroused nipples. He kissed her throat, nipping at it and her jaw, tackling her mouth again as her hands roamed all over his muscular body. She felt she was being uplifted, higher, the sensation of climax just out of reach, there, just...a... little...bit...aye! She cried out, loving that he could work her to a climax in such a wonderfully adept way. Then she slid her hands around to his buttocks and pulled at him to join her. This was it—the mating between wolves that would be forever.

"Are you ready?" he asked, being ever sensitive to her feelings.

"Yes, for sure, forever and ever."

He pressed his heavy arousal into her, slowly, deepening

their joining, penetrating all the way, and then he began to thrust. She met his thrusts, raising her pelvis so he could go deeper and kissing his mouth with appreciation and love.

Their hearts were beating so hard, as if they were racing to the moon and back. Their blood was on fire. His gaze connected with hers for a moment, lust-filled but loving too, while he continued to pump into her, taking her all the way to a cataclysmic orgasm.

She cried out, and he groaned with completion, and then he settled against her body like a heavy silken blanket. She wrapped her arms around him to keep him there. She knew she needed to make sure she made it to Heather's photo shoot in time, but for now, she just wanted to hold on to her mate and revel in the fact that he was all hers.

He didn't seem to want to let go of her either and just hugged her tight. "I'm not squishing you too much, am I?"

"No. You feel just perfect."

"So do you."

"I want to just stay here for the rest of the day."

"I want to also."

"Just don't let me miss Heather's photo shoot."

He glanced at the clock. "You have another half hour before you have to go."

She sighed. "Good. What are we going to do about tonight?"

"Do you want to have dinner and then run as mated wolves? We can tell the families we're mated after the photo shoot."

"That sounds good. Don't be mad at me if I let it slip

when I see Heather though." She was just so excited about it. She thought she would be careful about not sharing it, but if Heather asked her, Maisie wouldn't be able to lie and wouldn't want to either. She wanted the whole world to know.

Robert chuckled. "I won't be. We could tell our families now."

"No. Way. I want this moment of mated bliss to last for a few more minutes, and then I've got to shower, dress, and run." Maisie would have to show Colleen her pictures *after* Heather's shoot now.

As soon as she headed into the bathroom, she said, "Whoa, I love your bathroom. This whirlpool bathtub is fantastic."

He walked into the bathroom. "Do you want to take a bath?"

"Another time. I've got to get to work, so it's shower time. I love your glassed-in shower too. It's big enough for two." She pulled him into the shower with her, and he shut the door.

She was so ready to stay here in her new home with her sexy mate. It was the greatest.

As she pulled her bra and panties on, she said, "Oh, I need to move my clothes from the inn to the house!"

He laughed. "Okay, before dinner we'll pack up your things and bring them here."

She finished dressing while he did too, and she glanced in the closet, figuring he would have to move his clothes over to give her some room, but she was astounded at what she saw. The closet was fitted with rods for his and her clothes, shoe shelves, even drawers, and, on the very top shelf, room for hats. His clothes were confined to his side of the closet, leaving the rest for her. He was astounding, and she was thrilled. She appreciated his sensitivity in considering his future mate's needs. Not that he knew that he was going to find Maisie in particular, but for just any she-wolf he might have taken for a mate. She was so glad that she was the one who had totally lucked out.

"You are amazing," she said, wrapping her arms around him and kissing him. "I've never seen such a beautiful closet for two. And you didn't even spread your clothes out all over it until you found a mate."

He hugged her tightly. "I was just waiting for you to come into my life."

"Well, it's much appreciated, believe me. When Anne sees it, she'll wish you had caught her in the ocean instead."

"It wouldn't have been the same. Once I met you, this is where we would have ended up. You and me just like this."

"I agree. I can't wait to move everything in, and it will feel much more official that we're together now. Plus, we need to get it all put away before your open house. We probably should have waited until after your open house to mate." She didn't want to mess up his beautiful house.

He laughed. "There was no way I could have lasted that long."

She chuckled. "I agree." Then they kissed again, and she had to go! Heather would be at the castle gardens soon, and in her condition, she didn't need to be waiting for Maisie to show up! "I've got to go. I love you."

"I love you too."

Then Maisie was off to do the last maternity shoot that she had scheduled for a while.

———

Not only was Robert glad that he'd saved all his boxes from his move here in the garage and they could use them to move Maisie's household items to her new home, but he was also so thrilled that he had considered a home that was set up to beautifully accommodate a mate. Maisie had been so cute when she was so enthusiastic to see the closet's setup, and he knew he'd done it right. His sister had said his mate would love it, but when Maisie showed how much she did and that the bathroom was set up to accommodate a couple too, he knew his home design had turned out perfectly.

In anticipation of Maisie moving in, he began moving the packing boxes into the car. He was ready to move his mate into their home and enjoy the place with her as a mated couple. He was glad their packmates would see that he didn't have a half-empty closet, but that it was half-filled with his beautiful she-wolf's things too.

The master bathroom also had double sinks and enough empty cabinet and drawer space for anything Maisie needed to store in there. She hadn't even noticed that yet, and he knew she would really be pleased. He made room in the coat closet and then looked in the kitchen cabinets. He could move things around to accommodate anything she would bring to the house, but he would wait to see what she had.

He glanced out the window at the backyard. Would she like a garden like Edeen had? He didn't have time to grow and raise plants, not once he opened his clinic. But if Maisie wanted a garden, he would sure help her set it up. He imagined Lachlan would help him too.

Another delivery of supplies for his clinic showed up, and he went out to put them away, thinking about how he couldn't wait for Maisie to return so he could get her moved in for good.

Chapter 16

When Maisie arrived at the castle garden, Heather was already there wearing a pretty blue, silky, medieval-style gown. Maisie wasn't late, but she hadn't wanted Heather to have to wait for her even for a moment.

"Your gown is amazing." Maisie loved the long sleeves and all the handiwork in the form of embroidery on the front of the gown and around the neck and sleeves. Really pretty.

"Aye, Edeen does lovely work." Heather was rubbing her belly as she sat down on a garden bench to rest.

Maisie got her camera set up, and Enrick hurried to join them. He was wearing his kilt and looked handsome while he was posing with his mate. Maisie took photos, some of them kissing, holding each other, and some of just Heather. They were a beautiful couple, and she loved that they wanted her to take these pictures. She felt honored.

After they finished up, Maisie said, "I'll share these with you tomorrow at your shop. How about before you open? That'll give me time to find the best ones and do a little touch-up."

"That sounds great. Come a couple of hours before we open," Heather said.

"I can't wait to see them," Enrick said.

"Well, I was honored to do them. Thanks. I'm going to see Colleen and Grant and show them their photos. I'll see you tomorrow," Maisie said.

"We'll see you then," Heather said.

Maisie met with Colleen and Grant inside the castle, and she had tea with them in the library while she showed them the photos.

"Oh, these are all beautiful," Colleen said.

"I agree," Grant said. "It's hard to pick from all of them."

But they finally did and ordered the ones they loved the best. Then Maisie pulled up their animal photos in case they wanted to order any of them, which worked great. She'd taken them for Robert's clinic, but they loved the animal photos also.

"Photos of the dogs are going in the kennel and on our Irish wolfhound website. Some of the images of the Scottish fold cats will go in the kennel too since they slip in there to visit with the dogs all the time and sleep with them. Of course, some of the prize Highland cow photos will be added to the library walls," Colleen said, Grant agreeing with her.

After marking down the ones they wanted, Maisie said, "Okay, I'll order them and give them to you at the open house."

"That sounds great," Grant said.

Smiling, Colleen nodded.

Then Maisie left and returned to Robert's house.

"Are you all done?" Robert asked, opening the door for her immediately, smiling appreciably, pulling her into the house at the same time and kissed her.

"Yep." Maisie wrapped him in her arms with a warm embrace and continued the kiss. "We need to tell Anne and Edeen that we're mated. We need to decide what to do about housing arrangements. I mean, yes, I'm staying with you here no matter what, but with the guy who killed Gus on the loose? I'm not sure about leaving Anne with only William to guard her because if he has to leave for any reason, then she'll be alone."

Robert agreed. "William and another wolf from our pack can stay with her to make sure there's always someone there. We won't leave her on her own, given the situation."

"I want William's brother to join them then."

Robert laughed. "You feel sorry for him because his brother got to stay with Anne and he didn't."

"I do. I think the brothers would like to be together."

"Okay, I'll call Lachlan and tell him to send Edward over."

"But first, we should call my parents and then tell our sisters, or Lachlan will know why we have to have another guard there," she said.

"Okay, we'll tell your parents first." Robert sighed. "Maybe I should have met them and talked to them about a mating beforehand."

"No way. This was between us. We're wolves. We know when we find the right one for us. We don't need anyone else telling us who we should mate," she said.

"Let's do it then." Still, Robert seemed a little nervous about it.

She gave him a hug. "They'll love you." Then she called her mom and dad and put them on speakerphone. "Robert and I have some news, but we want to share it with you both before we called our sisters. We're both on speakerphone."

"You're going to mate each other," her mother said.

Maisie smiled. "We're mated."

There was silence for a moment, and then her dad said, "Finally, one of our girls is mated."

"We haven't met him yet," her mother said, her voice a little surprised.

"He is wonderful."

Her mother sighed. "Sorry. I was just a little taken aback that it had happened so suddenly. I'm sure he is just right for you. You wouldn't settle for less."

"We are delighted," her dad said.

Maisie was thrilled they were supportive. She knew her mother would feel even more comfortable about it once she met Robert. He was the kindest, sexiest, most loving wolf Maisie had ever dated.

"Aye, we sure are," her mother said. "You're mated." She sounded like she still couldn't believe it. Not that they were courting, but they were forever mated.

"You will love him," Maisie said.

"I will do everything in my power to prove to Maisie how much I love and cherish her," Robert finally said.

"I know you will," her mother said. "She would never mate someone like the guys she has dated in the past."

"I've told Robert about them, Mom," Maisie said.

"They weren't good for her," her mom said.

"No, they weren't," Robert said, "and I'm not anything like them. She comes first, and I would never keep her from her family. She told me you were worried about moving to this area until you were sure your daughters would set down roots permanently here. Between Maisie's photography work, my vet practice, and the inn's income, we'll keep their business going no matter what. We'll want you to be close by also."

Maisie was so glad, and she knew she had fallen in love with the right wolf. She hugged and kissed him, tears filling her eyes.

"Well, it's decided then." Her father sounded pleased. "We were just waiting to learn if the girls would actually stay and give the inn their all or eventually sell and return to Glasgow. When can we visit?"

"We have an open house at my place on Saturday, as well as a viewing of the vet clinic before it opens," Robert said. "We'll be having a lovely celebration. You can stay with us while you visit. It's just down the road from the inn and next door to the MacQuarries' Farraige Castle."

"Or we can stay with Anne, if you're not using your room at the inn any further," her father said to Maisie.

Maisie would like them to get to know Robert better, and if her parents stayed with them, they would.

"Okay, well, we have a son finally." Her mother was cheerful.

"And another daughter," Robert said. "My sister is eager to meet you also. And so is her mate, Lachlan MacQuarrie."

"The MacQuarries. They had that movie filmed at their castle, didn't they?" her mother said.

"They sure did, and they were featured in it. The wolves in it were wolf shifters," Maisie said.

"Wow, okay, great," her mother said. "So we're part of a famous wolf family then."

Robert laughed. "Yeah, you could say that."

"Okay, we will be there for your open house, and then?" her father asked.

"You can have dinner with Anne and us, and then you can decide which place you want to stay at," Robert said.

"That sounds like a good plan," her mother said. "We're so glad you found a good wolf to marry, Maisie."

"Yeah, me especially," Robert said. "Maisie is sure that for me."

"Oh, oh, marriage! When are you getting married?" her mother asked.

"We haven't discussed it yet, Mom." Maisie glanced at Robert to see what he thought of the matter.

"My sister will be having her wedding up at the castle, but we can have ours here at the house or the inn." Maisie knew Robert didn't mind where it was held.

"Or the castle?" Her mother sounded hopeful.

They laughed.

"I'm sure that they would be honored to have it there," Robert said. "Their chef is providing the food for the open house. I'm sure he would do the same for our wedding. Speaking of which, Edeen and Lachlan's wedding is in a week. You'll have to come with us, since you're family now too," Robert said.

With everything planned, they said goodbye.

Robert breathed a sigh of relief. "Well, it seems they're okay with me mating you."

"Yes, of course. They can't say anything but." Maisie laughed.

He laughed too. "Yeah. We're mated for life, so that's true."

"Alright, next up: we have to tell the rest of the family. Why don't we call our sisters on a conference call, and since Lachlan is your brother-in-law, we'll have him on too. We'll call Lachlan's brothers afterward." Maisie couldn't believe that mating the wolf meant gaining a whole bunch of family in one fell swoop.

"That works for me."

She called their sisters and Lachlan. "Robert and I are—"

"Mated!" Edeen and Anne screamed at the same time.

Maisie and Robert laughed.

"Aye, so we're going to ask Lachlan if he can arrange for Edward to join William to watch over you, Anne," Maisie said.

"Yes! William will be glad, I'm sure, and I'm so happy for the both of you," Anne said.

Lachlan agreed. "I know Edward will be, and congratulations, you two."

"Me too. Welcome to the family, both of you," Edeen said. "I'm so excited to have two more sisters. Now you'll be part of the wolf pack."

"Absolutely," Maisie said.

"I'm so happy to have a brother. I guess several—Grant, Enrick, and you too, Lachlan," Anne said.

"Exactly. This calls for a celebration," Edeen said. "But

also, if you don't think it's too late for you to be part of the wedding party, I would love to have both you and Anne as my bridesmaids, Maisie. Lana Cameron is also going to be one. Colleen and Heather were supposed to but can't because of being so close to delivery."

"Oh, we would love to." Maisie was just thrilled. "What would we wear?"

"I already have gowns made. You'll be beautiful in them."

"Aye, we would be delighted to take part in your wedding," Anne said.

"We called Mom and Dad to tell them first, so they're coming to visit and maybe they'll be staying in my room at the inn," Maisie said.

"Oh, oh, I guess you'll be staying with Robert from now on. It's just sinking in," Anne said.

"Yeah, Anne. Like a mated couple," Maisie said, beaming. Not that the notion had completely sunk in with her yet either.

"What about Conan?" Anne asked.

"We'll have to have him stay with us sometimes and you can have him sometimes, unless you want to keep him there for company, especially after William and Edward are no longer needed to guard you."

"We'll see how it all works out. What about the wedding?" Anne said.

Maisie realized it was all kind of overwhelming. She was just so happy about the mating. For wolves, that's all they needed to say I do. "You, Mom, Edeen, and I need to plan that."

"I'm ready," Anne replied.

"Me too," Edeen said.

"We'll have to tell the rest of the pack," Robert said.

"Call Colleen, Grant, Enrick, and Heather, and then they can share it with the rest of the pack," Edeen said. "But I can tell you right now that everyone suspects this was where this was headed from the day you and Maisie were stuck on Eilean Tioram."

Robert smiled, and Maisie chuckled.

"Alright and then we'll all have a special celebration," Maisie said.

"But if you invite your new brothers-in-law and sisters-in-law, do it quickly," Edeen said. "I keep thinking Colleen and Heather will have those babies at any moment."

Maisie laughed. "Yes." She wasn't used to being around women who were due to have babies any day. "Maybe we could meet at Heather's pie shop after it closes for the night to have a special family dinner celebration."

"Absolutely. I'm sure Heather would be thrilled. Her brothers will be there to do all the cooking and serving too, and they can join us," Edeen said.

"Okay, then we'll see if we can have it tomorrow night before the open house the next day." Maisie squeezed Robert's hand.

"I think that will work great," Robert said.

"Well, congratulations, you two." Edeen sounded as delighted as Anne.

"Congratulations," Anne said. "I'm thrilled for you and for us. We went from just the two of us and our parents to a huge extended family and a wolf pack."

"The same for me when I mated Lachlan. It had only been Robert and me for so long," Edeen said.

Lachlan said, "Everyone will be thrilled to hear it."

"After Robert and I call our parents about the dinner for tomorrow, Anne," Maisie said, "Robert and I will come over and pack up my stuff."

"We'll see you soon then," Anne said, and they ended the call.

Then Maisie called Heather to clear having the dinner at her place. Heather was ecstatic. "Can you let all the family know about it? I still need to call my parents," Maisie asked.

"Aye, I sure will."

Then Maisie called her parents back and invited them to the dinner. They said they'd pack up immediately and be there tomorrow.

Maisie ordered the pictures for printing for Colleen and Lachlan. Maisie needed to show Edeen her pet photos too. Then Maisie and Robert headed over to the inn.

When they arrived at the inn, Anne gave them each a hug. "I can't believe you left today to have lunch with Robert and mated him. I mean, I can. If I'd been in your shoes, I would have too, but I'm still getting used to the idea."

"Believe me, I am too. Not about being mated to Robert, but it seems strange to be moving to his place now."

"I bet. Other than clothes, what else do you want to take, and I'll start packing things up for you?" Anne grabbed a box.

"I don't need anything from the kitchen. We purchased all of it for the inn, and it needs to stay here for you and our guests." Maisie shrugged. "The same with the living room. Really, just my clothes and personal items need to go with me. The bedding and everything stays. I'm happy with Robert's bedding." She was more than happy since he was sharing the bed with her.

"Okay, well, you know if there's anything you change your mind about, you can have it," Anne said.

"Thanks." Maisie began pulling all her clothes from the dresser drawers while Anne removed Maisie's clothes from the closet and put them all on the bed to pack.

Robert opened a drawer to start packing Maisie's clothes and paused at her colorful lace underwear. Anne glanced at him and laughed. "I think he likes your undergarments."

Maisie turned to see what Robert was doing, and his face was red. She laughed. "You're so cute, you know."

He grabbed a handful of her bras and panties and smiled. "I can't wait to see you in these."

Maisie knew she wouldn't be wearing them for long once he saw her in them.

They finished packing all her clothes, and then she packed up her stuff from the bathroom.

William and Edward carried the boxes out to Robert's car, and when they returned to the inn, they all had a glass of wine and clinked them together. "Cheers!"

Edward looked thrilled to join his brother there at the inn to look after Anne.

"I'll be back in the morning to help with the inn." Maisie didn't want her sister to believe she was abandoning her now.

"Nay, the brothers are going to help me. You two need

the time together, especially before the open house and all. Then after that, you can help again." Anne winked at her.

"Are you sure? I hadn't planned to leave it all up to you to do."

"Mom and Dad will be here, and we have the celebration dinner tomorrow night, the open house the next day. Yeah, I'll be good. Both William and Edward have been a real help. They won't let me do it all alone."

The brothers smiled.

"I always help out when anyone needs some assistance," Edward said. "William's just like me."

"Yeah, I agree," William said.

"Okay, well, thanks for all the assistance. We're going home to have dinner and then go for our mated wolf run."

Anne smiled. "That will be me someday."

"Me too," Edward said, William agreeing.

Maisie embraced her sister, and Robert hugged her after that, and they said good night to everyone.

When Maisie and Robert returned to Robert's, well, her place now too, they carried in all the boxes and set them against one wall in the bedroom.

"Why don't I start dinner and you can begin unpacking? Then I'll come in and help you put the rest away," Robert said.

"Sure, that works." She started to put her personal items in the bathroom first, wanting to get everything sorted right away. Neither she nor Anne liked clutter, and Robert seemed to be the same way as tidy as his place was. Besides, being able to see her clothes hanging in the closet or folded in her drawers made it much easier to choose from rather than trying to sort through cardboard boxes to find anything. Then she noticed a box that said: *Unpack first.*

It was in Robert's handwriting, and she opened the box to find all her undergarments and nightwear. She laughed.

Chapter 17

ROBERT WAS SO GLAD THAT MAISIE WAS REALLY SETTLING in here now that she had all her clothes at the house. She probably wanted to put her clothes in some kind of order, so he would assist her in any way that he could, but for now, he was making their dinner.

As soon as it was done, he called out, "Steaks, chips, and salads are ready." He really liked being able to cook for Maisie.

"Coming!"

She hurried out of the bedroom and gave him a hug and a kiss. "I feel like I'm home now. I'm so comfortable with you—and now that I have my clothing and my personal items, I feel I belong here permanently."

"Aye, exactly. And I'm glad for that. It's like living out of a suitcase at a hotel without the suitcase."

She laughed. "Right."

They sat down to eat their dinner. She took a bite of her juicy steak seasoned to perfection. "Oh, this is divine."

"Thanks. We need some protein for our jaunt as wolves."

"I can't wait to go for our run, though I really want to unpack my clothes and put them away."

"We can do some of that tonight afterward." He thoroughly enjoyed running as a wolf with her.

She laughed. "Yeah, but you know what I want to do instead of putting my clothes away after our wolf excursion?"

"Aye, me too." He was glad that she wanted them to make love after the run. If she wanted to unpack her clothes after that, he would certainly help her.

"We have most of the day to sort out the clothes, or I do," she said.

"I'll help you with everything you need me to do."

"Thanks."

They finished dinner, and she helped him clean up. But while he was still cleaning the grill, she was stripping off her clothes, shifting, and then she went outside to nose him on the leg to hurry him up.

He laughed. He loved her. "Someone wants to run." He finished cleaning the grill as fast as he could, took off his clothes, and shifted into his wolf. As wolves, they greeted each other, nuzzling each other's faces as if they were just meeting for the first time in ages. Then they took off running. They were on their property, heading past the clinic, then to the end of the acreage. But when they turned, to his surprise, she tackled him.

He loved it. She raced off before he could catch her. She was quick, but he enjoyed the challenge. He tore off after her and nipped gently at her tail. She yipped in shock and barked joyfully at him. He stopped, lifted his chin, and howled, telling her how much he treasured being with her as a wolf and letting all other wolves out there know it. Other wolves howled in the distance on the MacQuarries' property, show-ing their comradery. She stopped and turned to face him, lifted her head, and howled too. Instantly, Robert charged her, and she smiled, turned tail, and tore off!

He tried to reach her and finally tackled her. She folded onto the ground as if playing dead, but she was really eager to play with him. He nipped at her neck, and she bit at his mouth in play. They were growling and having a ball. He let her up, and scrambling to her feet, she dashed off again.

He was feeling great and was glad they hadn't skipped running as wolves before they made love tonight. Exercise released endorphins and made them feel even more joy. It was always such a pleasure to stretch their legs as wolves and enjoy the other half of their persona.

They ended up running to the dike and onto the MacQuarrie castle properties and seeing other wolves up there. They howled and greeted them, then kept up with some of them for a while. Finally, Maisie woofed at Robert, telling him she was ready to return to the house.

He would have enjoyed a jog as a wolf much longer, but being with Maisie meant he wanted to be with her in an inti-mate way even more. They dashed through the dike and back down the hill, where they saw Edeen and Lachlan return-ing from more of a leisurely wolf lope. Robert and Maisie woofed at them, and they woofed back, then went into the manor house. Robert and Maisie reached their home and headed in through the wolf door, her going in first. It wasn't a race until they shifted inside the house, and she gave him a quick hug and kiss and then sprinted off for the bedroom.

"I'm not in a race to put away my clothes," she assured him.

He hadn't thought that was the reason for her running off. He rushed after her and swept her up in his arms, making her squeal in delight. Then he carried her the rest of the way into the bedroom and set her on the bed. The nice thing about making love after being a wolf was that they were already perfectly naked!

The next day, Maisie took her laptop to Heather's pie shop before it opened to ask her which of the maternity photos she wanted printed while Robert had offered to hang up her clothes in the closet in the meantime. She much appreciated it and would sort her clothes out the way she liked them later, but it helped to just remove them from boxes and put them up on hangers. Maisie opened her laptop on one of the tables. Heather's three brothers were there also, just in case she went into labor.

"Oh, this is like what Colleen said. The photos are all so good, it's hard to decide. Enrick is on his way to see them too," Heather said.

Callum, Ethan, and Oran were looking over their shoulders, amusing Maisie. "Good. I can't wait to see how he likes them."

"I love the ones where he's kissing my belly or behind me with his hands under my belly," Heather said.

"I love those shots too."

Then Enrick walked into the shop and joined them,

hugging Heather. "Sorry I was running late. Oh, those look great."

"No problem. We're not open for another hour and a half, and my brothers would be handling things with the other ladies when they turn up while we looked over these anyway," Heather said.

Half an hour later, they'd chosen all the pictures they wanted, and Maisie placed the order to have them printed and shipped. Then Enrick had to leave to get back to the castle, and Heather asked Maisie, "So how do you want us to decorate for the family dinner for tonight?"

"Oh, how about something that shows the MacTavishes joining the Campbells and MacQuarries?" Maisie asked.

"Sure. We can do something about that."

"We'll just pay for anything that anyone wants to eat in the line of pies, drinks, and desserts." Maisie figured everyone would love the food there like it was without needing to ask Heather to create new dishes for them.

"Okay, well, this will be simple then."

"Yeah, I think the main emphasis is just everyone meeting everyone and getting to know them, especially my parents, and making them feel comfortable. I'll bring your photos to the open house."

"Wow, that soon. Great!"

"I'm going to run home then"—Maisie still couldn't get used to the idea that she wasn't living at the inn any longer, but with Robert now at his home—"and we'll be seeing you tonight."

"That sounds good." Heather hugged Maisie, and Maisie left to go home.

"Hey, Robert." Maisie entered the house. Mittens immediately rubbed up against her legs. "You're so cute."

Robert walked inside the house, and she was surprised he hadn't been at home. He gave her a hug and kiss while Mittens greeted him too. "I was stocking the clinic with supplies and heard your car pull up. How did it go with the photos with Heather and Enrick?"

"They loved them. The prints are ordered. We talked about the celebration tonight. We're all good. Do you need me to help with anything at the clinic?"

"I'll have more stuff coming in next week and you can help with it, if you have time."

"Sure, I can. But I would really like to see what else we can do." Once Robert was working at the clinic, he wouldn't have as much free time for this, so she wanted to take advantage of it every time they wanted to.

"You read my mind," he said, and they chased each other to the bedroom.

━━━━━━

That afternoon Robert and Maisie put away the rest of her clothes and found the perfect place for her photography equipment in the office. "We'll set up another desk in here, and you can put your scuba equipment in a special storage closet in the garage with mine."

"Thanks. That works."

"Until you have a desk, feel free to use mine for your work."

"Okay, great. Shoot, I need to show Edeen the pictures of her animals and see which she wants to order."

"Alright. Do you want me to go with you?"

"Sure. I'll call Edeen and see if this is a good time for her."

Robert was so glad Maisie and Edeen got along so well. He hadn't been so sure to begin with, when Edeen was watching over him when he was hypothermic and trying to get warmed up in bed. Little did they both know that Maisie would be his mate after a couple more wild adventures. He was ready to settle into a routine with Maisie and hoped she would be fine with the long hours he put in while taking care of his animal patients. Likewise, he would always try to do something special for her when she returned from her photo shoots or working at the inn when they were together again.

Once Maisie confirmed that Edeen would be happy to see them at the manor house, they walked over, Robert carrying Maisie's laptop and holding her hand. It was little things like that that showed how much he cared about her, and he always wanted to be that way with her.

"You know, I don't think we could have a nicer setup than this unless the inn and Mom and Dad's home were sitting on the property too. Just a short walk to your sister's house and a little longer walk to see most of the MacQuarrie in-laws at the castle, which is really nice," Maisie said.

"Do you want to offer some land for your parents to build on? We have fifty acres, so plenty of room."

"We can ask them."

"I had another thought. Colleen and Edeen love their gardens. Would you like to have one also?"

Maisie stopped, smiled, and hugged him. "Aye! I love working in the inn garden. Anne does too. But I would love to have my own here also. I love photographing everything during the different seasons also."

"Just let me know how you want your planting beds and I'll work on them until our wedding. That will give me time to finish it, hopefully, so when we return from our honeymoon, your garden will be ready, and my clinic will be open for business."

"That sounds great. I'm sure I can gather some seeds from Edeen's, Colleen's, and the inn's gardens too."

Then they reached the manor house, the dogs all barking, and Edeen opened the door for Maisie and Robert and let them in.

The fox terriers, Jinx and Rogue, greeted them, and Ruby, the Irish wolfhound, did too. Even their Scottish fold, a blue named Silky, had to say hello before she returned to her windowsill to watch the birds at the feeders.

"I need to get some of those too." Maisie looked out the window and petted Silky. "We don't have any birdhouses, bird feeders, or birdbaths, and that would be a fun addition to the inn. At the house here also."

"Silky watches the birds for hours on end. I love hearing their songs." Edeen made heather tea for them while Robert opened Maisie's laptop.

"Mittens would love that too." Maisie pulled up Edeen's animal photos on her laptop. "Here they are."

They sat down to drink their tea while Edeen perused the photos. "Oh, I love all these. It was amazing how we got them to look at the camera and they sat so still even though they were excited."

"Dangling the treats as an incentive really helps," Maisie said. "So we're going to also build a garden, and I wonder if I could gather some flower seeds from yours?"

"Absolutely. Colleen shared plants and seeds with me. We can both do that for you. I would offer Lachlan's help with building it because I know he'll do it, but I'll let him offer to help on his own. I'll help you plant your seeds and plants." Edeen narrowed down her selection of photos. "I love them all and would buy all of them, but I wouldn't have enough room on my walls for them."

Maisie laughed. "I know what you mean." She ordered them right away from the printing company.

"When I first met you, I wondered if you were the one," Edeen said.

"The one?" Maisie asked.

"Aye. Despite Robert's hypothermic condition, when you came to see him in the guest chamber, his expression brightened. I thought you just wanted to make sure he was alright, yet my instinct told me there was more to it than that. Still, you threw me off when you needed a first aid kit and a pair of pliers. I figured either Robert had hooked himself with one of his fishhooks or he'd hooked you and you were being so sweet not to mention it in front of anyone and embarrass him. You barely knew him, yet here you were protecting him, not to mention you had gotten help for him and had assisted him in the cold water," Edeen said.

"He saved me from drowning when the boat knocked me

unconscious." Maisie slid her hand over Robert's hand and then squeezed.

Edeen smiled. "See? You're always protective of him. And he's just as protective of you. Everyone figured you were meant to be together after the second mishap when you were with each other on Eilean Tioram, but I knew it was from the moment Robert reeled you in on his fishhook."

"You knew right away. I mean, that he'd caught me with the fishhook." Maisie smiled at her.

"Yeah. That was what the pliers and first aid kit were for. But for a moment I was disappointed that was why you were there instead of just a need to see how he was doing. Then I realized what I would have been feeling like if I had wanted to get a fishhook out of my arm, and I knew you wanted to see how Robert was doing too, though you were being quiet about it." Edeen got them a refill for their tea.

"Exactly," Robert said. "I was as worried about her head injury, so I was glad to see her come to the guest chamber, besides the fact I needed to rectify the fishhook issue."

"Lachlan put off the fishing trip until later," Edeen said, "if you've been wondering about it."

"He probably wants to be in a different boat when we fish after my last fishing experience." Robert drank some of his tea. "Do you want to go with me this time, Maisie?"

Maisie laughed. "Riding in the boat with you might be safer. But sure, it would be our first fishing trip together, and I would love to go. We can see who can catch the most fish."

"It sounds like Maisie has a good competitive spirit," Edeen said.

"You bet, and I love a challenge," he said.

Lachlan came inside the house then.

"Stay for lunch," Edeen said to her brother and Maisie.

"Absolutely," Lachlan said. "I planned to cook. Come on, Robert. Let's put some chicken on the grill."

Edeen said, "Good. I thought you'd forgotten that you'd offered. Robert and Maisie want to go fishing with you."

"Good. We'll do it as soon as we can." Lachlan took the chicken outside, and Robert went with him. "So you want to go fishing. I was waiting for you to say when you were ready to do it."

Robert laughed. "Yeah, and what makes it even better is that Maisie wants to go with us."

Lachlan got the grill started. "That's great. It'll be safer than her scuba diving when you're fishing."

Robert chuckled. "That's debatable. But with any luck I'll only catch fish this time."

"Hopefully we all will. Edeen will be expecting it."

"That's what Edeen thought when I went fishing the last time and caught Maisie."

Lachlan chuckled. "She was your greatest catch in the world."

"That's for sure."

Once Lachlan was done cooking up the chicken, he carried it inside on a platter, and they heard the ladies laughing in the kitchen. Robert was so glad that Maisie and his sister really liked each other. They sounded like sisters and best of friends.

Chapter 18

"I bet you're excited about going to Bali," Maisie said to Edeen in the kitchen while they cooked the vegetables for lunch.

"Aye. I had to buy some maternity swimsuits and flip-flops and other beachwear that I don't often need. I have bathing suits, but for when I'm *not* pregnant."

"Oh, sure. I figure you wanted to get married as soon as possible after learning you were pregnant."

"Yeah, we should have done it sooner. I didn't want to have to worry about making a wedding gown with a lot more fabric, but I can still take it in after the babies are born and I lose the extra weight."

"It's good that you're such an extraordinary seamstress. Speaking of which, Anne and I each want to order a medieval gown for Christmas activities at the inn. We already picked them out on your site."

"Oh, wonderful. We can look at them and you order after we eat." Edeen dished up the beets, potatoes, and broccoli as soon as the guys came in with the chicken. "Do you know which gown Anne wants?"

"Yeah, the same one I want, but I went ahead and picked out something different that I loved just as much."

Edeen laughed. "That must be a problem when you're sisters. My brother and I have never had that problem."

Robert said, "I should hope not."

Everyone laughed, and they sat down to eat lunch.

"This is great," Lachlan said. "I didn't think we would have such excellent company for lunch."

"They came by to show me our pet photos. They're beautiful."

"I'm so glad. I can't wait to see them," Lachlan said.

"I can show them to you," Robert said, "while Maisie orders her and her sister's Christmas gowns."

"Sounds good."

"This is great chicken," Maisie said.

"All the veggies are too," Lachlan said.

Once they finished eating lunch, Robert showed Lachlan their pet photos, and Maisie ordered the gowns from Edeen. Now they were all set.

Then Lachlan and Edeen had to get back to work while Robert and Maisie walked back to their home.

As soon as they entered the house, Maisie got a call from her mother. "Hey, Mom."

"Can we meet Robert and visit a bit with you both at your house in a couple of hours before we go to the dinner at the pie shop?" her mom asked.

"Yes, absolutely. That would be great. We can't wait for you to get here. See you soon." Maisie put her phone on the kitchen table.

"Your parents are coming to see us?" Robert asked.

"Aye, in a couple of hours. So we might need to straighten up the house a bit. I'm sure they'll want to see my new living accommodations."

He laughed. "I hope they love it."

"They will, but even if they didn't, all that matters is that we both love it. I wouldn't want to stay anywhere else."

The house was really pretty neat. Both of them tended to like things organized, she'd discovered, though Edeen had asked about how he was doing in that regard. But maybe with his new house instead of a smaller apartment, he had more room to put everything away. Neither of them had to pick up after each other yet, so it worked out great. So far, they had helped each other prepare meals and clean up afterward. Now, they broke down the packing boxes, since all her clothes were put away.

Once Robert was working long hours at the clinic, things would probably change, but both of them were extremely flexible, and she was ready to prepare meals for him, no matter the hour, if he was busy working. She would have breakfast early with him, and then she would help Anne prepare breakfast for the guests. They would figure it all out.

For now, she just hoped that he got along with her parents and vice versa. It was really important to her that they accepted each other as family, but Robert was her mate, so she just hoped it all went well.

———

Robert was looking forward to seeing Maisie's parents.

"Are you worried about meeting them?" Maisie gave Robert a hug.

"No. They have to be wonderful to have raised you and your sister so well."

She laughed. "Thanks. They are pretty wonderful. I have to say thanks so much for talking to them about moving here too."

"That's what family does for family."

They laid out string to mark off where she wanted her garden beds and paths. He figured tomorrow was the open house, so they would be too busy to start working on it. But the next day, they would begin to build it.

As soon as they had it all figured out, Maisie ordered a couple of birdbaths, two birdhouses, and six bird feeders. "I'm putting half of them at the inn and half here at home. I like the way Edeen's and Colleen's gardens have stone paths, like the inn too, and stone flower beds."

"We have a lot of stones on the acreage that we can use as retaining walls anywhere you want them."

She smiled. "I can't wait to fill the planters with flowers."

———

Late that afternoon, Anne and their parents dropped by Robert and Maisie's house a couple of hours before the celebration dinner with the rest of the extended family so they could meet Robert and see the house and not have to wait until the open house. They would come back for the open house tomorrow, of course.

Robert gave the sisters' mother a hug and then the father. Mittens greeted everyone. Anne ended up cuddling her.

"Does anyone want cocktails or a glass of wine before we go to the pie shop?" Maisie asked.

"A glass of wine, sure," Frederick said.

Their mother also wanted one.

Robert poured everyone a glass of wine and then took them on a tour of the house. Her mother was impressed with the main bedroom's closet. "Now I want one just like that," Janet said to her mate. "And the tub with the jets? I really could use one of those."

Her husband laughed. "Maybe in the new place we get, we can have renovations to include them."

"I was telling Maisie that you could build a home on our acreage. We have fifty acres." Robert walked them outside to show them the patio and the area where they planned to put the garden.

"Oh, if we can't find a place to buy, we might take you up on it," Janet said.

"Right. But for now, we've found some good possibilities," Frederick said.

Anne was still carrying Mittens, rubbing her cheek against the cat's.

"Your house is really lovely. Can we see the clinic also?" Janet asked.

"Aye, sure." Robert led them over to the clinic, holding Maisie's hand like they were newlyweds.

"Are you going to stay for a while and look for a place to buy?" Maisie asked.

THE WOLF OF MY EYE

"Yeah. We're planning on staying at the inn for about a week and while we're there, we'll look for a place to live," Frederick said.

"I'm so glad." Maisie gave her mom and dad a hug.

"We were only just waiting to hear how you and Anne were doing financially with your business and if you were happy to be here. We really didn't expect you to meet a wolf and mate him anytime soon." Janet smiled.

"I was just photographing marine life when it happened," Maisie said. "I certainly wasn't looking for a wolf for a long-term commitment at the time. But you know how it happens when it's supposed to—if you're lucky, that is."

"Aye, your mom and I met like that. We didn't have any notion of finding each other either." He turned to address Robert. "Janet and I were both stranded on an uninhabited island after the fishing boat we were on sank, but we hadn't met each other before that. There were maybe thirty-five people on the boat, but she was the only other wolf. We had to wait several hours for a rescue boat. We were able to rescue some of the fishing equipment that was washed near the shore. I thought I was a damn good fisherman, but here comes this pretty she-wolf, and I swear she was catching fish left and right while I was still trying to catch my first one."

"I'm sure it had all to do with the currents, dear," Janet said.

Frederick chuckled. "She caught so many pollock and coalfish, she shared them with me and several other people who couldn't catch any. We cleaned and cooked the fish to sustain us until help arrived. She and I got to talking. The connection was instantaneous. As soon as we were off the island, we made plans to see each other again. Two weeks later, we were mated," Frederick said.

"Yeah, you know when it's right and you can't live without the wolf you've met," Janet said. "That's why we knew you had found the right wolf for you this time, Maisie."

"Did you meet the other wolves Maisie dated?" Robert asked.

"Oh, we sure did. We knew right away they weren't the ones for Maisie. But she had to do her own thing until she realized for sure they weren't right for her," Janet said.

"I so appreciate you for it," Maisie said. "By knowing who truly wasn't for me, I found who truly was. I'm so glad I met Robert."

Then they took a tour of the clinic and all its rooms, and her parents loved it.

"This is a really nice layout," Janet said.

"Thank you. It's similar to the one I worked at in Edinburgh, with the exception of the delivery room," Robert said.

Frederick looked at the pictures of the Highland cows on the walls. "This is great. You work with large as well as with small animals, I take it."

"Yes. There are lots of cows, sheep, goats, and horses in the area. But I'm also caring for working dogs and pets," Robert said. "And wolf shifters, of course."

"I didn't know Veronica had finished framing some of the photos," Maisie said.

"Yeah, she dropped them by when you were doing a

photo shoot, and I hung what she'd finished up," Robert said.

"Your photos?" Frederick asked Maisie.

"Aye."

"They're really nicely done," her father said.

"Thanks."

"Well, this is a beautiful clinic to work out of, and it's so nice that your home is right next door," Janet said.

"My sister has the manor house back that way." He pointed out of one of the clinic windows. "Up the hill is the MacQuarries' castle."

"Just down the road is the inn." Anne cuddled Mittens still.

"We want to live nearby too," Frederick said.

"Yeah, we're going to do it." Her mom sounded so confident.

Robert knew they would manage it. "We're so glad for it."

Then they all returned to the house and took seats in the living room.

Frederick asked right away, "Okay, what about the guest at the inn who was murdered?"

Robert had wondered when her parents would ask about it. "We believe it was a wolf who was after the same woman as the murdered man."

Frederick shook his head. "Doesn't the wolf who killed Gus realize he has just signed his death warrant?"

"He probably doesn't believe he will get caught at it," Maisie said.

"Anne showed us the security video," Janet said. "I swore

it looked like that one guy you ditched after you and Anne caught him kissing another woman."

"You mean Jude Springer?" Maisie sounded as though she couldn't believe her mother could identify him when neither she nor Anne had been able to. "He did lose his phone in our flower bed."

"Aye, Jude. He had a rip in his pocket on his trousers in the back. The same exact place that the man in the video had. When I saw that, I immediately thought of him. What would be the odds?" Janet asked.

"How did you even notice that?" Anne was incredulous.

"She always notices things that need to be repaired," their dad said. "If she sees someone wearing those expensive jeans that are ripped—"

"Distressed," Anne said.

"Yeah, distressed alright," her dad said. "When Janet sees someone wearing a pair of pants like that, she always wants to recycle them, sew them, patch them up, or toss them. When she saw Maisie's boyfriend wearing pants that were torn, Janet bit her tongue and didn't say anything until Maisie and he left on their date."

"You would have made a great police detective," Maisie said.

Janet laughed, but then her expression turned serious. "I can't believe that guy you dated could have murdered your guest."

"We learned his name is now Jack Wolfson and he was dating the same woman as Gus," Maisie said.

Robert said, "Jack had no other reason to be at the inn

that we know of. If he was there to talk to Gus and things got out of hand, he could have been motivated to get rid of what he saw as another wolf encroaching on his she-wolf."

"Then we have to take him down," Frederick said.

"Aye, but only after we've proven he murdered Gus," Robert said. "Even if that was him in the video, it doesn't mean he killed Gus. If he has an alibi that proves he wasn't there at the time when Gus was killed based on the results of the autopsy and the video of Gus's last sighting, then we'll have to look elsewhere."

Frederick changed topics then. "Do you think Anne's chances of finding a mate will be affected by having a couple of bachelor males staying with her for security? While we're staying at the inn, no, but when we're not there, other wolves who might be interested in her could be put off."

Anne laughed. "William and Edward and I are keeping each other company, enjoying the time since Maisie left to join Robert. We're not dating. They're just there for my security."

Janet raised her brows. "Any bachelor wolf who has a chance to stay with a female wolf could have designs on her."

"Okay, rest assured, we've talked about it." Anne sighed. "You worry too much. They know while they have a job to do, I'm not dating them or anyone else. Anyway, don't worry about it."

Maisie glanced at the clock in the living room. "Oh, it's time to go to the dinner."

Anne looked relieved that she was off the hot seat as she put Mittens on her cat bed.

Everyone got up to go, and then Anne drove her parents to the dinner at Heather's pie shop while Robert and Maisie followed behind in his car.

Maisie smiled at Robert. "I'm so glad I have you and my parents are no longer worried about who I'm dating."

"You just needed me."

"Aye! Just like you only needed me."

"Very true. I'm glad they seemed to like me."

"They adored you."

Robert smiled.

When they arrived at the shop, all the wolf families were already there: Colleen and Grant, Heather and Enrick, Heather's three brothers, Lachlan and Edeen, and now Robert and Maisie and her parents and sister.

Everyone cheered Maisie and Robert and welcomed her family as they showed them to their seats.

Little flags showcasing each of the clans represented— the Campbells, MacTavishes, MacQuarries—were on display on the walls. Each of the tables was adorned with a vase of roses.

Heather's brothers took everyone's orders, and then they were busy in the kitchen, preparing the meals. Everyone there was dressed nicely to celebrate Robert and Maisie's mating but also to welcome Maisie's parents and sister and Maisie herself to the pack.

Grant stood. "Our pack is growing by leaps and bounds with the addition of Maisie, Anne, and Janet and Frederick. We welcome the MacTavishes, and if you need anything, you only have but to call on any of us."

"That's for sure," Maisie said. "We've had to count on the pack a number of times during our wild adventures. Robert and I met in the most unusual way, but it was a beautiful beginning to something that will be forever."

"I feel the same way about being part of the pack and for certain about Maisie. I will never believe I'm not very good at fishing once I caught the greatest treasure of all. And I'll never regret the path we took to get here." He leaned over and kissed Maisie, and she kissed him just as enthusiastically back, just like they always did.

Everyone clapped and cheered them. Maisie's parents and Anne cheered the loudest, and Robert was so glad he had become part of their family.

Frederick said, "Janet and I are thrilled to have our first-born daughter mated finally and to a wolf who is perfect for her. We haven't ever been a part of a large wolf pack, and we look forward to Robert's open house, Edeen and Lachlan's wedding, Maisie and Robert's wedding, and other celebrations that you have coming up. We haven't had so many wolf-run activities to go to ever. We love it."

"That's for sure," Anne said. "We have never had this much wolf fun."

"We want to also mention you can run as wolves on our land anytime," Colleen said. "It's truly a wolf's paradise."

"Our land too," Edeen said. "It's not as much acreage as Grant and Colleen have, but we are connected to theirs at the dike, and we still have plenty of land to run on."

"That will be great," Janet said. "It's been a long time

since we've heard wolves howling with each other and since we've taken a wolf run."

"After dinner, we can run as wolves," Robert offered.

"That would be great," Anne said.

Janet and Frederick wanted to do it too. Grant frowned at Colleen. She smiled. "I can do a wolf walk."

"Me too," Heather said. "The more walking we do, the sooner the babies will come."

"Yeah, that's exactly what we're worried about," Enrick said.

Everyone laughed.

"But Robert will be with us," Colleen said, as if that would make a difference if they suddenly had to deliver their babies far from the castle, on open land or in the woods.

Then everyone began having conversations at their tables.

Callum, Oran, and Ethan started serving up the meals, and then they took seats with Heather and Lachlan, and they all began eating.

"The food here is delectable," Janet said.

"It is. I look forward to moving here and eating regularly at Heather's pie shop," Frederick said.

"We all feel that way," Colleen said. "Her food is the greatest."

Everyone agreed.

"We need to marry and go on our honeymoon the week before Robert opens his vet clinic," Maisie said.

"And your gown?" Edeen asked, as if she was going to make it for her.

"Oh, gosh, you all are having your own wedding and then going on your honeymoon, so I don't want you to worry about making anything for me."

Edeen smiled. "I can do it. I have the fabric for it if you want it to be white. I have just the perfect design for it if you want a medieval gown. Robert already had me start on a Campbell tartan shawl for you. If you have a MacTavish shawl and shoes, we should be good."

"We can make a crown of wildflowers for you from flowers from my garden and Edeen's," Colleen said.

"That sounds terrific." Maisie had thought she was going to have to order a gown online that could take weeks and not even get there in time or drive two and a half hours to Glasgow. She wanted to support Edeen's business, but she also adored the garments that Edeen made. She could wear them over and over in different ways to make them look really unique.

Edeen showed her the gown she had in mind on her phone.

"It's perfect."

Robert tried to see it, but Edeen pulled her phone away and frowned at her brother. "You're not supposed to see it until the wedding."

He laughed. "But we're mated."

"Chef will make whatever you want for the wedding feast," Colleen said.

"It's our treat," Grant said.

"If you would like, you can use the ancient chapel we have and we can provide flowers from Edeen's and my greenhouses and gardens." Colleen glanced at Edeen to see if she was good with it.

"Absolutely," Edeen said. "I never thought I would be growing flowers for weddings, but it makes them even more worthwhile."

"Same here," Colleen said.

"Thanks, everyone. It will be the perfect wedding," Maisie said.

Edeen glanced at Robert. "What about you and your wardrobe for the wedding?"

"I'm good. I have just what I need for the wedding."

"We all want to know where you'll be going for your honeymoon," Heather said.

"Not beachy kind of islands," Maisie said. "Somewhere that wild wolves run in the forests."

"How about going to the United States? To Glacier National Park in Montana?" Robert pulled out his phone and started searching for honeymoon vacations. "How about the Lodge at Whitefish Lake?" He showed her pictures of the lodge and the honeymoon suites.

"Oh, it's beautiful." Maisie smiled. "A Tiki Bar and Grill, Viking Falls Grill and Bar, a coffee bar, a beautiful swimming pool with a view of the lake, steam room, hot tub, hmm. We're going to Glacier National Park for our honeymoon."

Everyone cheered again.

They would have so much fun there, enjoying the comforts of the lodge while having fun foraging in the forest where they could fish without fishhooks and just enjoy dinner as wolves. It would be just perfect, and she couldn't wait.

After that, she would be doing her photography and helping Anne with the inn, and Robert would be busy at the clinic, so they would be more tied down. She was glad they could take a whole week to enjoy being with each other before that.

Then everyone ordered their desserts, and Maisie said to Robert, "What about the guest list?"

"We'll invite everyone in the wolf pack. Do you have anyone else in mind that you would like to invite?"

"Bruce and Mary Abercromby. They can stay at the inn."

"Alright. No ulterior motive, right?"

She laughed. "Like getting one of Lady's puppies? You should have said for sure that you wanted one."

Anne chuckled. "I told you Maisie would want one."

Maisie smiled. "The white Westie would be so cute with Mittens."

"Then you could take pictures of them," Anne said.

"Of course."

After dinner, Maisie and Robert thanked Heather and her brothers for having the celebration at her shop, then some of them drove to the castle while Maisie and her family and Robert went to his house. All of them stripped, shifted, and ran as wolves to join the other wolves up at the castle.

A chorus of howls erupted from the growing pack. It was beautiful, Robert thought. He loved hearing Maisie's howl, but her sister's was similar and just as pretty. Her parents howled, the mother first and the father after that, so now everyone would know the new pack members' howls.

Since Heather and Colleen were so pregnant, Robert

needed to stay with them and walk, just like their mates were doing. He had to, but he didn't want Maisie and her family to feel they had to take a leisurely walk with them.

Anne barked, and her parents took off with her, the three of them joining wolves who were more mobile—Colleen's cousins, Iverson, Veronica, and others.

Edeen was more mobile than Colleen and Heather because her pregnancy wasn't as far along, but she was carrying twins also, so she joined the expectant mothers on their journey, along with her mate.

Robert was glad to see his sister's and sisters-in-law's mates sticking by their sides when he figured they would enjoy a good long wolf run otherwise.

They were so glad to have the wolf pack to run with, everyone howling for joy.

Chapter 19

THE DAY OF THE OPEN HOUSE HAD FINALLY ARRIVED. Robert had made sure everything was cleaned up. Maisie and Anne had come with him after making sure their new wolf hire of the MacQuarrie pack, Jeanette Sanderson, was managing the inn for now. Their mom and dad were staying at the inn but had been looking at homes for sale in the area and were arriving at the open house later. Anne hadn't planned to be here for longer than three hours, so she could return to work at the inn. But Anne and Maisie wanted to help Robert hang up the rest of the animal photos first thing this morning, now that Veronica had finished framing for him. Maisie had brought her camera with her to take photos of the clinic. She would photograph the open house celebration at Robert's house later. She had received the print photos for Colleen and Heather and had them at the house.

Chef wouldn't be here for another hour with the food and beverages. Half an hour after that, they would be open for viewing the house and the clinic.

When Anne, Maisie, and Robert entered his clinic, Anne

noticed right away that picture hangers were on the walls. Maisie smiled at her sister.

Then she and Anne began to hang the pictures that would fit the spaces the best while Robert took a couple of the photos of Colleen and Grant's Scottish fold cats and Edeen's fox terriers into the exam rooms and hung them up in there.

Maisie peered into the room he was in. "Oh, those look good in there."

Then she went to the next room that was set up to be a labor/delivery room and for surgery. "You won't have families in here, will you?" Maisie asked Robert, Anne peering into the room.

"Wolf-shifter families will only be in here when we have a wolf shifter in delivery. When we have customers' pet patients in here? No."

"Then we need really cheerful pictures in here," Maisie said.

"All your photos are cheerful," Robert said. "Let's put Mittens's playful pictures in here. Maybe you can take some photos of the wolf pups after Colleen and Heather deliver and we can showcase those in here."

"Sure, that would be fun."

Maisie started taking pictures of the clinic. It was so nice and new. She hoped all his patients would be happy there. She loved it here.

"Hello," Colleen called out, walking through the front door of the clinic.

"Hey," Robert said, and Maisie went with him to see her while Anne finished hanging the pictures in an exam room.

Glancing at the photos hanging on the lobby walls, Colleen smiled. She was dressed in a pretty yellow-and-green sunflower dress that made her look summery and cool. "Aww, the pictures look beautiful in here."

"Thanks," Maisie said. "Veronica did a wonderful job framing them. I need to talk to you and Heather about taking your baby pictures. Do you want me to do new birth ones?"

Anne came out to join them and said hello.

Colleen greeted Anne and said to Maisie, "Um, once the pups are born and after I shift back and am settled, you can take pictures. I would like to have some done with Grant, but not while giving birth."

"Okay. You can call me after you've delivered, and I'll grab my camera equipment and come."

"That will be perfect. I spoke to Heather, and she said she wants it done that way too. I'm so glad that your parents will be here too. I wanted to come and see how everything looked before everyone got here. It's beautiful. Everyone will love coming here with their pets. You said you would have the maternity photos and the animal photos ready for me at the open house also, right? I can't wait to have them framed and hung up."

"Yes. They are in the office at the house. I can give them to you now, and—"

Colleen's face suddenly turned ice white, and she quickly grabbed the check-in countertop in the lobby, looking like she was about to faint.

Robert immediately seized her arm. "Colleen, are you okay?"

"I think I was wrong about the false labor pains for the last few days." Colleen grimaced, holding her stomach. "Man, that contraction was strong, and it's not letting up."

Then Maisie saw water dribbling down Colleen's legs, and she grabbed her free arm. "Your water broke."

"Uh, yeah, I think you're right," Colleen said. "You do realize we have a full moon out right now, don't you?"

Smiling, Robert shook his head. "It figures. Let's get you into the delivery room. I have a special bed for you ladies and other delivery options." Robert sounded as though he was talking about Anne and Maisie too.

He was so endearing.

"What about a water bath for a delivery?" Colleen asked.

"Aye, if you want. But I thought you wanted a wolf's delivery." Robert helped her toward the delivery room. "It's your choice. That's why I set it up that way, to give my expectant mothers several options."

"I do want to shift. I've got my bag with a change of clothes and baby items in my car. I've been taking it everywhere with me, just in case," Colleen said.

"I'll go get it," Anne said.

The special delivery room was set up for wolf shifters who wanted to have their babies as wolves. But it was also outfitted with a tub and a birthing chair if the mother changed her mind at the last minute and wanted to deliver as a human, which Maisie thought was an excellent idea.

"So you deliver human babies too," Maisie said, in awe of him.

"Robert didn't tell you? He was a family physician before

he switched to being a veterinarian," Colleen said. "He was working only with humans, but now that he's with a wolf pack, he can perform either kind of delivery safely. We were going to kidnap him and force him to be part of our pack if he hadn't decided to do so himself. He just didn't know it."

Robert smiled.

Maisie chuckled. "That's great for the shifters in the area." She loved how humble he was. If she had been a family physician and a vet and she was dating a new wolf she really, really liked, she would have told him all about it to impress him.

Anne walked in with Colleen's bag. "Wow, I overheard Colleen saying Robert was a family physician before. We are *so* lucky to have you. I'll call Grant to let him know the babies are on the way," Anne said, since Maisie and Robert were taking care of Colleen.

Colleen groaned. "I don't want to mess up your home and clinic open house."

"Nonsense. If you're ready to deliver these babies, I'm ready," Robert said. "This is a perfectly good time for me."

Maisie wasn't sure *she* was ready. Robert's vet tech, Tiffany Moore, was a wolf, but she wasn't going to start working there until he opened the clinic, so she'd decided to take a vacation before that happened. Maisie wondered if Anne was any more comfortable with the idea.

Anne said on her phone, "Hey, Grant, it appears Colleen's in labor. She's here at the vet clinic with Robert, Maisie, and me. Her water just broke. Uh, okay. We'll see you in a few minutes."

Maisie was helping Colleen take off her sandals and then

her dress. "I just can't wait for the babies to be born." Maisie was so excited for Colleen.

"Thanks. Me too. I just didn't think I would do it during the open house." Colleen still sounded regretful that the babies had to come right at this time.

"This makes for the absolute perfect open house. You are christening the opening of the vet clinic before we're open." Robert was getting everything out that he needed for the delivery and then setting up the large, disposable pad on the floor for Colleen for when she delivered her pups as a wolf.

Maisie admired him for being so flexible, patient, and caring.

"How far apart are the contractions?" Robert gently felt Colleen's belly before she finished stripping off her clothes and shifted.

"A couple of minutes apart, and they're strong and consistent," Colleen said.

Maisie helped her out of her bra and panties, and then Colleen shifted into her wolf.

They heard a truck engine roar up to the clinic. That had to be Grant. He must have torn down the road from the castle to reach the clinic so quickly.

Truck doors opened and closed. "Colleen!" Grant roared as he opened the front door of the clinic.

"Back here, Grant! Colleen has shifted," Robert called out.

Colleen woofed. She was pacing around the delivery room. Robert made more of a bed for her to lie down on when she needed to rest and brought out a dish of water for her.

Grant and Enrick quickly entered the delivery room.

"Lachlan and Edeen are on their way," Grant said. Maisie had never seen Grant look that worried about anything. He appeared anxious as he frowned and hurried to crouch down next to Colleen, then hugged her. She licked his cheek, and he smiled.

Enrick was on his phone right away. "Heather, Colleen's going into labor. Have one of your brothers bring you to the vet clinic... Aye, that's where Colleen is right now, and Robert, Grant, and others are here to assist her. I don't want you driving to the clinic alone... Alright." Enrick sounded worried that his own mate might go into labor any minute too, not that Colleen's labor could trigger Heather's delivery.

"It could still take hours for Colleen's first wolf pup to be delivered," Robert said. "These things can take time. She's having hard contractions, and I sure don't want to risk that the first baby comes quickly someplace where Colleen's not comfortable though."

Fifteen minutes later, Edeen and Lachlan arrived and peered into the delivery room. "Hey, how are you doing, Colleen?" Edeen asked.

She woofed at them.

Edeen smiled. "I'll be in your place in a few months. Chef is getting ready to set up refreshments for the open house at your house, and Lachlan is going to take charge of it in your absence, Robert."

"Okay, thanks," Robert said.

"I'll assist them," Enrick said, though a bunch of wolves would be helping out by serving food and drinks.

Everyone was anxiously waiting to learn of their pack leaders' babies' deliveries.

"I've helped my brother before with puppy births," Edeen said, and Maisie felt relief wash over her.

"I'll help in any way that I can," Maisie said. "I watched Robert assist with Lady's pups, but that's as far as my training goes."

Robert smiled at her. "You also had a sprained ankle at the time, or you could have assisted me more." He lifted Colleen up onto the exam table and then he checked to see how far apart her contractions were. "Her contractions are coming closer together and getting harder."

"For three days, she's been saying she's having them, but she said they were false contractions, just getting her ready for the real thing." Grant sounded like he thought she'd been mistaken.

"They could have been," Robert said.

"If you don't need me to assist in here, I'm going to help with refreshments." Anne appeared as though she wanted to make a quick escape.

Maisie smiled at her sister.

Then Heather rushed into the delivery room wearing one of her long, historical tartan skirts and a peasant-style blouse that she wore for the pie shop, and she gave Colleen a hug around her neck. Colleen licked her face. "You're finally doing it. Woohoo. Me next."

Robert glanced at Heather, appearing a little concerned.

Heather laughed. "Don't give me that look, Robert. I'm fine. You should have seen the expression on my brothers' faces while we were working at my shop when I got the news from Enrick that Colleen was in labor. I told them that one of them had to bring me here to the vet clinic right away. All three of them brought me as if two had to watch me while the other drove, even though I told them several times that Colleen had gone into labor, not me."

Enrick joined them in a hurry. "You're okay, right, Heather?"

Heather chuckled and gave him a hug and kissed him. "Do you need me in here, or is it getting too crowded?"

Maisie stepped up and said, "Heather, you look like you're ready to deliver any minute. Why don't you go enjoy the refreshments and rest?" Maisie was certain Heather should be just relaxing and visiting with the other wolves, unless she felt she had to stay for the delivery. But it could take hours.

"Yeah, I agree," Robert said.

Edeen agreed too. "We've got Colleen covered with Robert, Grant, and the rest of us here. We'll tell you when the babies are here."

"Alright then." Heather took Enrick's hand, and they left the clinic to go to Robert's house for refreshments.

Not long after that, Callum and Oran came with refreshments for everyone in the delivery room to sustain them, including a bowl of ice chips for Colleen. "The open house is going great," Oran told Robert. "Everyone feels this is the perfect celebration for the babies coming too, since we are all gathered together. Ethan's helping out too."

"I'm glad everyone's having a good time," Robert said.

"Thanks so much for the food and drinks. Tell Chef he outdid himself again."

"We sure will," Callum said.

Then Heather's brothers left to continue to enjoy the open house with the other wolves.

Colleen got up and started walking again, waiting for the inevitable, when Callum suddenly rushed back into the delivery room and announced, "Heather's water broke!" He sounded like their greatest enemy was ready to breach the castle walls.

Enrick was bringing Heather into the delivery room, and she was saying, "It will probably take hours for this to happen. Everyone, quit panicking."

Robert smiled at her. "Come join the party."

"See? Colleen hasn't even delivered her first pup yet." Heather motioned to her sister-in-law.

"What do you want us to do, Doc?" Enrick asked.

"You're still having your babies as a wolf, right?" Robert asked.

"Aye," Enrick said.

Heather poked at him as if to say it was still her decision to make. "Aye. I know either way can have complications, but I want to do this as a wolf."

"I know we remove our clothes and shift in front of each other," Edeen said, "but maybe Heather wants a little privacy while Maisie and I help her undress."

"Aye, thanks," Heather said, and then Enrick kissed her and he, Grant, and Callum left the delivery room.

Robert got things ready for another delivery while Edeen and Maisie helped Heather remove her clothes.

"Do you realize we have a full moon?" Heather asked.

"Not until Colleen mentioned it," Robert said, "though it's true that there are more wolf-shifter births then. For humans, it's just an unproven myth that there are more births during the full moon, since there's no real evidence to corroborate it."

Once Heather was undressed, she shifted and licked Colleen's face while she was lying down, panting.

Then Heather circled the room at a slow pace, which was good for her until she felt she couldn't walk any farther and was ready to deliver.

Robert said, "The guys can come in just as long as it doesn't get too crowded in here."

As soon as Maisie let Enrick and Grant in, Grant sat down next to his mate and began rubbing her back.

Colleen moaned.

"Good, right?" Grant asked.

Colleen woofed at him and licked his nose, letting him know she really appreciated his rubbing her back. Then Heather nudged Enrick, telling him he could do the same thing for her.

Enrick laughed. "You got it." He sat down on the floor, and she rested her head on his leg. He immediately began to rub her back.

She looked like she was getting ready to go to sleep, but then she groaned, and Robert timed her contractions.

"Okay, lassies, no races now," Robert said.

"Whose pup is coming first?" Edeen asked.

Everyone but the she-wolves in delivery laughed. Though they both licked their mates, appearing amused.

Maisie was sure both Colleen and Heather wanted to deliver first just to get it over with.

Then Colleen began to groan, and it sounded more noticeable than before. Maisie thought this was it.

"Okay, Colleen, you're doing it." Robert crouched beside her. "You're doing well."

Heather added her two cents' worth and woofed at her, offering encouragement. Enrick continued to rub Heather's back.

Grant was doing the same for Colleen, appearing as though he wanted to do anything to take the pain away from her.

Maisie knew how he felt. She felt like that for Colleen and Heather too.

"It can take fifteen minutes to a full hour for the first pup to come," Robert said, assuring them everything was alright.

Half an hour later, Colleen pushed out the first pup while Heather had gone back to pacing.

This could be an all-day-and-all-night affair, Maisie was thinking, but she was going to remain here until it was done. Anne had planned to stay here until eleven and then go home. But with the pups on the way, she'd decided to stay and help with the open house. William was staying at the inn, watching over things, though his brother, Edward, was swapping with him so William could enjoy the refreshments at the open house and visit with the other wolves too.

Robert was taking care of the first pup, setting the little male against Colleen to nurse. Colleen looked worn out already. It was a good thing she wasn't having more than the twins.

Heather suddenly lay down and began panting hard. Maisie smiled as she saw Heather's first pup emerge. Maisie was glad now that she had taken maternity shoots of both the ladies before the open house. Who would ever have thought they would both deliver during the celebration?

Edeen said, "It's the full moon. I'll have to remember that."

William suddenly peeked into the delivery room. "Maisie, Ike, Gus's brother, is here to speak with you. He talked to Anne, but he wants to talk to you also because you saw his brother last."

"Not last," Maisie said.

"Uh, yeah, that's true. I told him that whoever killed Gus had used a man's strength to strangle him," William said, "but that Gus had been with another woman. Ike just shook his head."

Maisie hurried out of the room, assuring everyone she would be back.

Robert said, "William, you stay with Maisie at all times while she's talking to Gus's brother."

"Yeah, Lachlan is there with Anne, and several others are watching out for her, and they'll be there for Maisie too. No worries," William said.

"Good." Then Robert continued taking care of Heather's first pup.

Chapter 20

"HOW COME IKE IS HERE?" MAISIE ASKED WILLIAM AS SHE went with him to the house and found them on the patio out back where Anne and several male wolves were watching out for her.

"He received word from Stuart about his brother and wanted to speak with both of you. My brother told him you and Anne were here and that you had gone out with Gus the night he disappeared," William said.

Then they saw Ike, who looked so much like Gus that, without seeing them together, Maisie really thought it was Gus. Maisie quickly introduced herself. "I'm so sorry that I didn't know you weren't Gus at Heather's pie shop. I just thought you were him and I couldn't understand why you didn't remember me."

"I'm sorry I didn't talk to you about it. Though at that point, I didn't believe his disappearance had anything to do with foul play," Ike said. "He could be rather inconsiderate at times about leaving me hanging concerning where he was going and why. I didn't want to make a big deal out of nothing and sound like an alarmist. I have done that before—twice. Gus would take hikes into the wilderness and never tell me or any of our friends, and we wouldn't have a clue where he'd ended up. Twice, he got himself into trouble doing that, getting lost, then running out of food and water, so he had to turn into his wolf to find his way back. So when it happened this time, I just figured he was doing his usual thing. Except we had an important meeting to buy a piece of property in Glasgow, and he was really excited about the prospect. I knew he wouldn't ditch the opportunity. I'd tracked him to this area, and because I hadn't eaten all day, I stopped by Heather's pie shop and ordered one to go. I was shocked when you approached me and said my brother had lost his driver's license at your inn."

"Yeah, I was gardening and found that, Lady's collar, and a guy named Jude Springer's cell phone."

"Lady? Bruce's Westie?"

"Yeah, he and his wife were out hiking with the dog when she ran off. Do you know if Gus was supposed to be meeting anyone? When he and I were having dinner out, he was watching the clock most of the time. It made me wonder if he was meeting with someone. He seemed really nervous about it. When we checked the security video, we saw Gus return with a woman to his guest room later."

Ike's eyes widened.

"But then he left with the woman again. On the security video, we thought we observed him return to the inn. What we witnessed was a man wearing a hoodie, black boots, and a wrist splint. Your brother wasn't wearing the same clothes; plus, he didn't have a splint. We believe the man we saw was Jude Springer, but he's going by Jack Wolfson now."

"Crap, I knew it." Ike's eyes filled with tears, and he sounded defeated that he hadn't found him before he got himself into trouble.

"Your brother was strangled. Someone—who was wearing a splint on his wrist, because it was either broken or sprained—couldn't manually strangle a full-grown man, I wouldn't think."

"Hell."

"Do you know if Jack was wearing a splint recently? We know he had a grudge against your brother. Stuart mentioned Jack was angry with Gus because they liked the same she-wolf named Chelsea Bowers."

"Yeah, they got into a bit of a row at a club over her. I don't have anything to do with Jack, so I don't know if he has been wearing a splint or not. Can I see the video of the man wearing the splint?" Ike asked.

"Aye. We have it back at the inn. Why didn't you talk to Anne about the license and your missing brother when you picked it up at the inn?" Maisie asked.

"As I told your sister, I just didn't know what to think. I teach art at an elementary school. Gus's car wasn't at the inn, so I assumed he'd left. I was also impatient. I was going to have to make the decision to buy the property without him, and I was running out of time. Your sister was busy with guests. I didn't want to wait or intrude. I left and began searching the area for him. But I couldn't find any scent of him. Just of Robert, you, and your sister as you headed for Eilean Tioram. And Lady, which confused the whole issue. Anne said you found my brother in the ocean."

"Right," Maisie said.

"Can I see the room where Gus stayed?" Ike asked.

"If we don't have a guest in there any longer, absolutely. Otherwise, you'll have to wait until after they check out," Maisie said.

"Where is my brother's body?" Ike asked.

"He's in refrigeration at the vet clinic. Robert is the vet there, and he's delivering wolf-shifter pups right now," Maisie said.

"I can take you to see your brother," William said. "Maisie already identified him, but everyone wanted to get ahold of you so you could see him. Robert has done the autopsy, so you can talk to him about releasing your brother's body so you can take care of his remains, if the doc can spare a moment."

Anne said, "If you want to return to the inn with William and me afterward, we'll show you the video and see about the room, Ike. I need to check the reservations first though."

"Yeah, I would like that," Ike said. "I'm sorry for not talking to either of you ladies further when I first saw you. I just really didn't believe anything bad had happened to my brother."

"That's no problem. I just hope we get this resolved soon," Maisie said. "If we learn anything more or you do, we'll need to share the information so we can catch this guy."

"Certainly."

William escorted Ike to the clinic, while Anne waited for their return so they could go to the inn. Maisie saw their parents visiting with some wolves, and she hurried over to see them. She gave them each a hug. "I've got to return to the delivery room in case I'm needed. It shouldn't be too much longer." She hoped. "I feel guilty for not being here for you though."

"Don't be. We're having a great time, and we are so proud of you," her mother said.

"Robert and the moms are doing all the work, truly."

"We're still proud of you," her dad said. "Believe me, everyone has been truly welcoming, so don't worry about us."

Maisie smiled. "Okay, good. I hope to be out in a little while." She hurried back to the clinic and saw Ike and William leaving. Ike's eyes were filled with tears. She felt bad for him, knowing how much the loss of his twin had to hurt. Then she entered the delivery room to see where the ladies were at in their stages of delivery. Colleen was panting hard, and she appeared to be having her second pup.

Heather was eating ice chips, then resting.

"You're almost there, Colleen, keep going," Robert said while Grant continued to pet her.

Then they saw the second pup's head breach, and Robert waited for her to finish delivering the pup. Once she cleaned him up, Robert took care of the umbilical cord and cleaned the pup further. He set him with his sibling, and the second little male began to nurse.

Edeen rubbed her own back, and Robert said, "Why don't you rejoin the others and just enjoy the party? Maisie will help me if I need assistance. You need to rest."

"Alright." Then Edeen left the room.

Maisie hoped if she was really needed, she wouldn't mess

up anything. But the next thing she knew, Heather was delivering her second pup.

"Where do we go from here, Doc?" Grant asked.

"Colleen and Heather can stay here for the night and I'll watch over them, or they can go home with the two of you and you just let me know if their conditions change at all. Make sure they don't have any fevers, the pups are eating well, staying warm, and moms are feeling fine, then that's good. The ladies can shift anytime they want, but they should do so when someone's with them to be able to help them with the second baby," Robert said. "Colleen and Heather can eat now too."

Colleen was sleeping right now, and Grant said, "I'll take her home after Heather is ready to go home. We'll be going to the castle, all of us, so if you need to check on them, that's where we'll be. Besides, we have a ton of wolves in the pack who will be helping to take care of them and the babies. We don't want Heather and Enrick to be at their home alone right now."

"That sounds like a winning plan," Robert said.

They stayed with the new mothers in the delivery room until they were ready to leave with their mates. Welcoming the newest members of their pack was important to the wolves, though the moms and dads would have all the bonding time in the world with them too.

Then Heather finally rose to her feet, her pups sleeping. Colleen's pups were sleeping also, and she stood up. Everyone knew they were ready to go.

Edeen suddenly returned with Heather's bag. "In case you

wanted to shift and dress." As soon as the mothers shifted from wolves to humans, their pups would shift into babies too.

Heather shifted and opened her bag. She pulled out a change of clothes and started to get dressed. "Thanks. I'm starving." They even had clothes and diapers for the babies in their bags, and Maisie and Enrick each started dressing the babies.

"Do you want to shift also, Colleen?" Grant put his hand on the zipper of her bag.

She quickly woofed and nodded, and he opened her bag and began to get her clothes out for her and then the babies' diapers and onesies.

When the kids were older, they would have control over the shift themselves, but when they were young, the mother would, which was best for both of them. Otherwise, a pup could shift into a baby on a wolf run, or a baby could turn into his wolf while at a store, and what a disaster that would be.

Colleen shifted, and Edeen began dressing one of the babies, and Grant put a diaper on one of his twins. "You're doing great." Colleen started to dress, watching him.

"Aye, well, you made me practice enough."

Everyone laughed.

"How do you both feel?" Maisie was amused that Colleen had made Grant practice changing a baby's diaper. There were no other babies in the pack right now that she knew of, so she figured he had to have practiced on a baby doll and not a wriggling baby.

"Tired. I want to sleep for weeks," Colleen said. "But I'm starving too."

Heather agreed with her and held her firstborn in her arms for the first time, while Enrick was holding their other baby; both of the babies were happily sleeping. "Now my brothers can work at the pie shop to their hearts' content without annoying me about leaving to deliver the babies."

"I'm just so glad to have these babies." Colleen was fully dressed now, cuddling with one of her newborns wrapped in a green baby blanket decorated in wolf pups playing. Grant was holding the other, looking like he was getting used to it, his tiny tot wrapped in a blue baby blanket featuring wolf pups sleeping.

"Are you ready? I would suggest you use wheelchairs until you feel more steady on your feet," Robert said.

"Yeah," Enrick said, "let's use them."

Maisie was glad Robert had thought ahead and purchased two of them.

The ladies didn't object, and Maisie and Robert brought them out and then helped the women sit. They pushed Heather and Colleen through the clinic and outside along the walkway to the house. As soon as they went inside Robert's house, everyone came around to greet them, but they were wolf quiet, no one wanting to disturb the babies.

Everyone was thrilled. Maisie's parents were just as excited as the rest of the pack to see the new babies.

Lachlan gave Edeen a hug. "Our turn next."

She smiled. "Yeah. It was wild to see two of our she-wolves give birth at the same time."

"That's for sure," Lachlan said, giving her a kiss.

Robert wrapped his arm around Maisie's shoulders and

leaned down and kissed her too. "Well done," he said to Maisie.

She laughed. "I was going to say that about you."

"Yeah, but I'm used to delivering pups and babies. This is new for you."

"I'm getting more used to it," Maisie said. "I loved seeing the wolf pups come. When the ladies are settled, I'll photograph them all. I'm going to take pictures of the open house for now."

She took pictures of everyone at the party, groups of wolves eating and drinking, some of them posing for the camera. Colleen and Heather ate their fill before Colleen's and Heather's babies woke. Grant and Enrick enjoyed the food too. They were smiling from ear to ear, looking like proud fathers. The mothers looked tired but happy.

Robert brought a plate of food over to Maisie because she hadn't taken the time to grab a bite to eat. Then the two of them enjoyed talking to everyone as a newly mated couple. The open house had turned into theirs and not just Robert's. Maisie was amazed at how things had turned out between them.

When Colleen told Grant she was ready to go home, Heather agreed with her and was ready to take it easy, and Grant and Enrick took the new mothers and their babies home to the castle.

"Are you going now too?" Robert asked Maisie.

"Yeah, to photograph everyone. But I'll be back."

He smiled. "Yeah, of course. We're mated now."

"I'm so glad." Then they kissed. He loaded her camera equipment in the car. "I'll see you in a little bit," she said.

"I'll keep your parents company," Robert said. "Since I was so busy with delivering the wolf pups, I feel like I neglected them."

"It couldn't be helped, and they know it. They'll be as proud of you as I am." She kissed him again, and then she drove off to the castle.

———

Robert went back to the house and saw Janet and Frederick visiting with Lachlan and Edeen and several other wolves. They were having a great time, and he overheard them saying they were moving to the area as soon as they found a place to buy and sold their home. He was glad they were letting everyone know they wanted to be part of the wolf community, and he knew the sisters would love seeing them more frequently. Their parents would be invited to all the pack functions.

Frederick and Janet saw Robert, and they hurried to speak with him. "We are proud to call you our son," Janet said.

"Exactly, and when Maisie needs a doctor for any occasion, we know you'll be there for her," Frederick said.

"Anne too, when she finds a mate," Janet said.

"I sure will be." Robert smiled. He was glad her parents seemed to really like him as well as Anne and Maisie did. And he couldn't wait for Maisie to come home to him. Once everyone left, he would be ready to take her to bed. Unless she wanted to run as a wolf first. He enjoyed everyone's company, but he was ready to be alone with his mate.

He wanted to get ready for Maisie's return before she got there and make it really special, but he felt many of the wolves didn't want to leave him alone until she came home. He didn't want to be rude, but he was ready to spend the rest of the night alone with his mate.

As if Anne finally realized how he was feeling, she gave him a hug. "We'll see you later. It was a really lovely open house, and congratulations on the beautiful deliveries."

"Yes, thanks for everything," Janet said, giving Robert a hug too. "We're going to be spending the rest of the week looking for a home. We'll get together with you both whenever we all can."

Frederick likewise gave him a hug and a slap on the back. "Great job on everything. We're really looking forward to being here permanently and dropping by to enjoy time with you and Maisie and Anne."

"Me too," Robert said.

Thankfully, once Anne and her parents left, others began to leave—all except Veronica, Iverson, Lachlan, Edeen, and a few others who helped clean up after the party. Chef was packing up his kitchen tools and grills, and some were helping him with that.

Once everyone but Lachlan and Edeen had left, Edeen said, "I know you so well, Robert, and because of that, I'm sure you want to get ready for Maisie to come home and need the time alone with her. The open house was fantastic. Everyone had such a great time. I'm glad you got to visit with everyone and enjoy the feast too." Edeen laughed. "The pup deliveries delighted everyone, and for both Colleen and Heather to deliver practically at the same time, that was unbelievable and wonderful. It couldn't have been more perfect."

"I know, right? If they hadn't, I know it wouldn't have been long for the other one to deliver," Robert said.

"Not with the full moon here," Lachlan said.

"Yeah, I hadn't taken that into account." Robert laughed.

"None of us had," Edeen said.

Lachlan said, "Well, this will go down in the history of the pack."

"You couldn't have kept me away for anything. Not when you and Edeen are expecting too," Robert said.

"I looked on the calendar, and my due date isn't near the full moon," Edeen said.

Robert laughed. "That's a good thing."

"Do you want us to stay or let you relax before Maisie gets home?" Edeen asked.

"Why don't you go home and take it easy? I know you need to rest. I have some plans for the roses you decorated the house with," Robert said.

"You are a romantic at heart," Edeen said. "I never would have guessed it. I'm so glad I set the roses up for you for the open house."

"I'm going to have to learn a trick or two of yours," Lachlan said.

Edeen laughed. "You are also so romantic."

Robert smiled. Then he hugged Edeen and Lachlan, and they returned to the manor house.

He took the red roses from one of the vases of flowers his

sister had brought for the open house, then began pulling off the rose petals and scattering them on the bed. After that, he took more rose petals and scattered them from the garage door through the house to the bedroom.

He was going to make Maisie a Whisky Mac made of Scotch whisky and ginger wine, her favorite, according to her sister, as soon as he heard her car drive up. Hmm, or he could draw a warm bath and toss some rose petals on top of it, with a chilled bottle of champagne sitting next to the tub. She hadn't had time to drink anything but water before she went to take photos. He hadn't had any alcohol himself yet because he wanted to have a drink with her.

He put the chilled bottle of champagne on the tile surrounding the tub and started the bathwater, hoping it would still be hot by the time Maisie came home, though he would start it over if he had to.

He snapped his fingers. "Candles." He got some of the cinnamon-scented candles that Edeen had placed throughout the home and set them around the tub as he heard Maisie's car pull into the garage.

He quickly lit the candles and then scattered rose petals on top of the water. Then he ran to get a couple of the remaining vases of flowers and set them around the tub also.

"Hello!" Maisie called out. "Did I mate a romantic wolf or what?"

He came out of the bedroom to meet up with her in the hallway and hugged and kissed her, smiling. He was so thrilled to see her and so glad they were finally alone. "You deserve the best."

"I am so lucky."

"So am I. I have the bathwater going, but if you want to take a wolf run first instead, or…" He was totally up for doing anything she wanted to do—whatever her heart desired to make this open house finale the best.

"The bath sounds superb as long as you're in it with me, sharing the hot water, the jets, the bubbles from the jets." She grabbed his hand and headed for the bathroom.

"That's exactly what I hoped you would say." In the bathroom, they began stripping their clothes off in a hurry.

"Good. I suspect that's exactly what you had planned. Wow, scented candles and chilled champagne, just…wow."

"Naturally."

Chapter 21

EARLY THE NEXT MORNING, MAISIE SNUGGLED WITH Robert, not wanting to get out of bed for anything. She couldn't believe how he'd been so romantic after the long day and delivering the wolf pups, then visiting with the rest of the guests while she had taken the newborn pictures. She absolutely adored him.

He kissed the top of her head, his hand stroking her back. "Do you have anything scheduled today?" she asked him.

"Nope. Everything's unpacked and put away. I'm still getting more supplies in for the clinic, but otherwise I'm free. I thought we might start working on setting up your garden. What about you?"

"I need to go to the inn and help Anne with the morning meal. I'll help her clean the rooms too. I don't have any photography sessions for a while, but we have Edeen and Lachlan's wedding coming up that I need to photograph. What else are we giving them for their wedding present? She said that the photography was enough for her, but—"

"We paid for their airfare to Bali, and Enrick, Grant, and their mates paid for the rest of their excursion for their honeymoon," Robert said, "so we're covered. Speaking of which, Lachlan and his brothers and their mates are paying for our flight, lodging, and meals for our honeymoon."

"Ohmigosh, that's wonderful."

"I should have mentioned we'll be taking care of Edeen and Lachlan's three dogs and the cats while they're gone, and they'll reciprocate for our honeymoon. We'll also be taking their pets for the first couple of weeks after they have their babies."

"I'm looking forward to it. I won't be here all the time, but I'm sure between the two of us, we'll give them plenty of loving, and you know I love animals."

He smiled. "Yeah."

"Okay, so if neither of us have anything else to do today—"

"We'll return to bed and make love once you're done at the inn?" he asked. "In the meantime, I'll start to work on the garden."

She laughed. "We'll catch a killer."

Robert raised a brow.

She sighed. "We could try and get in touch with Chelsea and see what she has to say about Gus and Jack. We need to resolve this."

"Iverson is looking into it since he has had homicide training, though he has been unable to reach her. We do have her phone number, address, and email, but no response."

Maisie smiled. "I've got an idea."

Robert kissed her forehead. "I'm not surprised."

"I like to solve problems. Okay, so how about we say that Gus put Chelsea's name in a box at the inn for a chance to win a free photo shoot and she is the winner?"

"What if she was involved in Gus's murder?"

"He could have entered her name in the contest before he got together with her," Maisie said. "But if we can get her to come to the inn, I could question her."

Robert smiled. "Now that might actually work."

"I'll call her in case she doesn't check her emails very often." Maisie grabbed her phone off her bedside table where it was charging and called the number that Iverson had given them.

Robert cuddled with her as she made the call, and she loved it.

As soon as a woman answered the call, Maisie couldn't believe it! "Hi, Chelsea Bowers? I'm Maisie MacTavish, part owner of the MacTavish Inn where Gus Anderson was an overnight guest. I'm also a professional photographer for magazines and for other clients—weddings, pet photos, maternity, and newborn photos, you name it—and Gus put your name in for a contest for a free photo shoot. I'm pleased to announce that you are the winner, and if you can come here this week, I can do your photo shoot."

"Oh, wow. I haven't heard from Gus since he stayed at the inn. He didn't tell me he had done that. That was so sweet of him. Do I need to make an appointment? Would two this afternoon work for you? Or is that too soon?" Chelsea asked. "I've got work for the next two weeks after today and I don't know if I'll have time to do it after that otherwise because of the way my jobs come in."

"Yes, that would be perfect." Maisie pumped her fist. "I'll see you this afternoon then. I can't wait."

Robert smiled.

Maisie ended the call and said, "I wonder if one of our former homicide detectives should be there to do the questioning, and I'll do the photo shoot at the same time."

"She might feel more open talking to you. You could speak with her first about Gus and then if you don't get anywhere with it, the guys can talk to her. I'm going with you. I can be helping Anne, visiting with your parents if they're around, or acting as your photography assistant."

She smiled. "Good. I was planning on asking you if you wanted to go with me. You can definitely be my assistant photographer-in-training."

"I'm totally at your command."

"Now that's what I like to hear. I need to call Anne and tell her what we're doing so she's not blindsided."

"Good call."

When Maisie told Anne what they had planned, she said, "I'll tell William and Edward that they'll need to question her unless you can get what we need out of her first."

"Okay, we'll see you after we have breakfast then. Mom and Dad will be out looking for houses or land for sale again. I'll let them know what we're doing. I hope they don't hang around to make sure that we're okay."

"I agree. I'm afraid if there are too many of us there, we'll spook Chelsea."

———

After they finished the call, Maisie and Robert dressed, had breakfast, and then drove over to the inn.

Iverson was still in Glasgow in search of Jack Wolfson. Jack had been missing since Gus's death, he'd learned. Was Jack also dead? Or just in hiding because he was responsible for Gus's death?

On the way over to the inn, Robert called Iverson to let him know that Maisie had gotten hold of Chelsea and the scheme they had planned.

"Good. Let me know if you learn anything useful."

"I sure will, Iverson. Good luck on tracking Jack down."

"Thanks. I would still keep an eye out for him in case he doubles back there for any reason," Iverson said.

"We are. Thanks."

When they arrived at the inn, Robert saw that the sisters' parents' vehicle was gone.

"That doesn't mean they won't return for lunch and then decide to stay," Maisie warned.

They walked inside the inn, and Anne greeted them with a smile and hugs. "I'm so glad you're going to be with Maisie the whole time, Robert."

"Like we wouldn't be there to protect her," William said, watching them.

Nearby, Edward smiled.

Anne shook her head. "You know what I mean. He's her mate."

"Are Mom and Dad coming back to have lunch with us?" Maisie asked.

"No. I told them what was going on, and they agreed that too many of us hanging around might make Chelsea shy away from telling anyone anything," Anne said. "They really loved Heather's pie shop, so they're going there to eat. Besides, they dropped by the castle to give baby gifts to the new mothers, and when they went to see Heather, mentioning they were having lunch at her place, she gave them the mission of making sure her brothers were doing a good job. They were invited to a free lunch at the castle too, but they had their heart set on steak pies and dessert at the pie shop."

"I'm sure Heather's brothers are doing a great job," Maisie said.

"I agree. I need to figure out what to give the babies," Anne said. "Everything has been happening so quickly, I haven't had time to think about it."

"I'm taking portraits of the two sets of twins each month for free until they're a year old," Maisie said.

"You are so lucky you have such a great gift to offer," Anne said.

"Edeen's making them some clothes with the MacQuarrie tartan," Maisie said.

"Edeen's got a great talent also that she can share," Anne said.

"Something personalized would be nice. Maybe their own bowls, plates, and sippy cups with their names," Maisie said.

"I'll look into that, though they'll be on bottles for a while, well, and nursing."

The first of the guests arrived in the main dining room for breakfast, and Maisie and Anne got to work while Robert spoke with William and Edward in the inn's private quarters.

"So where is Maisie doing the photo shoot?" William asked.

"Maybe the gardens or with a view of the ocean. The guests should be off exploring by then, so it should be just us there," Robert said.

"We figure you and Maisie will set up the camera equipment, and then once Maisie begins taking pictures, she can start talking to her," Edward said. "If Maisie isn't able to get anywhere, we'll try to handle it carefully so Chelsea doesn't leave."

"What if she tries to leave?" Robert asked.

"We take her into custody. We have to know the truth. Does she know if Jack murdered Gus? Does she know where Jack is? Did she have any part in this? We've talked to Grant, and he said that if she cooperates during the questioning, we can just do it here. But if she stonewalls us, we'll take her to the castle."

"Alright. That sounds good," Robert said. But who knew how wrong the plan could go?

Chapter 22

AFTER THE LAST OF THE GUESTS HAD EATEN THEIR BREAK-
fast and left the dining room, Maisie and Anne finished
cleaning the kitchen. Then Robert and the brothers sat
down with Maisie to go over the plan. "Have you decided
where you're going to do the photo shoot?"

"In the garden. It's close to the unit where Gus stayed.
Since Chelsea saw Gus there, it should bring back more
memories when I question her. She did appreciate that he
put her name in to win the photo shoot but said she hadn't
heard from him since she'd seen him last. I didn't pry because
I didn't want her to go silent on us."

"I agree. Besides, seeing her face-to-face is much better
because we can see emotions and smell them too," Robert said.

"I've got a couple of rooms to clean," Anne said. "But
during the 'special event,' I'll be manning the desk."

"I'll help you with the rooms," Maisie said.

"I'll be glad when this is resolved and we don't have to
have all this additional security," Anne said.

William and Edward clutched their hearts as if she'd
wounded them with her comment.

Everyone laughed.

Once they had done their chores, the birdbath, bird-house, and bird feeders came in for the inn, and the guys all helped Anne and Maisie set them up in the garden. Robert and the brothers returned to the inn after that. Once Anne and Maisie filled the feeders with birdseed and the bird-bath with water, they returned to the inn to find the guys had grilled hamburgers flavored with steak sauce, onion, and green chiles, with french fries on the side—totally the Texans' menu—for them for lunch. Maisie and Anne loved it.

Robert was smiling. "It was fun cooking with these guys and learning something new to fix."

Maisie took a bite of her burger. "Wow, this is really good. We'll definitely have to make this back home."

"Yeah, this is delightful," Anne said.

"Now I know their secret," Robert said.

Anne and Maisie thanked the guys for a delicious meal.

"So what happened concerning Ike and his brother's body?" Anne asked.

"He had it moved to Glasgow for a memorial service," Robert said.

"I'm so glad he was able get some closure," William said. "When he looked at the video, he believed right away that the man in the splint was Jack because of his clothes."

After they ate, Maisie made sure she had a fresh battery in the camera and figured out her lighting in the garden. She'd taken lots of pictures here, and they turned out beautifully, so she knew that this would be a good spot for it.

The men had cleaned up after cooking while Anne was taking care of the check-in desk.

A pretty woman with chestnut-brown hair and bright-blue eyes arrived, and Maisie said, "Hi, are you Chelsea Bowers?"

"Yeah. Are you Maisie?"

"I sure am. Congratulations on winning the photo shoot contest." Maisie almost felt guilty about the lie, but if they could find out what they needed to—and she was actually giving Chelsea a free set of professionally taken photos—they had to do it.

The guys were in the house, and she saw Robert watching her from the window. Maisie nodded to him, letting him know that this was Chelsea.

He came outside. "Hi, I'm Robert, Maisie's mate and assistant."

"Hi," Chelsea said. "I'm so excited to do this. So we're doing it in the gardens? They're beautiful."

"Thanks, they are, and perfect for photography. I'm going to take some shots, check my lighting, and then we'll go from there." Maisie was trying to make sure Chelsea was really enjoying the photo shoot before the questioning began. She captured several shots of Chelsea then. "Great. Nice smile. Perfect. Aye, I like that."

Robert was waiting for Maisie to direct him to do something, but she was so focused on photographing Chelsea and she normally never had anyone to help her, so she'd nearly forgotten he was there. Chelsea didn't seem to notice, thankfully, but Maisie finally motioned to the spot she wanted the light to shine. "Robert, can you move that one light over this way just a wee bit?"

He obliged, and she said, "Perfect, thanks."

He smiled.

"I'm so thrilled to meet up with other wolves. Gus never said that the owners here were wolves," Chelsea said.

"Oh, aye. We love it when wolves stay here." Maisie was trying to figure out a way to approach Chelsea about the murder. "So you said you and Gus met up here, right?"

"Yeah. We've been dating on and off. I've also been dating another wolf, and he has been seeing other she-wolves, but he doesn't like the idea that I'm seeing anyone else. That was the deal we'd made when we first met, that we were not dating exclusively, but if you ever see Jack Wolfson, please don't say anything about my meeting up with Gus here."

Maisie nodded, unable to say the poor guy was dead. "Do you want to crouch behind the roses and smile?"

Chelsea did what Maisie asked.

"Good. Looks nice. Now if you can sit on that bench, that would be perfect. I have a vase of flowers, if you can get them, Robert, on the check-in counter. Chelsea can hold a bouquet."

"Coming right up." Robert went inside the inn.

While Robert got the vase of flowers, Maisie said to Chelsea, "I know what you mean. I've dated a couple of wolves like that. Two of the guys tried to keep me from seeing my family and friends even. The one guy kept accusing me of seeing other wolves behind his back."

Robert returned with the vase of wildflowers and handed them to Chelsea.

"Oh, yeah, that's like with Jack. I have a twin sister and an aunt and uncle that I'm close to who he didn't want me to be around any longer."

Maisie nodded and took some more shots of Chelsea holding the bouquet of wildflowers. "Well, I told both of my former boyfriends who were controlling that I wasn't about to neglect my family and friends. With Jude Springer—"

"Wait, Jude Springer?" Chelsea asked.

"Uh, yeah. I met him at a club in Glasgow, where I used to live." Did Chelsea know Jude and Jack were the same person? She couldn't believe it. This couldn't be a more perfect way to lead into the circumstances surrounding Gus's death.

"Glasgow," Chelsea said.

"Aye," Maisie said.

"I saw his—Jack's—expired driver's license one time, and his name had been Jude Springer from Glasgow. He said he changed his name because he'd used that name for so long that people were getting suspicious about why he was aging so slowly," Chelsea said.

Maisie stared at her. "Have you seen Jack recently?" Maisie was trying to tread lightly. She noticed Edward and William were watching them out of the window, the window open so they could hear what was being said.

"No. It's so odd. I had the date with Gus here, and it was so nice. He is always such a sweetheart. I still can't believe he was so thoughtful to enter me in this contest. But I haven't heard from him since the date. I would have stayed with him that night, but I had a job to do the next day early. Gus had dropped me off at a petrol station where I'd left my car. Before I returned home, I had to get some petrol, and I saw Jack. I don't know if he saw me or not, but he left, never saying a word to me, so I suspected he didn't see me. I sure didn't want to talk to him because he would have smelled Gus on me because we had kissed and hugged before I left him. I did worry that he might have witnessed Gus dropping me off there. But Jack didn't confront him, so maybe he didn't. I haven't seen Jack since then either."

"How far is the petrol station from here?" Maisie asked.

"About ten kilometers."

Maisie wondered if that was where Iverson had found Gus's car. "Do you think Jack knew you came to see Gus?"

Then it would have just been a weird coincidence that Maisie and her sister owned the inn and it had nothing to do with him stalking Maisie, which was a relief in part.

"I...I sure hope not. I don't want to see Jack any longer, but before I saw him at the petrol station that night, he kept dropping by my place. I swore he had followed me before when I went to meet up with my family or friends—not for dates or anything even. Anytime I tried to see Gus, Jack would always show up, and the two would get into a fight. I wasn't even sure about dating Gus any further because I didn't like the way he'd act around Jack either."

"Is that why you met Gus here? To try and ensure Jack wouldn't show up and get in his face?" Maisie took some more photos.

Chelsea nodded. "Aye. We kept trying to get together, but

Jack always seemed to catch us wherever we went and start a fight, so we decided to meet here. We knew if we were well outside Glasgow, he wouldn't happen to run into us. I mean, we can't keep leaving the city to meet up. It's not sustainable. But when I'm just with Gus and we don't have to deal with Jack, Gus is a really nice guy. I keep hoping Jack will find someone else to date on a steady basis and give up on me." She bit her lip. "So what happened between you and him?"

"I caught him having dinner with another woman when Jude and I were supposed to be dating exclusively. I don't think he was all that into me and liked the other woman better since he continued to date her. I was glad for that. When I dumped him, he didn't pursue me any further, thankfully. That was back in Glasgow. I didn't realize he had changed his name. I did date someone else, but Jude never learned of it or didn't care if he knew about it." Maisie sat down on the bench next to Chelsea and showed Chelsea the photos she had taken. "I'll do some touch-up work on them also at no extra charge."

"I love these. They're beautiful."

Maisie didn't have the heart to tell Chelsea that Gus was dead and that Jack might have been the one who killed him. It sure sounded to her like Chelsea was the motivation for the murder. Not that it was her fault in the least, and Maisie didn't want her to feel that it was.

Robert was taking down Maisie's lighting equipment, being a good assistant cameraman. She was sure he was waiting for her to say something about Gus's death.

"You can have my deluxe photo package for free. Do you

have time to go inside with me and I can show the photos to you on my laptop? You can see them better that way and pick which ones you want in print in which sizes," Maisie said.

"Yeah, sure, that would be great."

"Perfect." Maisie wanted her inside so that, once she told her Gus was dead, Chelsea would be in private if she got emotional.

They went inside, and Edward and William smiled at Chelsea, and both said, "Howdy."

"Oh, boy, you're not from around here, eh?" Chelsea said, smiling.

"No, we're from Dallas, Texas," William said.

"Wow, that's cool. What brings you here?"

"Our cousin, Colleen, inherited Farraige Castle and mated the wolf who was managing it. She wanted us to join her, and we love it here, so we just stayed," Edward said.

"That's so wonderful," Chelsea said.

Maisie and Chelsea sat down on the couch in the living room. William joined Anne at the check-in desk, mainly to stay out of Chelsea and Maisie's way.

Edward was in the kitchen putzing around but listening to Maisie and Chelsea's conversation.

Robert was packing Maisie's photographic equipment up in the car, trying to act like an assistant. Maisie was sure he was past ready for her to talk about the murder. She was still trying to come up with a way to speak with Chelsea about it.

But once Chelsea had picked her photos out, Maisie didn't have any time left. She ordered them from the print company and said, "I can mail these to you when they come in."

"They are just beautiful. Thanks so much." Then Chelsea said, "I have a question for you though. Why did you ask me how far the petrol station was from your inn?"

Maisie sat back against the couch. "I...I have some bad news to tell you."

"What? Just tell me. It's Gus, isn't it? Something's happened to him." Tears filled Chelsea's eyes. "I just knew it. I kept thinking he would get in touch with me. I kept trying to contact him to no avail."

In Maisie's peripheral vision, she saw Robert enter the house, but he tried to fade into the background.

"Yeah. When I was gardening, I found his driver's license. My sister and I tried to locate him to tell him we'd found it. Finally, I met his brother, who was looking for him too."

"Ike."

Maisie got her a box of tissues. "Yeah. Then later, Gus was discovered. He'd been murdered."

Chelsea sobbed. She was totally distraught. She wasn't faking it. "Where was he killed?"

"We don't know where he was actually killed." Maisie didn't feel the need to go into details about how they'd found him dead in the ocean unless Chelsea asked for them. "But after Gus drove off with you, I don't think he came back. Someone else did. My mother swore the man on the security video was Jude Springer because of the tear in his back pocket of a pair of black pants."

"But Jude Springer is Jack Wolfson, and aye, he lost his

wallet and his phone out of that torn pocket once. I told him he needed to get new pants or sew it up before he lost something important for good." Chelsea wiped away tears. "It was because of me, wasn't it? Jack knew I had been with Gus, and he killed him for it."

"If Jack killed Gus, it was because of Jack, no one else."

"Ike must feel really bad. He told Gus not to see me any longer because he thought Jack was capable of going berserk over it," Chelsea said. "Because of Jack, Gus and I weren't really together exclusively."

"Ike was torn up over it for sure," Maisie said, "but I don't think he blamed you. No matter what, you weren't at fault."

"That really scares me though. If Jack killed Gus, then I might be next. He must have known I was with Gus," Chelsea repeated.

"I know. Ever since we learned Gus was murdered, we've had a couple of men staying here to make sure Anne and I are protected from Jack, in the event he returns," Maisie said.

"Do you think he would?" Chelsea asked. "I mean, if there's a way to get him to come here—even using me as the bait—I'm all for it. It would be better than me worrying about returning home and him coming after me there when I'm alone. Or even him going after another wolf if I dated someone else. Then they can get him to confess and the pack leaders would deal with him—terminally."

"What if you posted something on Facebook, like a picture of you and me together?" William said to Chelsea, joining the conversation.

"But then *you* would be at risk," Chelsea said.

Edward walked into the living room. "We're both former homicide detectives from Dallas, Texas. We can protect you."

"I'll get ahold of Iverson and have him return," Robert said. "He's from here and a former homicide detective also."

"Do you really think this will work?" Chelsea asked.

"We can certainly try it. Let's take some pictures of you and your new boyfriend, Chelsea," Maisie said. "I believe it's worth a try if we can catch a killer."

Chapter 23

ROBERT WAS THINKING THAT THIS WAS A GOOD PLAN. "WE need to make up a profile for William on Facebook that doesn't say he's a former homicide detective of Texas. Where should we say he's living?"

The Playfair brothers, Robert, Maisie, and Chelsea walked around to the back side of the property that overlooked the ocean.

"Living at Castle Farraige might seem too formidable. What about if I'm working here at the inn as an assistant manager? I could say I'm a handyman or groundskeeper, but it might sound like I would be more capable of fighting him. So something more administrative that sounds not as—"

"Alpha?" Robert offered.

William smiled. "Yeah."

Maisie had William sit on a bench with the ocean at his back and had Chelsea sit on his lap. "Simulate a kiss, but make it look like you're really into each other," Maisie said.

William appeared to want to be a gentleman about the whole thing, but Chelsea wrapped her arms around his neck and gave him a really great kiss that made it appear they were really going somewhere with their relationship. When Chelsea finally pulled her mouth away from William's, he looked surprised, but then he smiled. "Hot damn. I knew Scottish lassies were the best."

Maisie and Robert laughed.

Robert liked Chelsea's sense of humor and the Playfair brother's playfulness. Robert was glad she could feel good about trying to catch the man who had killed her friend.

"Well, if that doesn't piss Jack off, I don't know what else would," Robert said.

Then they returned to the inn and let Anne know what they were doing.

Anne shook her head. "I would have loved to see all that."

"I'll show you the cute pictures," Maisie said.

"Mom and Dad shouldn't be here if we're trying to trap the wolf," Anne said.

"Aye, I was thinking the same thing. What if Robert and I stay in my room at the inn and Mom and Dad stay at our house? Robert should be here in case anyone gets hurt," Maisie said. "And before you say anything, I'm staying with you, Robert."

"I expected no less," he said.

"You're a doctor or a nurse?" Chelsea asked Robert.

"Veterinarian, but he was a family physician before," Maisie said before he could answer Chelsea, sounding so proud of him, and he smiled.

"Wow. That is so cool," Chelsea said.

Anne was on the phone with their mom and dad after that, filling them in about the situation. When she got off the phone, she said, "Okay, Mom and Dad are good with this. They'll drop by and get a bag each to take to Robert's place. Are you going to let them into your house?"

"Yeah, we'll have to grab a bag of our stuff from the house. Why don't we have dinner with your mom and dad when they arrive here? After dinner, we can return home, let them in, and grab a bag," Robert said.

"That sounds good," Maisie said. "William should say on his new Facebook page that his hobbies are weaving wool, reading books about oil painting, and his greatest fear is—"

"Spiders," William said.

Edward laughed. "That *has* to be on your Facebook page. William always makes me kill spiders of the venomous variety."

William began building his Facebook page on Maisie's laptop and Anne's. He used one of the photos that Maisie had taken of scenery all over Scotland to create his Facebook header.

"Okay, everyone can start friending you," Robert said. "I'll send the links to the rest of the pack, letting them know what you're up to, and you'll have the whole pack as friends before you know it so that it appears that you are real people."

"I'm going to make some posts that I haven't ever met a woman I care about like I do Chelsea," William said. "Woohoo, got ten friend requests already. Though I've set my profile to private for nonfriends so that Jack will just see Chelsea's dating a guy who works at the inn."

"Okay, I'm going to post pictures of both of you kissing me on my Facebook page after everyone's settled down. I can't wait. If we can catch this bastard and put him down, I'm all for it," Chelsea said.

After they had the Facebook pages set up, they posted about a bunch of different things—accounting stuff—and things about being an administrative manager, also making it appear to be boring. Neither sounded like wolves who would put up a good fight with another wolf who might try to take their girlfriend away from them.

Chelsea suddenly looked really sad, and Maisie gave her a hug. "We'll get him," Maisie said.

"I sure hope so. It's better to do that instead of just worrying about Jack coming after me when I'm defenseless or going after anyone else that I might even try to date," Chelsea said. "I just feel bad that Gus died."

"Me too," Maisie said.

Janet and Frederick arrived, and they met Chelsea, greeting her with hugs and heartfelt condolences. Afterward, they packed a couple of bags, and Maisie changed the sheets so she and Robert could sleep in there. Edward and William changed out the sheets on the guest room bed for Chelsea to use now.

The guys all went out to grill steaks on the barbecue while the women made salads and mashed potatoes.

"You girls stay safe," Janet said as she set the table.

"I've been thinking of how we can work this," Maisie said. "Once our parents are at our house, we'll do the Facebook posts. Of course, Chelsea will be posting all this stuff too, because if Jack sees anyone's posts, it will be Chelsea's. If our plan succeeds," Maisie said.

"Do you think it will?" Janet asked.

"It might take time," Maisie said. "We have to be patient. We have Iverson coming to join us. We have a cot we'll set up in the living room near the sofa bed for him. We'll have a full house at the inn." Then she asked her mom and dad, "How are things going on finding a place of your own?"

"We're still looking, though we've found a couple of places we like," Janet said.

"Oh, that's wonderful. If you want my opinion on a place you're interested in, just let me know and I'll go with you to check it out."

"Thanks, Maisie. We might just do that."

Then the guys came in with the steaks, and they all sat down to eat and had red wine with their dinner.

"I never expected to stay here like this when all I thought I would be doing was a photo shoot." Chelsea frowned. "Oh, what an idiot I've been. The contest wasn't even real, was it?"

"No, sorry, but Anne and I do own the inn, and I am a professional photographer. The pictures I'm having printed are yours for free. You just didn't win a contest for the package deal. We had to learn if you might know who had killed Gus."

"Did you think I had anything to do with it?" Chelsea's eyes filled with tears, but she looked angry at the same time.

"Stuart said you were seeing both Gus and Jack and both were perturbed about it. We figured that was your involvement. But a man strangled Gus, and we knew you hadn't done that," Maisie said. "As to your staying with us, we genuinely want to keep you safe. Since you don't have any clothes here or personal items, we have complimentary toothpaste, toothbrushes, shampoo, conditioner, and bodywash that you can have."

"You can borrow some of my clothes," Anne said. "You're the same size as I am, so they should fit you, and you can wash your things here."

"I want to wear one of your shirts, William. Nothing is sexier than wearing a boyfriend's clothes." Chelsea cheered up a bit despite the circumstances.

They laughed.

"If Jack is the one who killed Gus, he's going to want to kill you for sure," Edward said. "Let him come for you, and we'll show him what we've got."

"He won't stand a chance," William said.

Robert agreed.

Once they finished eating, Anne and Chelsea cleaned up while Edward and William pulled out the trundle bed in the guest room and moved it near the sofa bed for Iverson. Robert and Maisie returned home, and her parents followed behind them to play out the next part of the plan.

Maisie couldn't believe she and Robert would be staying at the inn again as they packed a bag to take there. He was so cute because he brought out his bag for both of them to pack their things in, and it reminded her they were truly together as mated wolves. But at least this time when they stayed at the inn in her bedroom, she would be with her mate, not just a wolf she was courting! She really hoped the wolves who were trained to take down criminals would be the ones to catch Jack, but she knew if Robert was needed, he'd be in the middle of the action, and she didn't begrudge him for it at all. He wouldn't be her mate if he didn't want to help.

She sure hoped they would be able to trap Jack and take him down for everyone's peace of mind.

"Are you sure you're going to be alright, the both of you?" Janet set her bag down in the guest room.

"Aye, we will be. We'll make sure Jack doesn't get to any of the women, if he shows up at all," Robert said. "We don't know if he'll take the bait. He might just wait for Chelsea to return to Glasgow. But if he really doesn't like that she's dating another guy and he learns he lives here, he might attempt to come after him. Or her."

Frederick dropped his bag off in the guest room and returned.

"We're off to the inn." Maisie motioned to the fridge. "The kitchen is yours—you can make this your home."

"Just be careful, Maisie. You and Anne don't need to take unnecessary risks," Frederick said.

"We have another former homicide detective coming to join us, so that will make four male wolves providing extra security, and we should be able to manage Jack if he shows up." Robert rolled his bag to the door. "If we have any trouble, we can call on the wolf pack and get additional support."

Frederick cleared his throat. "It's good to have them as a backup."

"It sure is," Robert said.

"We're heading back to the inn if you both feel you're settled in," Maisie said.

"Aye, your home is so comfortable, and the guest room is so nice. Let us know what's going on, and we'll keep looking for a home in the meantime," Janet said.

"We will," Maisie said.

"Like Maisie said, feel free to have anything in the kitchen. Our home is your home." Robert gave them an extra set of keys to the house.

Robert and Maisie gave her parents hugs, and they left to return to the inn. When they arrived there, Iverson was grabbing a ham sandwich for dinner, and they were ready to start posting messages on Facebook.

"Are we ready then?" Chelsea held up her phone.

"Yeah, go ahead and post," Robert said.

Chelsea sighed. "I've got my post up that I'm seeing a new guy named William and he's so much fun."

"Let's take a selfie." William motioned to the ocean view. "The sun is beginning to set over the ocean. We can get a good shot before it's too dark."

They headed outside to watch William and Chelsea sitting on the bench with their heads placed together and smiling as the sun was setting. It would make a really pretty picture.

Then Chelsea posted the picture. "I'm saying it's a picture of us at the MacTavish Inn on a moonlit night."

"Okay, let me take one of us and I'll post it on my fake Facebook page." William took a picture of him draping his arm over Chelsea's shoulders while she was smiling up at him.

"You said Jack hasn't been in touch with you for a while, right?" Maisie asked Chelsea.

"Right. Maybe he has already given up on me. Or maybe he has been by my apartment looking for me and I haven't been there," Chelsea said. "That doesn't explain why he hasn't called or messaged me though."

"What about the work you had to do? You said you were going to be tied up with it for a couple of weeks." Maisie didn't want her to lose her job.

"My sister is taking on the job for me. She hasn't had work for a while, so she was grateful. It's hospice care at a home, and she and I are both trained for it. Jack doesn't know that I had that job, so he won't be after my sister. I've told my aunt and uncle and sister where I am and what we're doing. They're worried about me, but they said they would be more anxious if I returned to my apartment and I was all alone if Jack wanted to hurt me."

"Exactly," Iverson said. "If he has decided you're only supposed to see him, he might just figure no one has discovered that Gus died at his hands. If he believes he got away with murder, he could believe he will be able to do the same to William and get away with it. I've seen so many cases where a guy feels if he can't have a woman, no one else can. Sometimes, the man will kill both the girlfriend and the new boyfriend, but other times, just the new boyfriend because he still wants the girlfriend."

"Do you always catch them?" Chelsea asked.

"Yeah. Being a wolf helps with the hunt for sure," Iverson said, "but when I ran into some of the MacQuarrie kin and learned they had a wolf pack out here, I left my job and joined them. I do whatever they need me to do, and I love it here. It's great being with a pack."

"I bet," Chelsea said.

"It's late, and Maisie and I need to make breakfast early in the morning for our guests," Anne said.

"Can I help?" Chelsea asked.

Anne and Maisie smiled. "Sure, if you want to," Maisie said.

"I would love to. I'm used to earning my keep, so that would be great," Chelsea said.

Then they all said their good nights. Tomorrow would be a busy day—taking pictures of William and Chelsea and then sharing the photos on various social media networks of the newfound friendship between William and Chelsea.

But then Maisie had a thought. "Oh, oh, Chelsea and I need to see Gus's car," she said to Robert.

"To smell the scents there," Robert said. "Hell, I hadn't thought of that. Let's get Chelsea and take a trip to the castle. I'll call Grant and tell him we're on our way."

Chapter 24

As soon as Maisie told Chelsea what she and Robert were going to do, Iverson said he was going with them. William and Edward would stay behind with Anne.

Of course everyone who had planned to go to bed couldn't now, as they wanted to hear what Maisie and Chelsea discovered.

"I'll make us some green tea," Anne said, wearing pajama shorts and a shirt and a robe. "Be safe, all of you."

"We will be," Robert assured her, and then they took off in his car for the castle.

"I wish I'd thought of this earlier," Maisie said.

"If Gus's car was found near that petrol station where I saw Jack, that has to confirm that Jack was in the same proximity," Chelsea said. "How far was Gus's car from the station?"

Iverson said, "Just a mile. It was on a farm road, sitting mostly hidden by some old sheds so it wasn't really visible, but I saw the back of the car, and it was black, so I drove down the road to check it out. It looked as if someone had parked it there to hide it. The sheds were practically in ruins, so the farmer probably doesn't even use them any longer and might not have come across the car for a long time."

"So Jack tailed me to the petrol station from Glasgow," Chelsea said, "and Gus picked me up from there. I never saw any sign of Jack at that time. Then Gus and I went back to his room while I left my car at the petrol station. We visited for about an hour, and then he drove me back. When I got in my car and moved it to a pump to get some petrol, I saw Jack. I wonder if Gus did too. Well, worse, that Jack saw Gus leaving me off. I left, irritated that Jack was there, not wanting to have any kind of a confrontation and worried he would smell Gus on me. I hadn't considered that Jack had followed me there. But then why not follow me to the inn and confront Gus there? So I figured at the time that it must have been a coincidence."

"Too much of a coincidence," Robert said.

Maisie and Iverson agreed with him.

"Aye. I should have assumed it was. I thought Gus had just left and returned to the inn. After we said our goodbyes, I didn't watch him leave. But if he saw Jack there or Jack could have followed him, then maybe the two of them got into an altercation once I had left. I didn't see Jack leave either."

"I didn't see Gus on the security video fighting with anyone at the petrol station," Iverson said. "What did Jack's vehicle look like?"

"A blue car. Something new. I don't know vehicles that well. It was a two-door. I hadn't seen him drive it before, actually."

"That would explain why only Gus's car ended up back at the inn and some other guy was driving it. He had Gus's room key, got the bags, returned to the car, and left again," Maisie said.

"After he got the garden stone and rope from the shed," Robert said.

Maisie sighed. "Right."

Iverson said, "Jack's car is a five-door hatchback, Nissan, silver. He must have used another car for his trip there."

"Unless his car was in the shop for repairs or for some other reason, it sounds like this was planned," Robert said.

"Aye, just what I thought," Iverson said.

"What I don't understand is how we wouldn't smell him in the room or on anything, except his phone. He should have left his scent in the room when he grabbed Gus's bags," Maisie said.

"Hunter's concealment," Iverson said. "If he planned this out—like driving a car unknown to either Chelsea or Gus— he wouldn't want either of them to smell him coming. He most likely didn't know the inn was owned by you and your sister."

"Until he smelled our scents around the place," Maisie said. "It sounds like he didn't follow Gus and Chelsea to the inn, or we would have seen his car on video, but instead waited at the petrol station for both of you to return."

"Unless Jack parked somewhere close to the inn but out of sight of your security cameras and then followed Gus and Chelsea back to the station after they left his room," Iverson said. "In any event, once Gus dropped off Chelsea, she saw Jack. Jack had to have seen Gus there and then followed him and confronted him, maybe ran him off the road, had a fight with him, and then killed him."

"I should never have joined Gus there," Chelsea said with regret.

"If you had seen Gus at a different location or even had been with someone else instead, the result could have been the same," Maisie said.

Robert and Iverson agreed with her.

When they arrived at Farraige Castle, several people greeted them in the inner bailey, including Enrick, Lachlan, and Grant.

"How are Colleen, Heather, and the babies?" Robert asked Grant and Enrick as they walked to Gus's car.

"They're good," Grant said, "and they're eager to learn what we discover about all this business."

That was the thing about a wolf pack. They all wanted closure for each other.

Maisie checked out the car on the driver's side. "I smell Iverson, Gus, and Chelsea and the heavy odor of bleach, which is burning my eyes. No one would have been able to ride in the car if it had been covered in bleach, so the killer had to have cleaned it out after leaving it on the farm. But I don't smell any sign of Jack."

"Which means that he must have worn concealment. It's the only explanation for how he could enter Gus's room, pack his bags, and remove them without leaving his scent behind," Iverson said. "But nothing proves he actually murdered him."

Which was true. He had motive. He'd been at the station at the same time that Gus and Chelsea had been, so he didn't have an alibi.

"I'll check the petrol station's video inside the store. I didn't before because Gus was never seen going into the store. But if I can find Jack entering it and maybe buying bleach inside the store, that would help confirm that he was the one responsible for Gus's death," Iverson said.

"Was Jack wearing a wrist splint when you saw him at the station?" Robert realized no one had asked Chelsea about it. And they needed to have her see the video of the man wearing the splint.

Chelsea's eyes widened. "Aye. Jack had hurt his wrist about six weeks before I went to see Gus. He made a big deal of it because he wanted me to baby him and I didn't. I'd learned that he had struck a wall with his fist and broken it in a fit of rage when he was angry with someone at a pub. So I figured he had kind of deserved what he got for losing control. But he wasn't wearing the splint when he was at the petrol station. I would have noticed it."

"If there's nothing else that you ladies want to look at with regard to the car," Iverson said, "let's go home and get some rest."

"I want to see the security video you have of the man wearing the splint," Chelsea said.

"We'll show it to you when we return to the inn," Maisie said.

Robert really hoped she could identify that the man with the torn pocket was Jack. "Were Gus's bags in the car?"

"Yeah, in the trunk," Iverson said. "What about Gus's cell phone? Were you able to ever get it to work?"

"No. Too much salt water," Robert said.

They said good night to Grant and his brothers and to the others who had come out to learn what they could about their murder investigation.

On the way back to the inn, Chelsea said, "We have to prove Jack did this and take him down."

"We will. He won't get away with it," Robert said.

Iverson agreed. Maisie was quiet.

Robert glanced at her. "Are you okay?" She looked pale too, and he suspected just seeing the car and thinking about the scenario had gotten to her. Especially since she'd seen Gus's body. He reached over and gently rubbed her shoulder.

"Yeah. I'm sorry that Jack wore hunter's concealment, though it's possible it was someone else. But I bet it was him. I wanted to know for sure that he had been in Gus's car though."

"Me too," Iverson said, "but it shows he fully intended to kill him all along. I just texted the petrol station and asked them if they had any sales of bleach that evening and if they had hunter's concealment. They don't carry hunter's concealment, but yes on the bleach."

Everyone practically held their breaths to hear what Iverson had to say.

"A blond-haired man bought the bleach before he got some petrol. He used a credit card," Iverson said.

"Yes!" Robert said.

"His name was Jude Springer," Iverson said.

"Ohmigod, he probably thought no one would connect him to the name Jack Wolfson, the man who had the beef with Gus," Maisie said.

"We've got him then." Tears spilled down Chelsea's cheeks.

Iverson gave her a hug.

"We just need to physically catch him now." Robert hoped their plan to get him to the inn would succeed.

When they got back, they found everyone waiting up for their arrival. Robert could understand that. If the roles had been reversed, he would have been sitting up, waiting to learn what they'd discovered too.

"We need to see the security video and show it to Chelsea." Iverson walked through the door first.

"That's exactly what I told Edward and Anne," William said, "as soon as you all left."

They had Chelsea review the video after that, and she carefully studied the man in the hoodie. "That's Jack. That was the wrist he injured, though he hasn't been wearing a splint for a long time, but I'm sure he knew there would be security videos. If any of them caught him, it would look like he was an injured man, and no one would figure he could have murdered anyone. And that hoodie? He wore it a lot when we went on hikes. The pants with the torn pocket? No wonder he lost his phone in the garden."

"He had to have been grabbing the paving stone when he dropped it and didn't realize it," Maisie said.

"Aye, in too much of a hurry," Robert said.

"I suspect he removed Gus's driver's license and stuck it in the pocket with his phone, intending to get rid of it so if anyone had discovered Gus's body, they would find his wallet but no ID," Iverson said. "Since Gus's wallet didn't contain anything else, not even a credit card, Jude must have gotten rid of whatever might have been in it at some other location. But before he disposed of the driver's license, he'd accidentally lost it in the garden. Now we have confirmation Jack was the one wearing the hoodie also." Iverson stretched.

"There's no doubt about it," Chelsea said.

"Okay, well, let's get some sleep." Robert took hold of Maisie's hand, ready to take her to bed. "Now all we have to do is catch him."

"And eliminate him." Chelsea sounded like, if she could, she would take him down herself.

———————

Early the next morning, Maisie woke to see Robert smiling at her as she snuggled with him in bed at the inn. She wondered how long he'd been awake. She really didn't want to get out of bed. She was always ready to get up and go first thing in the morning, but when she had such a hunky wolf to wake up to, she really had a hard time letting go of him.

He kissed the top of her head. "Ready to get up?"

"No. I'm so happy to be here with you like this."

"I know. Me too."

Then they heard Anne and Chelsea talking in the kitchen and starting breakfast and a shower running in one of the bathrooms.

Maisie sighed. "It's time to get up. I'm glad we went to see Gus's car last night and had Chelsea look at the security video. I had thought of it earlier, but we didn't know if she was in on the murder initially. Though I had no intention of telling her that we had ever suspected she could have been involved in his murder."

"When we started to set up the boyfriend situation between Chelsea and William, I just didn't think about it again." They kissed and got out of bed. "I can't wait to see if Chelsea or William had any response to their posts." Robert pulled on some boxer briefs.

"What if Jack's a sneaky bastard and doesn't say anything, just comes for William and/or Chelsea?" Maisie slipped her shirt on over her head. "And he'll be wearing hunter's concealment too."

"There's a chance he'll just wait for Chelsea to return home and then attack William. But he fought with Gus before he killed him, so there's a good chance Jack will come out here and take William to task for dating Chelsea." Robert finished dressing.

Maisie pulled on her shorts. "I agree. I'm going to help the ladies with breakfast so we can get that cleaned up before we start on the guests' breakfasts."

"What do you want us to do?" Robert asked.

"If you don't mind, maybe you guys can clean up the guest room. One of our guests is checking out by ten. So we can get that ready for the next guest coming in at three. I'll take William and Chelsea out to capture some more fun boyfriend/girlfriend pictures after the guests' breakfasts are done," Maisie said.

"Okay, Iverson and I can do that, while William and Edward watch over you ladies."

"That sounds perfect. First, I want to know if Chelsea or William got any messages."

"You and me both, Maisie."

They left their bedroom and checked on everyone else, telling them the plan.

"Jack didn't contact me yet. I wonder if he's anxious about returning here, afraid he might just get caught," Chelsea said.

William looked at his phone and smiled. "Jack sent me a friend request."

Everyone just stared at him, waiting to hear more.

"Okay, I accepted."

"Let's wait and see if he responds once he sees your selfie with Chelsea," Robert said.

The ladies had made eggs and haddock and brought them to the table. They began to eat, and William got a comment on his post.

Everyone stopped what they were doing to see what he had to say.

William laughed. "Janet said she met Chelsea and she's such a nice woman. She hopes that the two of us enjoy spending time together."

Chelsea smiled. "Your mom is so sweet, Anne, Maisie."

"She's funny. I didn't expect her to get involved in this charade," Maisie said.

"Me either," Anne said.

After breakfast, they got busy with their other jobs. Robert and Iverson took care of the vacated guest room while the ladies took meal orders and began making breakfast for the guests.

After they were done, Maisie went out with Chelsea and William to take photos in the woods while Anne stayed with Iverson at the inn and Edward and Robert watched out for Maisie and the "couple."

Maisie photographed them hand in hand in the woods, and then they took selfies to make it look like they were on their own.

After they returned to the inn, Chelsea and William posted their pictures on their Facebook pages. Then they all had tea and waited to see if there was any response. Nothing.

"I would say Jack might not be monitoring your Facebook page, Chelsea. But since he friended William, I feel like he has taken the bait," Robert said.

"I got a message from him! Jack asked where I am. He is worried about me because he has been dropping by my apartment and I haven't been there." Chelsea smiled. "I'm glad I'm here. What do you suggest I say?"

"You're in the Highlands, enjoying a vacation because you don't have a hospice job right now and you have friends you're staying with?" Maisie said.

"That could work if Jack thinks Chelsea's got friends and is protected and so at least she would be safe," Robert said. "So he might think he could solely go after his competition."

"What if Jack thinks Chelsea's friends are really just one guy—William?" Iverson asked.

"That's a possibility," Anne said. "That could be good because he might think she is lying and want to get rid of the guy who has come between them. So he will come to take William out, and then we'll get him."

"He will think Chelsea isn't telling him the whole story anyway if she doesn't mention seeing William." Maisie finished her tea. "Does anyone want another cup of lavender tea?"

Everyone did, and she went into the kitchen to heat up some more water.

"Go ahead and post what Maisie suggested and see what happens," William said.

"It's interesting that he contacted me right after I posted the picture of me having fun with William." Chelsea typed in her message to Jack.

"Yeah, he's watching what you're up to," Iverson said. "Now we just need him to come here so we can catch him."

"He hasn't contacted you yet, has he, William?" Edward asked.

"Nope. Other than friending me. I'm sure he just wants to see my posts for now. Commenting or messaging me would leave a trail, so he might not do that. Especially if he has a plan to eliminate me. Then anyone investigating my disappearance would possibly put two and two together. He probably didn't want to even friend me, but he had to, to see my posts. That way he would get to know me better—learn what I was thinking about Chelsea, maybe more about me, my habits, my strengths, and my weaknesses," William said. "I had another thought. We've had homicide cases where someone is selling something like a car, for instance, and they'll put it in an ad. In one case, the supposed interested buyer took the car for a test-drive and killed the car's owner."

"Or you could say you're trying to buy something and maybe he says he has just what you're looking for," Edward said. "The idea kind of seems like a long shot, but something like that might give him a reason to come see you, and then we can watch what happens."

"Yeah, just make sure you take him down if I don't first," William said.

Chapter 25

Of course, with everyone waiting for Jack to show up at the inn—William even posting that he had a Porsche for sale—Jack never interacted with Chelsea or William further. They couldn't locate him either, no matter how many of the pack members tried to discover where he'd disappeared to. William had a lot of interest in his Porsche from other potential buyers though.

Maisie and Anne had done the transitional training with Conan up at the castle, and he was alternately living at Maisie and Robert's home and with Anne at the inn on different days. Conan was happy to live at both places, and he was so well behaved now. He also loved all of Edeen's pets, which was a good thing because he would be staying with them when Edeen and Lachlan went on their honeymoon.

All week long, other than taking care of the inn business, Robert and Anne had been working on her garden with additional heavy-duty support from several male wolves with the pack who were helping Robert to build the stone retaining walls for the raised beds and paths.

Then the big day arrived for Edeen and Lachlan's wedding, and everyone was thrilled to be there.

Because Maisie had mated Robert, Maisie and Anne were no longer just guests at the wedding; Edeen had made them bridesmaids. They couldn't have been happier. Maisie and Anne's parents had found a home and had returned to Glasgow to get ready to sell their place there, but they had returned to attend the wedding. Both Anne and Maisie had seen the house and loved the cottage that was only a couple of miles from the inn and had a lovely garden and some acreage.

William and Edward continued to stay at the inn with Anne while Robert and Maisie had returned to their home. William and Chelsea continued to pretend they were seeing each other online, but she had moved into the castle so that if Jack had any plan to go after her, he would be out of luck. Iverson had returned also. Chelsea was thrilled to be able to attend the wedding today too.

Robert was excited about his sister and Lachlan's wedding. Not only was Robert serving as a groomsman, but he also had the honor of giving her away to Lachlan since their father had passed away a decade earlier. William and Edward Playfair were serving as two of the ushers and escorted Colleen and Heather to their seats. Two nanny wolves were there with the week-old pair of twins also, the babies well fed and sound asleep.

As groomsmen, Grant and Enrick escorted Anne and Heather's baker, Lana, to their seats. In the meantime, Maisie was taking photos of the whole wedding.

Wearing a wedding gown that she'd made for herself, Edeen was beautiful. Robert's own mate, her sister, and Lana were wearing pretty green medieval Celtic bridesmaid gowns. The groom and groomsmen were all wearing kilts—Lachlan and his brothers wore the MacQuarrie tartan, and Robert wore his Campbell tartan.

Robert felt like this was a rehearsal for him and Maisie. The groomsmen would be the same, except Lachlan and Robert would switch roles and Edeen and Maisie would swap places as the bride. At least Maisie's father would give her away to Robert. Chef was delighted to prepare feasts for both weddings.

Robert hugged his sister before he walked her down the ancient stone castle chapel nave. He was so glad she had found Lachlan to mate. They were just perfect for each other.

She smiled brightly at him, and he hadn't ever seen her look so excited and pretty. Six flower girls from the ages of three to eight scattered rose petals from their baskets in front of them. Robert loved giving his sister away to Lachlan, and then he took his seat with the others while Lachlan and Edeen said their vows. When Robert sat with the rest of the wedding party, he wished he were sitting next to his mate. But he was so proud of her for taking the photos of the wedding that he knew everyone would cherish.

Once the vows were made and Lachlan and Edeen kissed, everyone cheered them, a few of the shifters howling with joy.

Then Maisie had the wedding party gather so she could take pictures on a timer, and she joined the group. Then she did some separate photo shoots with family groups—including the couples with their new babies, the bride and groom, of course, and even herself and Robert.

Everyone else headed to the great hall where the feast would be held.

Once the others were there, they waited for the bride and groom to enter, and when Lachlan and Edeen came inside, everyone cheered. They would make toasts, then have dinner before they danced.

"To the bride and groom," Robert said, Maisie photographing the toast. "My twin sister has always been my best friend, but with her mating to Lachlan, we were no longer just the two of us. I've gained brothers and sisters galore. Wishing you all the best, both of you."

"Here, here," a chorus of cheers went up.

"We never thought our youngest triplet would find a mate, but our next-door neighbor turned out to be just the one to set him on the right path. We love you both and are so grateful your brother joined us as part of the family too," Grant said.

Lachlan echoed the sentiment with his own toast, and then the meal was served—a warm asparagus and goat cheese salad first. The main entrée was baked rainbow trout on a bed of green beans and roasted cherry tomatoes with a horseradish-and-walnut sauce served with new potatoes. For some, they opted to have roast fillet of beef on a bed of spinach and porcini mushrooms with a red wine jus, served with roasted potatoes and honey-glazed carrots.

During the meal, Robert was glad to have Maisie at his side. Anne and their parents were sitting with them also. So were William and Edward, Chelsea, and Iverson.

"The wedding and reception are sure lovely," Janet said.

Frederick cut up some of his beef. "It was done really well. I couldn't imagine having it at the castle, so this was great."

"We'll have something similar," Maisie said. "I love how it turned out."

"The food is terrific." Janet took another bite of her trout.

"Aye, I love the beef." Frederick ate another slice of beef.

Anne sighed. "I just need a mate so I can do this too."

They all laughed.

After dinner, they had chocolate cake and homemade vanilla ice cream.

Robert and Maisie asked her parents how things were going with their house in Glasgow.

"We just got an offer while Edeen and Lachlan were saying their vows and sold it," Frederick said. "We'll be moving into our new home in three weeks, so when you return from your honeymoon, we'll be living here a week later."

"We can help you get moved in then," Maisie said.

Janet laughed. "Practically the whole wolf pack is helping us. We couldn't be more thrilled about how everything all played out."

"That's great," Robert said.

"What are we going to do about Jack?" Anne asked.

"I was just going to ask if there had been any other news about him," Janet said.

They hadn't brought the subject of Jack up in a while

because they hadn't thought of any other way to try to get hold of him.

"Not a word. I wonder if he has taken a new alias and has found a new girlfriend," Robert said.

"I wouldn't let your guard down," Frederick said.

"No. Certainly not." Robert and the others would definitely keep an eye out for him for as long as it took.

"I'm still trying to locate him with all the resources I have," Iverson said.

"Good." Frederick drank some of his champagne. "The guy needs to be dealt with terminally."

"Hey, I know you and Maisie planned to go fishing with Lachlan when they get back from their honeymoon, but by then you'll be getting married and going off to the woods for your honeymoon. Chelsea wants to go fishing, and we were wondering if you would like to go as a foursome? We'll take a separate boat, and we'll all go fishing," William said. "And of course, we'll take some photos of ourselves, in the event Jack's still monitoring our social network posts."

"I would love to do that. We finished the flower beds for the garden, and it's time to just take a break. This time we'll actually catch fish." Maisie kissed Robert on the mouth, and he deepened the kiss.

"Aye, that sounds like fun. You'll have to photograph all the fish we catch so Lachlan and Edeen know we really caught something." At least Robert hoped they would.

"How about tomorrow? After Anne and Maisie prepare breakfast for their guests?" William asked.

"That sounds good," Maisie said, "if you're alright with it, Anne."

"Yeah, and we can have a fish fry once you return." Anne smiled. The challenge was on.

Edeen and Lachlan had their first dance after the meal, and everyone loved watching them. Then everyone had a chance to dance.

Colleen and Heather were doing well, tired because of nursing the babies so much, but each of them managed one dance with their mates. The rest of the time they enjoyed the celebration while the babies slept in two separate bassinets next to the head table. Even Janet and Frederick were happily dancing with each other.

"Let's dance," Robert said to Maisie, standing and offering her his hand.

"I've been waiting for you to offer."

They danced for the rest of the night, working up the heat, and she whispered in his ear, "As soon as Edeen and Lachlan leave, you and I are taking this to bed."

"Most assuredly."

A lot of the wolves would run after the wedding, but Edeen and Lachlan skipped it to drive to Edinburgh to stay overnight and get their flight to Bali the next day.

Robert was happy to do anything that Maisie wanted to—a wolf run would be grand, or just going home to make love to his mate? He was all for that too.

"A wolf run?" he asked.

She smiled in such a sexy way, he knew she was too hot for that and was ready to make love.

Of course Maisie was always ready to run as a wolf with her mate, but he'd gotten her so worked up while they were dancing close that she really wanted to take this to bed.

Once Edeen and Lachlan thanked everyone and left, Maisie and Robert said goodbye, then headed home. They were newly mated wolves after all, and they had their priorities.

But once they arrived home, they were thwarted. They had to greet Ruby, the Irish wolfhound; Rogue and Jinx, the fox terriers; Silky, the Scottish fold cat; and Mittens. Anne was taking care of Conan for the week so they wouldn't feel too overwhelmed with the pet menagerie.

After taking the dogs out to relieve themselves, Maisie and Robert told the dogs to go to their beds, which they did. Mittens and Silky would do their own thing. There was no racing to the bedroom to make love now, not unless they wanted to start the dogs barking and chasing them as if they were playing with them.

Then they reached the bedroom and began stripping each other's clothes off, though Robert was having a difficult time unfastening Maisie's gown. She'd removed his sword and belt and was working on his Prince Charlie's jacket and pulled it off his shoulders.

"You look so handsome in this."

"Thanks. You look just gorgeous in your gown, pretty as a bride."

"I kept feeling like this was a prelude to our wedding." She unfastened his white shirt.

"Me too. I kept thinking it felt like a full-blown wedding rehearsal except for changing some of our roles. Our menu will be different too."

"Right." She ran her hands over his bare chest. "The first time I saw you like this was when you got out of the bed in the guest room at the castle to pull the fishhook out of my arm."

He smiled and kissed her head, then began removing the pins from the floral wreath she was wearing. "I felt more of a need to remove the fishhook than to worry about being naked. You didn't appear too shocked."

She laughed. "Nothing you do shocks me too much, Robert Campbell."

They finished undressing, then tossed the covers aside and climbed into bed. They ran their hands over each other's bodies, exploring, enjoying the sensory stimuli.

She kissed his cheek. "In that moment, you could have yanked off a sheet and covered yourself with it. But that wouldn't have been you."

He brushed her throat with featherlight kisses.

"I believe I fell a little bit in love with you in that instant," she said.

He combed his fingers through her hair, looking down at her with love and admiration.

She felt the same for him as she ran her hand over his cheek with a gentle caress.

"I couldn't believe I'd caught you in the ocean, your blue eyes spearing me with indignation, and I swore *you'd* caught *me* right in that second, like a mermaid drawing a sailor—"

"To his death?"

Robert's eyes were lust-filled, his heart beating harder, like hers was, and he kissed her soundly, deepening the connection. Then they separated for a breath of air, and he smiled. "I was under your spell. Right away, I wondered if you had a mate or someone you were seeing, and I wanted to date you in the worst way. But then we were fighting for our lives after that."

There was no more talking, just purpose in their actions. He slid his hand down and cupped a breast and massaged, making her nipples tighten with need. They were sensitive to his touch. He kissed her so expertly, she felt uplifted and needy at the same time. She couldn't get enough of his touching her, of feeling his bare skin against hers, of hearing his rugged sighs and beating heart, of smelling the musky scent of him when he was so into her. Their pheromones always laid the path to each other, shouting for them to complete the mission, to make love all the way.

He kissed her down her tummy, his fingers parting her curly hairs, and he began stroking her between her legs with skillful intent. She swore she melted under his caress and tensed with delight at the same time. Then he claimed her mouth with another hot, possessive kiss. Her bud was swollen and sensitive and was straining to reach climax. She loved what he did to her to make her feel so good.

His voice was husky as he whispered against her ear, "I love you."

"Oh," she moaned in delight, "me too." But that's all she could say because she was so wrapped up in his intense kisses and intimate strokes. Then a jolt of pleasure raced through her, and she was tumbling off the cliff into an exquisite climax. "Ohmigod, aye!" She shuddered as the orgasm pulsed through her and she was grasping at him, wanting him in her now.

He spread her legs farther apart with his knee, and then he inserted his arousal into her, pushing deep. Her breath caught, and she wrapped her legs around his as he began to thrust. She had him just where she wanted him.

He felt so good inside her, and she was so glad they had come together as mated wolves for this and so many other reasons.

———

Maisie was so easy to love and make love to. Her eyes had darkened with arousal as he slanted his mouth over hers and she began to explore his mouth deeply, tonguing him with her delicious kisses. He loved the way she caught him with her legs and claimed him as he thrust deeply into her.

Then he licked her nipples, mouthing them as he continued to thrust, delighting in the satiny feel of her lush breasts and the way she shuddered when he loved on them. He caressed her breasts and relished the way she arched against him, every close contact of the heated, rewarding kind. But then he began kissing her sweet mouth, and she nipped at his lips, her hands cupping his face, her mouth pursuing his possessively. He kissed her deeply again to taste her fully, their tongues tangoing in a sensual kiss.

He pushed fully into her, gliding out and surging deeply in again. She was clenching hard as if she was getting ready to have an orgasm again, and she did. As soon as he came with an explosive ejaculation, she cried out his name, and he realized she had climaxed at the same time.

"I'm so glad we didn't run as wolves first." She sighed heavily and kissed his chest. "When you were dancing with me, I was so primed for this."

"The same thing with me. I couldn't have run as a wolf as well until a particular part of my anatomy had settled down."

She laughed. "I love you, my hunky wolf."

"I love you, my beautiful mate."

———

The next morning after Maisie and Anne served the guests breakfast and cleaned up the three rooms that would have new guests later, Maisie, Robert, William, and Chelsea dressed to go fishing. They were launching two boats off the MacQuarrie beach, all ready to fish, excited. It was a beautiful day, overcast—perfect for fishing—and warm, though the wind off the water was always cool.

They had their life preservers, fishing buckets, flares—this time!—ice chests, fishing rods, tackle boxes, a gallon of water for each of them, beef jerky and granola bars in case of emergency, fillet knives, extra-long rope in the event they needed more for an emergency towing, and first aid kits!

Then they pushed their boats into the water and motored out to fish. Both of the boats were seventeen-foot unsinkable

Boston Whalers that were good and stable on ocean waves. These were equipped with GPS plotter/sounders, fix-mounted VHF radios that had a range of fifteen to twenty miles, and emergency beacons. They didn't plan to have any trouble, but they knew trouble could find them when they were least expecting it.

"This is so much fun," Maisie said to Robert as they motored out into the water, found the area where they wanted to fish, tossed the anchor in, and cast out their lines.

"It is," Robert said. "We've been so busy that it is nice to take a break and just relax, especially because the clinic will be open upon our return from our honeymoon."

"Aye. Do you think we'll catch any fish?"

"With luck, sure. Maybe between the four of us, we'll manage." Robert waved at William and Chelsea nearby.

Often fishing boats hunted the fish together, though they had to watch out that they didn't run into each other. But they should be okay, anchored some distance from each other.

Chelsea and William were taking selfies fishing and laughing. Even though it was all faked, they looked so real while they did it. They finally settled down to fish, too, when a large school of pollock began to swim under the boats.

"Oh, wow, unreal," Maisie said softly.

Everyone concentrated on fishing and began catching pollocks. For the area, they were some of the hardest-fighting fish, pound for pound. As soon as they began catching them, the pollocks were fighting to get back into the kelp. Maisie was trying hard not to lose the fish or her fishing pole.

"How many do we have now?" Chelsea asked, struggling to get her fish under control and William using a landing net to bring the pollock in.

"Six for us," Robert called out, helping Maisie with hers.

"Four for us," William said. "We're catching up. Got another one."

Then the school passed them by.

"That should be good enough for a feast for everyone," William said.

That's when they heard a boat coming toward them. They thought it was another fishing boat, wanting to cash in on their good fishing spot, but the boat wasn't slowing down, and the school of fish had already left.

"Pull up anchor!" Robert shouted to William, who was hauling his up right away, just like Robert was trying to.

Everyone had their life jackets on, but if the boat hit one of theirs, it could seriously injure them. That's when Maisie thought of Jack and how he must have used a boat to dump Gus's body. God, had he been tracking William's movements all this time, just waiting for the right moment to go after him?

William had posted about fishing with Chelsea, and the cliffs in the picture showed just where they were. "It's probably Jack," Maisie said. She got on her phone while Robert started the boat's motor and got them underway. "Grant, we've got trouble."

"Enrick told me you're fishing with Robert. What happened this time?" Grant asked.

"We have a boat headed straight for us. I'm sure he's after

William and Chelsea. But he'll want to take us out too, most likely, so there aren't any witnesses."

"Jack?"

"I can't make him out, but that's whom I suspect. He's not slowing down, and he's gaining on us."

"Hell, it will take us time to launch a couple more boats, but we'll do it. Just try to get close to our beach."

"We're headed that way now." But Maisie knew they weren't going to make it to shore before the faster, larger boat was upon them.

Chapter 26

ROBERT COULDN'T BELIEVE THAT JACK WOULD BE BARREL-ing down on them with his motorboat—he wasn't sure how fast it could go, but he was coming in hot. It looked like it would close in on them before they could outrun him. "We're going to separate from you guys and turn," Robert shouted to William.

"He's going to go after Chelsea and William," Maisie warned.

"Aye, and we're going to make a turn and toss the extra towrope, anchor, fishing line, everything we've got to try to wrap around his propellers," Robert said.

She picked up the flare gun. "What about this?"

"We'll use that as a last resort. Can you switch places with me?"

"Aye."

William pulled the same maneuver, making a sweep to the left instead. As soon as the motorboat followed him, Maisie had switched places and was driving her and Robert's boat as close as she could get to Jack's before it passed them by. Robert tossed the extra length of towrope, fishing net, and fishing lines at the motorboat. They were right near the propeller, but he was afraid they hadn't caught. Then suddenly, they heard a grinding noise, and some of the items, if not all of them, were tangled around the prop.

Jack was cursing a blue streak as his boat went idle in the water.

Robert and Maisie couldn't see William's boat until they headed back toward the beach, getting out of reach of Jack's wrath, in case Jack decided to shoot at them with a flare gun or rifle if he had one on him.

"What are you going to do?" Maisie asked Robert.

"Take him into custody."

"How?"

"Get closer to his boat. I'll use the transom to climb aboard. Then you head to the beach."

"No, Robert. He could shoot you as soon as you get on his boat."

But Robert had to stop him. He was afraid that the bastard would flee somehow and they would still have the issue of William and Chelsea's safety.

Despite Maisie's objection, she apparently trusted Robert enough to do this and he trusted her to get him close enough to Jack's vessel. He leapt onto the transom, made it into the boat, and saw Jack with his hands on his head, watching Chelsea and William get away. He was so shook up that his prey had evaded him that he seemed to have forgotten that another boat was still out there with Robert and Maisie on it.

Robert stripped off his clothes and shifted into his wolf, not having the luxury of time or any other way to sneak up on Jack. Robert sprinted to take Jack down, and in that instant, Jack turned and saw him.

"What the hell?"

Yeah, always watch your back with wolves. Especially when the hunter with murder on his mind was now the prey.

━━━━━━━━

Maisie wasn't one to sit and wait for an outcome. She cut the engine and used the short towline to tie the boat to Jack's vessel. Then she climbed onto the boat with the flare gun in hand, just in case she had to use it on Jack to save Robert's life.

Jack had a large knife in his hand and was trying to stab at Robert, who dodged him as a wolf. God, Jack was wearing the clothes he'd worn on the night he was on the inn's security video: the black boots, the charcoal-gray hoodie, the black pants with the torn pocket. Some people never learned. All that was missing was the wrist splint. He had more of a beard now than when she'd dated him.

"Throw down the knife or I'll use this on you," Maisie shouted. She was afraid Robert would look back at her, but he kept his focus trained on Jack. She hoped this would go down the way they needed it to and that both of them hadn't made a mistake.

"Hell, what are you doing here?" Jack asked her.

"Taking down a murderer."

Jack set the knife carefully down, but she didn't trust that he was truly giving up. He had to know murdering Gus and trying to do the same with Chelsea and William gave him an immediate wolf's death sentence, so there was no way out for him.

What she didn't expect was for Jack to begin to yank off his clothes and shift. Nay! She was afraid that Robert would do the more honorable thing and allow Jack time to shift and then the two of them would fight. Damn it!

As soon as Jack had stripped off his clothes, he shifted, but Robert had already gone in for the kill. He wasn't going to give Jack more time to prepare himself or go on the offensive.

Good. But Maisie couldn't use the flare gun without chancing hitting Robert, so she stripped off her clothes and shifted into her wolf. Two wolves on one should decide Jack's fate. She heard William's boat's engine returning and then two others. But they wouldn't get here in time to decide the way this was going to go down.

Robert had bitten Jack's face, and his cheek was bleeding. Robert had blood on his wolf coat too, but she didn't know if it was from being bitten or if it was Jack's blood. She raced across the boat deck and bit into Jack's flank.

He immediately turned to tear into her, but Robert grabbed at his neck, getting Jack's attention. A wolf's bite could crush the spine. Jack quickly shook loose of Robert's tentative grip. Both wolves' canines were painted in blood. That meant Jack had wounded her mate too.

All three wolves were panting, chests heaving, Jack's and Robert's steely gazes on each other while she kept her attention on Jack. One false move and that could be a wolf's demise. If Jack got ahold of Robert's neck and could kill him, she wouldn't stand a chance against the bigger male wolf.

She had to go for Jack's tail so the distraction would give Robert a chance to take Jack down once and for all.

The boats coming for them were still too far off to be of any assistance. She leapt for Jack's rump. Robert seemed to have anticipated her action and dove for Jack before Jack could attack her. She bit Jack's tail hard, missing his rump because he skittered out of her way, but then Robert grabbed hold of Jack's throat with the killing blow and wouldn't let go until Jack was limp on the boat deck, his heart no longer beating.

She went over and licked Robert's ear, but he wasn't letting go of the wolf, as if he was afraid Jack might still get up to try and hurt her. She listened to the wolf's heart again and then shifted. "He's dead, Robert. There's no heartbeat. He's dead, and he can't hurt anyone ever again."

Finally, Robert released Jack and shifted, then took her into his arms and squeezed her to his chest tightly. She hugged him just as hard. "I'm okay. We're okay. The other boats are coming. Let's get dressed."

They started to dress, but she was so shaky, he needed to help her. That was because of the adrenaline flooding their bloodstream after the fight. Once they were dressed, they watched as the boats arrived, filled with Highland wolf warriors ready to take down the murderer. But they were too late.

Robert climbed into their boat first, then helped Maisie into it next. He untied the rope.

"I can't believe our extra towline stopped his boat." She settled down on the seat while they motored away from the boat and Grant waved to them from another boat, William also. There was no sign of Chelsea. Maisie was so relieved that they would have no more trouble with Jack.

"Chelsea's at the castle," William called out.

They gave him a thumbs-up.

"He's dead," Robert said to Grant, sounding just as relieved.

"Good. We'll take care of the boat, him, all of it."

Maisie was glad they had a wolf pack to deal with matters like this. "Do you even feel like having a fish feast after all this?"

"In celebration of catching the bad guy and taking him down? You bet. We'll just need to get cleaned up a bit, and we'll have everyone come to the house. How do you feel?" Robert asked.

"I'm ready for it. Are you okay? Are you injured badly?"

"I'm okay. I have a few bite marks that will need some antiseptic and bandaging, but that's all."

"I'll take care of you when we get home." Maisie thought Robert might say something about objecting to her coming to his rescue.

He finally smiled at her. "You're a great wolf fighter."

"So are you. I didn't want you to be so honorable— though that's your nature and I love you for it—but under the circumstances, I didn't want you to let him shift first."

He nodded. "But you noticed that I didn't wait for him to charge me first."

"Aye, I was glad you hadn't."

"I wouldn't have. Especially when you were at risk of being injured if he had gotten the best of me. I knew just what you were going to do when you bit his tail. I love you, honey."

"I love you so much too. And I'm glad you figured out I was going for his rump and took advantage of his distraction."

They ended up on the beach, where a bunch of the pack members had gathered to see them, cheering them for taking down the murderous wolf. Howls rent the air. Even Chelsea was there and gave them a hug.

Grant returned to the shore on one of the boats and joined them. "You were lucky his towline got caught in his propeller."

"*His* towline?" Robert asked.

"Yeah, his boat was bouncing on the waves, and it must have flipped out and tangled around the propeller," Grant said.

"Well, damn, that's good," Robert said.

Maisie shook her head. "Here we had thought we'd stopped him."

"It's all good. The threat has been eliminated, and that's all that matters." Grant smiled. "Looks like someone's going to be up for a fish fry."

"Aye," Robert said.

"It's well deserved."

"We're going to our house to have the fish fry," Robert told William. "Iverson, you'll have to join us since you were so involved in trying to catch this guy too. We'll just need to have Edward bring Anne and we'll be all set."

"I'm calling Anne now," Maisie said.

"Thanks, Grant, and to everyone who has helped in dealing with Jack," Robert said.

"Aye, it's what we do for each other," Grant said.

———————

Maisie drove Robert home, and they brought in all the fish, but before they could take care of Robert's injuries or begin preparing the fish, they had to greet all of Edeen and Lachlan's animals and Mittens too.

Afterward, Maisie had Robert strip off his clothes so she could clean up his bite marks.

"Come on. Let's take a quick shower before everyone gets here." Robert grabbed up his clothes and put them in the laundry sink and poured water on them while she removed her clothes.

Then the two of them hurried to the bathroom to clean up. After carefully drying Robert and herself, Maisie applied antiseptic to his bite marks, bandaged him, and they both dressed.

"I'm so glad that your bite marks don't look too bad. If you have a fever or see red streaks around the wounds, let the doctor know at once," Maisie said.

He laughed. "I love you."

"Aye, just like I love you."

Not long after they began cleaning the fish, Chelsea, William, and Iverson arrived. That gave Maisie a chance to rinse the blood out of Robert's clothes. William and Iverson began helping clean the fish.

Chelsea was making them wine coolers when Anne and Edward joined them.

Hugs were shared all around. "I can't believe you and Robert took Jack down as wolves," Anne said to Maisie.

"I couldn't let Robert take care of him on his own if there was the slightest chance Jack could have gotten the best of him," Maisie said.

After cooking the fish and chips—served with vinegar and salt and ketchup for those from Glasgow and brown sauce for those from Edinburgh—they sat down to eat them.

"These are delicious," Chelsea said.

"I'm so glad you caught these," Anne said. "I just wish Edeen and Lachlan could have been here to enjoy them too, so you could prove you could fish."

"I took lots of pictures of our catch," Maisie said.

"Me too." Chelsea drank some of her soda. "I have never had so much fun, until the murderer showed up, but now I'm ready to return home, and I have a job for the rest of the week. My sister will cover for me when I come to your wedding."

"That's great." Maisie raised her glass of water to her.

"We'll miss you." Iverson grabbed a chip.

"I guess this is the end for us," William said to Chelsea, still playing along. "I'll be deleting my fake Facebook account now."

"Aye. I'm going back to dating guys in Glasgow, but hopefully no one who is like Jack again." Chelsea shook her head.

"I know what you mean." Maisie leaned over and kissed Robert.

Iverson sat back in his chair. "I contacted Ike before coming over here to tell him that Robert and Maisie took Jack down. He wanted to thank you both, but also to thank Chelsea and the rest of us for trying to catch him too. He also wanted to say he never felt it was Chelsea's fault that his brother died. That was all on Jack."

Tears filled Chelsea's eyes. "I still feel it was my fault for seeing him, but I'm glad Ike doesn't feel that way about me."

Then Robert got a call, and he smiled. "It's Lachlan." He put it on speakerphone. "Hey, we're all here having a fish fry. You're supposed to be relaxing—and other stuff—in Bali."

"Grant told me. You didn't think we wouldn't find out about you taking down Jack with Maisie's help, did you?"

"You're on your honeymoon!" Robert was really surprised Grant would call them and tell them about it. Then again, Grant was the pack leader, so it made sense he would call his packmates to tell them everyone was okay.

"Grant would never have heard the end of it if he hadn't told us what had happened," Edeen said. "We're so glad both of you are fine and that Jack is dead."

"I can't believe you took him down when you were fishing," Lachlan said.

"It was all in the planning," Robert said.

Everyone laughed.

"Okay, when you go fishing with me, we'll just catch fish, right?" Lachlan asked.

Robert smiled. "Truly, I can't make any promises."

"You know Robert hasn't been out there alone when he has been fishing," Maisie reminded them.

"Exactly," Edeen said. "It's the special combination of the two of you that make wild adventures happen."

Robert leaned over and kissed Maisie. "That is so true. I don't believe it will ever be the same without her."

"Oh, aye," Maisie said. "I don't believe I'll let him go without me. It seems when the going gets rough, we need to be a team."

Truly, that was just the way they looked at their mating. They were there for each other through the great times and the harrowing times. He couldn't be more fortunate than to have Maisie at his side.

"We'll let you get back to enjoying your well-deserved fish fry," Lachlan said. "Just know that when we return and you have time, we're doing this again, minus taking down a killer."

"We're all for it," Maisie said.

Everyone hoped their honeymoon in Bali was going great, which they said it was, and then the fish fry party concluded with deep-fried Mars bars for dessert.

After hugs all around at the conclusion of dessert, William drove Anne back to the inn and would stay there for one last night. Iverson, Chelsea, and Edward returned to the castle, and Chelsea would leave in the morning for Glasgow. Maisie and Robert would continue last-minute plans for their own wedding that would happen in less than a week now.

"First, we take the fox terriers and Ruby out for their potty time, and then..." Robert said.

"We run as wolves. I want to run as far and free as we can. I just feel that I still have so much adrenaline pumping through my blood after the fight, even though I'm sure it's mostly dissipated, but I just want to run it off," Maisie said. "As long as you're feeling okay. We'll have to rebandage your wounds after we return."

He smiled. "Aye. Though making love can relieve that extra adrenaline too."

She started to gingerly remove his shirt. "I want to run with you."

"But this time, no nipping at each other."

"You got it," she said.

Not long after that, they were running as wolves, tearing across their acreage and the MacQuarries', barking and howling with delight. Other wolves joined them in a chorus of howls. The pack was united. The bad guy was eliminated. Everyone was safe and sound.

Maisie and Robert had found the perfect mate in each other. The world was right again.

But who knew what adventures they would find themselves in as their mated journey continued?

Epilogue

In great anticipation, Robert waited to see his bride and her father enter the chapel filled with flowers from Edeen's and Colleen's greenhouses and gardens. Then he saw Maisie on her father's arm, and he smiled broadly as he watched them walking down the ancient stone castle chapel's nave. Everyone from the pack who could attend was there, excited to dress up for another celebration. Even Bruce and his wife were there, having brought Lady and her pups to show off to everyone because Robert and Maisie had made the miracle possible. But that wasn't the only reason. They were gifting one of the pups to them for their wedding present, whichever one they chose, though the pups were too young to go to new homes yet. Ike had even brought Chelsea to the wedding.

Maisie was smiling like Robert was. She looked amazing in her beautiful medieval wedding gown of white, a shawl of red-and-light-blue MacTavish plaid crossing over one shoulder and her body, fastened by a MacTavish clan brooch of a boar's head and the logo *non oblitus*—not forgetful. She was wearing a Gaelic crown of wildflowers, lavender, and ivy from Edeen's and Colleen's floral gardens.

He was so proud of his sister for making Maisie's wedding gown in record time before her own wedding. They had just returned from their honeymoon, and Edeen had done the finishing touches on Maisie's gown. She had also made a shawl out of the Campbell plaid of dark blue and green for Maisie. Robert had also purchased a clan crest for her, a boar's head with the logo *ne obliviscaris*—forget not. It hadn't worked for him with other women, but with Maisie, he never forgot any occasions that she was part of.

In truth, eighteen ancient Scottish clans actually had a boar's head on their coat of arms, but still, it was a gesture of taking her into his clan while she was still keeping ties with her own.

He'd always thought he would be nervous when getting ready to wed his she-wolf, but he realized he wasn't because he was already mated to her for life, and this was just a special, human formality to celebrate their mating. When her father handed Maisie off to Robert, he thanked his father-in-law. Robert didn't think anything could be better than when Maisie told him she wanted to mate him, that she loved him as much as he loved her, but seeing her at their wedding was just as amazing. She was beautiful. He couldn't wait to get her alone tonight in Edinburgh. Tomorrow, they would fly to Montana, their final destination being Glacier National Park for their honeymoon at the Lodge at Whitefish Lake.

But right now, they were saying their vows, he was changing out her shawl to the Campbell tartan, then kissing his beautiful bride and mate, and walking her back down the nave to enjoy the celebratory feast, to dance, and to run as a wolf.

When Maisie walked down the nave to join Robert, her mate looked so handsome in his Campbell kilt and Prince Charlie jacket and armed with his sword. She was so happy. Her sister had asked her if she was nervous, but Maisie hadn't been at all. She was so excited to go with Robert on their honeymoon and take wolf runs where wild wolves, grizzlies, and black bears actually lived.

She wasn't crying, but her father sure had misty eyes because he was giving his first daughter away, even though she was already mated. When he left her with Robert, she loved her mate for thanking her father for giving her away to him despite it being a little late for that. Her mom was shedding happy tears also, which almost made Maisie cry.

After saying their vows, he removed the brooch on her shawl, then pulled her MacTavish shawl off, and her sister came up and took them from him and returned to her seat. Then he secured the Campbell plaid over Maisie's shoulder with the Campbell clan crest brooch and kissed her—the very best part of the wedding!

She would save her MacTavish shawl as a keepsake, but she was officially now a Campbell. She so loved him. "I'm so glad I caught you with your fishhook," she said, smiling up at him as they headed outside to walk to the great hall for the feast.

He laughed. "Is that what happened? I love you."

"I love you too."

In the great hall, they had their own special table

decorated with a vase of roses, and everyone was having steak, chips, fruit, and salads. Champagne was served for everyone who wanted it, whisky for some, and milk for the nursing moms. Maisie couldn't believe that the babies had slept through the whole wedding ceremony. In the great hall, everyone was talking, and both Colleen and Heather ended up having to nurse their babies during the feast.

"So which puppy are we going to take?" Maisie asked Robert. She was so thrilled that Bruce and Mary had come to the wedding and were giving them their choice of puppy before they found homes for the others. They were still young, but they were weaning them now. They were furrier, their eyes open, stumbling around, and every one of them was adorable.

"I think you have your heart set on the little female. It's totally your choice," Robert said.

"Aye. Let's get the female. Hopefully, Mittens will love her too."

"She will. They'll grow up together. She'll always be a reminder of our special experiences on the island."

They told Bruce and Mary they wanted the little female pup, and she would be called Etta, which meant "pearl."

The toasting began, then dancing. She loved dancing with her father after she danced with Robert. Her mother danced with Robert, and Anne did afterward, while Maisie danced with Lachlan. Then the rest of the time, Robert and Maisie danced together.

The wolf run was after that, though Colleen and Heather weren't ready for a run with their young ones yet. Even Bruce and Mary were thrilled to go running since they didn't often run like that near Glasgow.

Once Robert and Maisie were done with their run, eager to get on their way, they shifted and dressed, thanked and hugged everyone, and then they headed home. It was time to pack up the car, drive to the airport, and start their dream honeymoon. The wedding had just been the cherry on top of the whole blissful affair, celebrating with the pack, family, and friends.

Discover how Enrick MacQuarrie met
his match in his feisty mate in

THE WOLF WORE PLAID

Chapter 1

"WE'VE GOT TROUBLE," LANA CAMERON, THE BAKER, SAID
to Heather MacNeill, motioning with her head to the big
glass windows of Ye Olde Highland Pie Shoppe in the village
near the MacNeills' Argent Castle.

Heather glanced out the window and saw Lana was right.
Heather had been hoping the rumors about having more
problems with the Kilpatrick brothers wouldn't come true.
But redheaded Robert and his equally redheaded brother
Patrick were climbing out of their truck, looking around to
see who was eating at the café tables outside and then speaking to each other before they entered the shop. They both
looked like wary gray wolves.

They should be. After Patrick had killed the wolf Heather
was going to mate, she'd wanted to end Patrick herself. The

only thing stopping her was that the fight had been her mate-to-be's fault.

Lana joined Heather behind the counter. "Did I tell you Enrick MacQuarrie came in when you were gone yesterday afternoon?" Lana raised a brow and gave her a smile.

Heather frowned. "On purpose?"

"Of course he came in on purpose."

Heather let out her breath in annoyance and folded her arms. "He came into the shop when he knew I wasn't going to be here?" As owner, manager, and general hand-on-deck, Heather was nearly always there, though she was training Lana to take over whenever she had to be away.

Lana let out a long-suffering sigh, placing her hands on her chest and looking heavenward. "Aye, if 'twere up to me, I would chase the hunky Highlander all through the heather until I had him pinned down to a mating. But alas, he doesna see me as a prospective mate."

Heather continued to frown. "Me then? Why come when I wasn't here? On purpose."

"He is a hardy warrior but with feelings running deep for ye." Lana was keeping in character with her role here at the shop. "'Tis you he wished to see, but he fears you're still in mourning over Timothy and doesn't want to approach you too soon for a courtship."

Heather didn't lose the frown. Lana couldn't be serious. Was she up to a bit of matchmaking where none would be possible? "He has never had time for me...ever. He's a workaholic. He doesn't believe in having fun. He's a...stick-in-the-mud." With her. Not with others. She folded her

THE WOLF WORE PLAID

arms and let her breath out in a huff. "Okay, so then what did he do?"

"He asked me how you were feeling."

"And you said?"

"Good." Lana laughed.

Heather curbed the urge to sock her.

Lana sighed again. "That you were ready to date if he would get on with it and start making an overture. Don't expect too much at first. I'm not sure he took me at my word." Lana smiled, then frowned. "Just think, if he were your mate..." She motioned to the windows where the Kilpatricks looked unsure about coming inside or not. "He would toss them out on their ear if they came inside. Or at least Enrick would make them shake a bit in their boots. They wouldn't be as cocky as they are otherwise."

Protective, oh aye. Enrick and his two brothers were protective of her when Heather chanced to go to the MacQuarrie castle. But the brothers thought she was too wild, too impetuous. And that irritated her. She'd overheard them talking to her brothers about it on different occasions, how difficult it was to keep her in check. She sure didn't need a mate who felt that way about her.

What was wrong with wanting to do things on the spur of the moment? To take a chance at doing something fun and whimsical? That was who she was, and she wasn't changing to fit some male wolf's concept of the perfect she-wolf.

Take her business here. It had been a risk to start something like this, and a few had said she couldn't do it. Well, she proved she could. She'd worked hard to make her dream come true. And it was her dream, no one else's.

"Oh, I've got to tend to the bread." Lana hurried off to check on it while Heather glanced back at the glass door.

She was seriously surprised Enrick had come to talk to her friend and feel her out about Heather's thoughts on dating again. As much as she'd had a crush on the wolf forever, he *wasn't* the one for her. She'd figured that out a long time ago.

Then she thought again about the current situation. Enrick wasn't here to serve and protect, so she was on her own for now.

As far as she knew, the Kilpatricks and their McKinley cousins had been furious they hadn't gotten the film contract to have a new fantasy film shot at the McKinleys' castle in the Highlands. They would be even madder once they learned the MacQuarries had gotten the contract to have it filmed in part at their castle and on their grounds *instead*. Since some of the MacNeill wolves would be participating with the MacQuarries as extras in the film, and the MacNeills were McKinley rivals, there was bound to be trouble at some time or another between them. Had the Kilpatricks already learned where the shoot was going to be held, and that was why they were here? She knew they weren't here to tell her they were sorry for Patrick killing Timothy. Patrick had felt perfectly justified, and truthfully, he had been.

The MacQuarrie pack leaders were keeping quiet about the film location for now, although they'd told Heather's pack leaders because they needed some of their men and women to sign up as extras. Heather knew because she was going to be in charge of the MacNeill female extras during the filming. She hoped the McKinley wolf pack would leave the pie shop out of their quarrels, though the Kilpatricks—members of that *lupus garou* pack—had been passive-aggressive of late with both the MacQuarries and the MacNeills at pubs or wherever they chanced to meet. That attitude was sure to escalate once word reached the world on where the film would actually be shot.

Heather had her cell phone out, just in case she needed to text her pack leaders for some Highland wolf muscle.

The aroma of fresh bread baking, of hearty beef stew bubbling in a cooker, and of sweet pastries filled the air as Lana brought out another loaf of Scottish soda bread from the oven. In full view of the customers, she made buttermilk bread and soda bread in a brick oven, just like in the old days. Originating in Scotland, the bannock bread made of oatmeal dough was cooked in a skillet, so it was made in the shop's kitchen. The ladies working in the shop were all wearing long dresses with narrow sleeves, long tartan overskirts, boots, and wimples. Lana's kilt was the Cameron tartan of red, green, and blue, while Heather's was the blue and green tartan of the MacNeill clan.

Heather's pack leaders—gray wolf cousin Ian MacNeill and his red wolf mate, Julia—had assisted Heather in establishing the shop a year ago to help some of their wolves remain gainfully employed and Heather achieve her dream. Julia had loved the idea of Heather sharing several of the clan's old-time recipes with the world because Julia was

American with Scottish roots and had fallen in love with all things Scottish when she joined them a couple of years back. Since the wolves lived such long lives, aging a year for every human thirty, many of them had been around for a very long time. Heather had wanted to own a shop like this since she was always cooking for Ian and his brothers, and she'd wanted to share the old-world charm of the recipes she'd personally prepared. She just hadn't had the means to do it on her own without the pack leaders' assistance.

Heather manned the cash register as a man and his wife paid for two venison and cranberry pies.

The woman said, "We've been wanting to come here since the shop opened. It's so fun, and best of all, the food is great. I love your costumes too."

Heather smiled. "Thanks, I'm so glad you enjoyed the visit." No one could accuse them of wearing costumes that weren't true to the late medieval period. Though about that time, some of the women were casting their wimples aside.

Agreeing with his wife, the man nodded to Heather and carried out the pies as the couple left.

The medieval Highland theme of the shop and the food brought in customers locally and from around the world for a unique dining experience. Who wouldn't want to try something different?

Everything was going fine, busy as usual, when the two men of the enemy wolf clan finally walked into the shop, making Heather feel as if they were turning her sunny day into something dark and dangerous. The brothers glanced around at the customers eating and visiting. Were they checking to see if any of her clansmen were there, ready to stop them from whatever they were up to?

She sure wished a whole bunch of men from her clan were sitting there eating right now. She suspected the brothers might have gone on their way then.

The *lupus garous* attempted to look easygoing, when she knew they were anything but. Their clan had been fighting with her people through the ages. They'd been pirates in the old days and were still trying to cheat or steal from others. Robert epitomized cunning and deviousness. He was a cutthroat who wouldn't hesitate to kill someone who got in his way. His brother went along with everything he did.

Heather wanted to tell them they weren't welcome here, but she didn't want to cause a scene in front of her customers. As long as the Kilpatricks were behaving themselves and had *only* come to shop, she would just have to deal with them and leave her feelings out of it.

Lupus garous had to take care of their own kind if they were involved in criminal acts. They didn't want a wolf incarcerated long term, even if the rogue wolf could control his shifting during the full-moon phase. So if the Kilpatricks caused any trouble, Heather couldn't call anyone other than her own wolf-pack leaders to handle it.

A chill ran up her spine as she eyed the brothers with a wolf's wariness. Sometimes, men worked in the shop, but not right this minute. Ironically, many of the clansmen who cooked and served there had sworn they would never want to work under medieval conditions again, but they got a kick out of the nostalgia at the shop. They did have modern ovens and stoves and fridges in the back to keep up with the growing business's orders and, of course, fresh running water instead of having to carry the water from a well like they did in the old days.

Three women were in the back cooking, and Lana was still baking bread, while two servers were filling trays with the meals. Another woman was handling takeout orders.

Robert Kilpatrick, the older of the two brothers, gave Heather a small smile. It wasn't warm or friendly or reassuring in the least. More calculating. She didn't trust him or his brother.

Even though Heather knew Patrick wasn't at fault in her fiancé's death, she still didn't like him. She was certain the men's appearance in her shop meant trouble. Anytime she or other pack members had dealings with them, there were problems.

Another couple of customers entered the shop: two men, all smiles, wearing New York City T-shirts from the Big Apple, jeans, and sneakers. Americans? Maybe.

The Kilpatrick brothers glanced at them, but the Americans ignored them and continued to the counter. "We'll take two of the steak pies," one of the men said.

One looked suspiciously like the star of the movie they would be filming at the MacQuarries' castle, Guy McNab. Heather smiled brightly at him. "Aye, sure." She rang up their orders and noticed Lana glance at the two men and her jaw drop.

Don't burn the bread or drop it, Heather wanted to tell her.

About the Author

USA Today bestselling author Terry Spear has written over
a hundred paranormal and medieval Highland romances.
One of her bestselling titles, *Heart of the Wolf,* was named
a *Publishers Weekly* Best Book of the Year. She is an award-
winning author with two Paranormal Excellence Awards
for Romantic Literature. A retired officer of the U.S. Army
Reserves, Terry also creates award-winning teddy bears that
have found homes all over the world, helps out with her
grandchildren, and enjoys her two Havanese dogs. She lives
in Spring, Texas.

Website: terrylspear.wordpress.com
Facebook: TerrySpearParanormalRomantics
Instagram: @heart_of_the_wolf

Acknowledgments

Thanks so much to Donna Fourier and Darla Taylor for beta reading and catching my bloopers, and to Lor Melvin for brainstorming with me so much on this book! I also want to thank Inge and Blaine Spear who have made over one hundred dives and gave me suggestions for the scuba diving scenes. Thanks to Deb Werksman for acquiring my books for over a decade! And to the cover artists who bring the story to visual life.